PRAISE FOR

"This is one addictively swoony book. At this point, I'm convinced Julie Murphy is personally trying to sweep me off my feet!"
—Ali Hazelwood, #1 *New York Times*–bestselling author

"No objections, but I will not hold my peace—*Student Union* is exactly what I want in a fake marriage plot. Julie Murphy reached into my soul and gave me just what I needed."
—Julie Soto, #1 *New York Times*–bestselling author

"Come for the bratty rich boy with a good-girl kink, stay for the post-sex midnight grilled cheese. I fell for this messy, horny, delightful book at page one but didn't realize it was true love until the Joe Pesci striptease. Now I will never be the same. There's only one thing left to do— Julie Murphy, will you marry me?"
—Ashley Poston, *New York Times*–bestselling author of *The Seven Year Slip*

"Julie Murphy proves she's at the top of her class! She aces the assignment, with a story so charming it deserves extra credit."
—Meghan Quinn, *New York Times*–bestselling author

"Julie Murphy writes bold, big-hearted stories that are unforgettable, and Student Union is no exception. 10/10, no notes."
—Amy Daws, *USA Today*–bestselling author

"Julie Murphy casts her magic spell yet again! No idea how she can make something this fun and sexy—a veritable trope-a-palooza—feel so grounded and real and unique, but that's why she's in a class of her own. A+!"

—Julia Whelan, international bestselling author of *My Oxford Year*

"*Student Union* is the college-marriage-of-convenience rom-com you have been WAITING for. Heartfelt, hilarious, and horny . . . Julie Murphy never misses!"

—Rachael Lippincott, *New York Times*–bestselling author

"This book has heart and humor out the ass!"

—Rebekah Weatherspoon, bestselling author

"In the syllabus of rom-coms, Julie Murphy is required reading."

—Nisha Sharma, author of *Dating Dr. Dil*

"Julie Murphy is an absolute treasure—
I'll read anything she writes!"

—Morgan Matson, *New York Times*–bestselling author

Student UNION

Student Union

JULIE MURPHY

BALZER + BRAY
New York

Balzer + Bray
An imprint of Macmillan Publishing Group, LLC
120 Broadway, New York, NY 10271 • us.macmillan.com

EU representative: Macmillan Publishers Ireland Ltd, 1st Floor, The Liffey Trust Centre, 117–126 Sheriff Street Upper, Dublin 1, D01 YC43

Our books may be purchased in bulk for specialty retail/wholesale, literacy, corporate/premium, educational, and subscription box use. Please contact MacmillanSpecialMarkets@macmillan.com.

Library of Congress Cataloging-in-Publication Data is available.

First edition, 2026
The text for this book was set in Adobe Caslon Pro, and the display type was set in Brix Slab and Relation Two. Designed by Aurora Parlagreco. Production was supervised by Celeste Cass and Jocelyn O'Dowd, and the production editor was Ilana Worrell, with support from Mariam Chaduneli. Edited by Alessandra Balzer, with support from Lavell Nero.
Printed in the United States of America

ISBN 978-1-250-42824-0 (paperback)
10 9 8 7 6 5 4 3 2 1

ISBN 978-1-250-42822-6 (hardcover)
10 9 8 7 6 5 4 3 2 1

To my pookie bears:
May we always turn left and may our glasses
runneth over with endless cream puffs

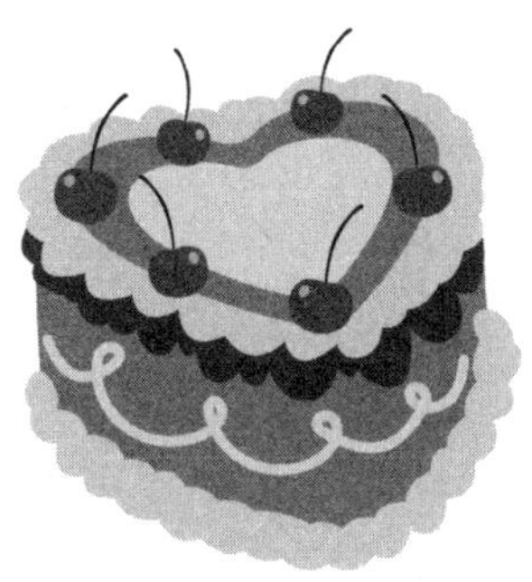

To make a prairie it takes one clover and one bee,
One clover, and a bee,
And revery.
The revery alone will do,
If bees are few.
—To Make a Prairie
by Emily Dickinson

"Mawage. Mawage is wot bwings us together today."
—The Impressive Clergyman,
The Princess Bride

Beverly Clearly
LIBRARY
MARINER
-HALL-
STUDENT
UNION
FOUNDERS
HALL
COMMODORE ELIAS
ROOK STADIUM
Keep Wesley Weird
WEXL
UNIVERS
Black Bear
Blvd
PIZZA TRAMP
TIPSY
BEAR
SPORTS BALL
Hemphill St

CANNON BEACH GOLF CLUB
HAYSTACK ROCK
HAYSTACK HALL
Student Parking
HOLLOWELL HALL
Dining Hall
THE GRAY IVY
Wavecrest St
POST OFFICE
WEXLEY MEDICAL CENTER
SHUTTLE BUS
inevich Blvd
Wexley-on-the-Sea
OREGON
W
S
N
E

PROLOGUE

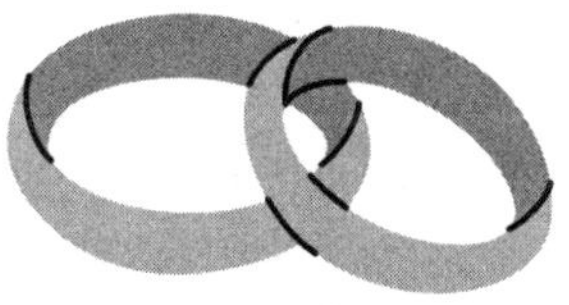

Clover

I'm all dressed up and fully prepared to be left at the altar.

Well, technically the judge's bench.

"Did he say he would be here?" asks Marianne. "He's probably just running late."

My stomach is swimming as I realize this isn't going to work. Bennett is going to be a no-show, and this absolute Hail Mary is about to sail right past me.

I wipe my sweaty hands against my thighs as I look up to Marianne in her polka-dot wrap dress. My mouth opens to thank her for taking the morning off work even if it was for no reason, when I hear the clicking of shoes. Expensive shoes.

"I've got eyes on the groom," whispers Marianne as she frantically smacks my shoulder.

I turn and there he is, briskly making his way down the hall toward me.

"Don't call him that," I tell her. Despite what we're about to do, I refuse to think of Bennett as my savior.

He wears a fitted navy tux and polished leather dress shoes. The black silk tie matches the lapels of his suit, and his crisp white shirt is simple and makes my mouth dry for reasons I have no plans to explore. My gaze lingers for a moment on his gold bumblebee tie pin. Leave it to Bennett to show me up on my own damn wedding day.

I traded in three of my old Reformation dresses over the weekend at Revived Threads, the secondhand store downtown. The dress I walked away with is a white raw silk shift with a boat neck and little white bows stitched all over in a scattered pattern. The back scoops down a little lower than I'm comfortable with. I also picked up organza wrist gloves and wore my hair in waves, half pulled back with a long, light pink tulle bow that Marianne's daughter wore when she was in *The Nutcracker* last December.

I feel silly for dressing up, but he's practically peacocking down the main corridor of city hall, so I guess this is better than underdressing.

He strides toward where I sit in front of the courtroom. A soft smile—the one that always has people forgiving him before they even know what he's done wrong—reveals his dimples as he tucks his sunglasses into his breast pocket.

"You were supposed to be here ten minutes ago," I tell him.

"Weddings never start on time," he says.

Obviously one of us hasn't spent the last two years getting paid hourly.

"Well, maybe this one could if the groom were on time." I wave at his flashy suit. "And this is just the Cannon Beach courthouse. You didn't have to come dressed as an Armani ad."

"Tom Ford, actually." He holds a hand out for me even though I have no intention of taking it. "I'm here now, Clo. You needed me and I'm here, aren't I?"

I stand up. God, I hate the way he says *needed.* It sounds so pathetic. "My *name* is Clover."

"Well, Clo is your nickname."

"Nicknames are reserved for close friends and loved ones."

He winces slightly but says nothing.

"The flowers are a nice touch," Marianne tells him, and I'm annoyed with her for even trying to cut the tension. I give her a *whose-side-are-you-on-anyway* look, but it's lost on her because she has been infected by Bennett's charm and dimples.

"For you," he says, presenting me with the bouquet of light green hydrangeas framed by eucalyptus leaves, with bright red berries and large peonies scattered throughout. Then I notice the small clusters of green peeking through. "Clover."

He clears his throat into his fist. "And, uh, those are rowanberries."

It's . . . kind, which feels suspicious. And it makes the fact that this day is probably nothing either of us expected when we imagined our future weddings that much worse. I'm frustrated with him for trying to make this anything more than what it is: a means to an end. "Thank you, Bennett. This—you didn't have to do this."

"It's nothing." He brushes the palm of his hand up the back of his head, and my fingers tingle a little at the thought of what the short, prickly hairs might feel like against my fingertips.

What the hell is wrong with me? He walks in here with a suit and flowers and suddenly I'm thinking about touching his hair full of overpriced products.

The three of us wait in the courtroom, watching a few other couples in front of us take the plunge. It's impossible to ignore the bouncing of Bennett's leg, and I think for far too long about whether I should reach over to still it. By the time I decide that I should, the clerk calls our names.

The judge is all smiles, with ruddy cheeks and thick white hair. "Marcy," he says, speaking to the clerk. "I think these two are the youngest I've had this month."

She doesn't look up from her desk but smiles all the same. "I think you're right, Judge Morris."

We turn to face each other, like two kids playing pretend, and it reminds me too much of when we were little and imagining scenarios that we were much too young for.

"I'll just go through the vows with you," Judge Morris says. "Then if you're planning on it, you'll exchange rings, and Mateo, our courthouse photographer—"

"Rings!" I gasp.

"Don't worry, baby." The pet name rolls off his tongue and the arch of his brow is entirely too smug. "I remembered them both."

"Oh." I turn to the judge. "Okay, sorry."

Judge Morris chuckles. "Just goes to show what a good match you both are. My Delilah was always trailing behind me, remembering all the things that would fall out of my head."

As the judge reminisces, the silence between us grows deep enough to fill a chasm.

With glasses sitting on the tip of his nose, Judge Morris begins. "People of the court, we are gathered here today to witness the joining of two souls in the bonds of matrimony. Bennett Andrew Graves—" He glances down at Bennett. "Of *the* Graves family?"

"That's the one," Bennett says.

The judge chuckles again and winks at me. "Lucky girl."

Bennett's dimples deepen as he takes my hands in his. "Oh, sir, it's *me* who's the lucky one."

"Of course, of course," Judge Morris says with a grin. "Let's see here . . . ah, yes. Bennett Andrew Graves and Clover Rowan Walsh.

Marriage is a serious, honorable matter. It should not be entered into lightly." He peers down at the two of us standing as far apart as possible while still holding hands. "I trust the two of you have taken the time to determine what marriage means to you, and that you stand before this court ready to offer each other a lifelong commitment based on love, trust, and respect?"

Bennett's throat works up and down as he gives one assured nod.

"Yes," I whisper, despite the distinct feeling that I am in danger of being sent to the principal's office or combusting into flames from lying in a courtroom.

What the hell are we even doing? I'm eighteen years old. Bennett is nineteen, turning twenty in just a few weeks. We have no business getting married. I don't even know what all the dials on the washing machine do. I count two Uncrustables as a balanced meal. I get nervous walking into a bank by myself.

I hardly comprehend the rest of the brief ceremony.

Faintly, I hear Bennett clear his throat and say, "I do."

"Clo?" he asks.

Then Marianne chimes in. "Clover? Sweetie?"

I blink. Once. Twice. And then look up from my black patent-leather platform Mary Janes and the sheer white socks I paired them with.

"Your turn," Bennett says with an unsteady smile.

"Right." A nervous laugh bubbles up like a spate of hiccups. "I do."

"And the rings?" Judge Morris asks.

Why do I feel like I'm lying to my sweet old grandpa right now? I don't even have a sweet old grandpa. Mom's dad is dead, and my dad's . . . well, he's even more of a mystery than my father himself.

From his slacks pocket, Bennett takes a smooth gold ring that is as thick as the band on a cigar. I can hear myself saying the words, repeating after Judge Morris. My hands holding Bennett's, his long fingers smooth and manicured, the wedding ring on his left and his family ring on his right, a G in an ornate script intertwined with a smaller B and A.

Then, he pulls my left hand closer and slides a slightly too-big ring on my finger, but that's not what I'm concerned with. What concerns me is the oval diamond framed in gold on a thin, delicate band.

Instinctively, I pull my hand back like I've been burned, but Bennett doesn't give me any space and instead leans toward me and whispers into my ear, "Calm down. It isn't real."

I nod and give him a weary smile. It's fake. Just like this whole marriage, but that's fine because this unholy union is about to provide me with some very real on-campus housing.

With a chuckle, Judge Morris says twelve words I'll remember forever. "I now pronounce you husband and wife. You may kiss the bride."

Bennett leans in for the kiss and I tilt my head just in time so that he only gets the corner of my lips. But I'm guessing Judge Morris has seen plenty of awkward kisses, because he's unfazed as he beckons us and Marianne, our witness, to sign the papers that legally bind me to the one person I swore I'd never speak to again.

CHAPTER 1

Clover

SEVENTY-TWO HOURS PRIOR

Three years ago. That was the last time I spoke to Bennett Andrew Graves.

I'm on my lunch break during one of my last shifts at Driftwood Diner. I've hardly eaten since cooking up this ludicrous plan, but I ordered a cup of chowder because for some delusional reason I think it makes me look less desperate.

Marianne delivers my cup with an encouraging smile and I resign myself to nibbling on oyster crackers because I feel like I could puke.

I rehearse the speech in my head again, and it takes shape, building logic and reason where there is none.

The air leaves my lungs as the wind chimes above the door jingle softly.

He wears a loose V-necked sweater with the sleeves pushed up to his elbows and the front French tucked into dark tan chinos that are rolled at the cuff in a near haphazard way that feels like the type of carefree look only money can buy.

His black Adidas Sambas are a change from the Italian loafers he wore to school most days at Calvin Prep. At least that's what he wore before Mom removed me from the most elite private school on the coast because my tuition was one of the many benefits we lost when Bennett's mother fired mine. Public school, however, was the exact right price at free ninety-nine.

Bennett points toward me when Marianne, my beloved work wife and single mother to a nine-year-old girl named Penelope and a high-needs Chihuahua, tries to seat him. She gives him a dizzy smile the moment he flashes his dimples. Marianne's an easy target, but they are also objectively very good dimples.

He slides into the booth across from me, and without even looking up to greet me or take off his sunglasses, he peruses the menu until Marianne approaches with her pen and pad. Before he looks up, she gives me a wink. She has been the firsthand witness to my sheer panic over the last few weeks and is the only person who knows about my potential solution.

"Tuna and chips," he tells her, and I'm not prepared for how his voice has deepened in the years since I've seen him. "Extra tartar sauce. And some of that banana pie." He blesses her with his dimples again and she pockets her notebook without writing down his order because Marianne never writes down orders. The notepad is just there for emotional support—more for diners than for herself.

"You got it," she says, and makes a show of reaching across the table, her breasts hanging between us like two (admittedly very nice) buoys. She looks down at me, her head facing away from Bennett, and mouths *hot*.

Bennett removes his matte black aviator Ray-Bans and places them on the table next to his key fob. He studies me with what seems like amusement, the blue of his eyes piercing and intrigued. The only sign that he is even the least bit anxious is the brief twitch along the sharp line of his stubbled jaw.

"Clover Rowan Walsh," he finally says.

"Bennett."

"Come on now." There are those fucking dimples again. "You've got me burning with curiosity."

"Is that all it took for you to remember that I exist? A bit of curiosity? How simple of you, Bennett. Did you get permission from Mommy to come out and play today?"

At the mention of his mother, he briefly grimaces.

I take a deep breath, filling my diaphragm. I hate this. I hate the fact that I have to even talk to him again, let alone ask him for something.

"I got an academic scholarship at Wexley."

His eyes widen slightly, but his features remain, otherwise, neutral. "Congratulations, Clover."

"Yeah." I clear my throat and crinkle the plastic of my cracker package between my fingers. "I got a full ride." I was nine years old the first time I visited Wexley and since then I have never been able to imagine a future for myself that didn't involve that lush, bluffside campus crawling with fog that always seemed to look right at home amid the late-1800s Gothic architecture.

"Your mom must be proud. How is she?" he asks, his voice teetering on genuine before he clears his throat. "So, I guess you wanted to meet up and split custody of the campus."

I don't look up, because I know that if he's nice to me—hell, even just cordial—I'll warm back up to him, and if I warm up to him, I'll fall for his charm. Bennett's charisma is powerful but rationed, and when he rewards you with it, it feels like the sun.

"No, actually, the family who finances my housing scholarship pulled funding after one of their grandkids was put on academic probation."

"That's shitty. I bet the kid's a prick." He cards a hand through his chestnut waves. "But aren't first-years required to live on campus?"

I nod my head as I prepare myself to be humbled, my heart racing. "Yeah, the only exception is for residents of Wexley-on-the-Sea, and we live in Cannon Beach."

It all comes down to numbers. A few years ago, I couldn't remember even looking at a price tag, but now all I see anywhere I look is numbers. And my first semester at Wexley is racking up.

Tuition . . . covered (Thank fuck.)

Housing . . . $6,400/semester

Textbooks . . . $874

Meal Plan . . . $671/month

Now, with the question on the tip of my tongue, I realize that the hard part won't be the ask at all. It will be the answer.

"Bennett, will you marry me?"

The pause is the longest of my life. At least ten breaths long. Maybe twenty or even a hundred.

Then . . . he *laughs*. The smug motherfucker laughs. Bennett nearly chokes, he's laughing so hard. He downs his glass of water and Marianne refills it as an excuse to eavesdrop. Her brows raised at me as Bennett chugs his freshly refilled glass, and I give her a short shake of the head.

She refills him once more, and then finally his knuckles wipe the tears from his eyes as he takes in the one hundred percent serious expression on my face.

"If you're finished, I can explain."

Marianne returns with his food, and he holds a hand out for me to go on, like I am his own personal entertainment, as he bites into a few fries at once.

"There's no way I can go to school without living on campus. I live outside of the waiver radius. And even if I were to get a fake address, I share a car with my mom. She needs transportation for work. When my housing fell through, I thought I was cooked. But then I read that newsletter that the housing office sent out last week." I give him a moment to confirm he knows which one I'm talking about.

He shakes his head, a smirk curled on his lips. "Sorry, you'll have to clarify. The last time I checked my email was April when I signed up for a VPN to access a Danish website that deals in . . . artistic films."

"I don't want to know about your weird Danish porn habits."

"Of course it's weird," he says. "It's Danish. And I wouldn't be surprised if less than six people open the newsletters from the housing office."

He is giving me an actual headache. I can't believe there was a time in my life when I saw him every day and didn't feel like splitting my brain open. "Excuse me for being invested in my future college career."

That elicits an eye roll on his part.

"Anyway, the newsletter you did *not* read was about a new initiative to integrate nontraditional students into the more traditional aspects of campus culture. Greek life. Sports. Student government. And . . . housing."

"How charitable," he says. "And you are a nontraditional student how?"

"*We* aren't," I tell him. "Not yet. But as of this semester, married couples can sign up to live in traditional gender-neutral dorms."

He leans back against the booth with his arms draped across. "I'm crushed, Clo. You mean to tell me that this marriage proposal isn't from the heart?"

He's needling me. Pushing for a reaction. But if I'm going to humble myself to this extent, then I'm not going to blow this opportunity on my short temper. Wexley is an exclusive school with an unusual history and quirky traditions, but it is one of the most prestigious schools in the country. In fact, it is often referred to as the Ivy of the Pacific Northwest or the Gray Ivy. My dreams of being a Wexley Bear rival some little girls' dreams about their wedding day. (Ironic, I know.)

"My *heart* is in attending Wexley, the school I have worked my ass off to get into. Listen, you're the only other person I know who's going to Wexley in the fall. I just need this one semester and I'll have something figured out by the spring. Trust me when I say that if I had any other options, I wouldn't be sitting across from you."

He flinches, and then turns rigid as he reaches into his back pocket and begins thumbing through his wallet. "Well, I wouldn't want you to settle, Clover."

In one swift motion, he slides out of the booth and stands, slapping two twenties on the table before he storms out.

Panic rises in my chest like water in a sinking car. *Fuck, fuck, fuck.*

Marianne's eyes widen as she frantically waves me after him.

"Shit," I mutter as I shimmy out of the booth with much less grace than he did. "I can't believe I'm chasing after that twat," I whisper to Marianne.

She glances down to the table I just left. "Well, that twat is a great tipper."

"And a rich boy piece of shit," I call over my shoulder as I run out into the constant Pacific Northwest drizzle.

"Can you just wait?" I yell after him and his stupid long legs that are already halfway down the block where his vintage Toyota Land Cruiser is parked.

He doesn't respond.

"Bennett!" I try again. "Just let me finish." He's reaching his car now, and I run across the street, darting out in front of a passing vehicle that responds with their horn.

That gets his attention, and he yanks me toward him as the back tire hits a puddle and splashes across the hem of my jeans. "Are you trying to get yourself killed?" he asks as I backpedal until I'm pressed against his driver's side door.

The rainwater from the car is seeping into my thin T-shirt and the back of my bra.

With his rearview mirror on one side and his fist braced against the doorframe on my other side, I'm hemmed in, and I think he's gotten even taller since the last time I saw him. He's hunched over so that even the rain can't find me.

"Why me?" he asks. "Why does it have to be me? You could ask any random person on campus."

A single rain droplet rolls off a rebellious curl above his ear and down the sharp line of his jaw until it disappears somewhere along the vein trailing the side of his throat. He's not just the haughty spoiled boy anymore. No, in this moment, he's absolutely predatory, and as he leans further over me, my head inadvertently tilts back to accommodate him.

"B-because you're the only person I know at Wexley."

His lips are less than an inch from mine, his gaze pinning me in place and then flickering down to my mouth. My silly little brain wants to know what would happen if I just closed the gap. If I let him kiss me.

But I can't. I'm willing to humble myself enough to ask him for help, but I won't stoop so low as to kiss him and let this potential marriage begin as anything more than what it is.

I shrink back against the car door as much as I can. I need space between us and I say the one thing I know will work. "Because you fucking owe me, Bennett Andrew Graves."

His jaw twitches and space exhales between us as he steps back. With one little wave of his hand, he shoos me out of the way and then gets in his car.

"You can meet me at the courthouse tomorrow morning for the marriage license," I tell him. "Ten o'clock. And if you're not there, I guess I'll have your answer."

With his gaze trained on the road ahead, he nods once and then shuts his door, leaving me in the rain.

CHAPTER 2

Bennett

TWO WEEKS LATER

"This is a great fucking town house." I plop down next to a slouched Tex on the worn leather couch he hauled up here from Oklahoma in the bed of his truck.

"Yeah," he says as he organizes the eco-friendly reusable moving totes he rented for the move so that they can be returned. "Too bad you're not going to be living in it."

My other would-be roommate, who is my cousin and sometimes best friend, Julian, lies on the island of our kitchen, hands held over his abdomen, feigning exhaustion as though he just carried each of his boxes up one by one instead of having a white-glove service move and unpack for him while he watched Tex wrestle with the freight elevator.

"At least you can always count on a Graves to pay their bills, so Auntie Sydney is still paying the mortgage while this idiotic motherfucker runs off and secretly gets married." Julian sighs. "It's like the first thing they teach rich kids with trust funds: Don't get married without a prenup."

"I've got to uphold my mantle as the Graves family fuckup," I tell him. "Besides I couldn't pay Clover to sully her hands with my money."

"Well, she's more than happy to use you for housing benefits."

Tex scratches his chin. "He's not wrong."

"The real concern," Julian announces, "is that the fuckability of this household has just dropped dangerously low." He turns to Tex with a wink. "Not that I don't still consider you highly fuckable, Tex."

"I got drunk and let you kiss me on the lips *one* time after we won a game of strip table tennis." Tex throws his head back, but it doesn't hide the ruddy color of his cheeks.

"It was more like a headbutt than a kiss," I say in his defense even though I have always thought the two of them would actually make a pretty good couple.

"Do you see the way he objectifies me?" Tex asks.

"That's just the cost of doing business with Julian," I tell him.

Julian and I have only known Tex for a year, but he's the glue we didn't know our friendship needed. In fact, after a big fight last spring, he was the one who brought us back together. Tex's actual name is Miles Eugene Barrows III, which is a much stuffier name than is appropriate for him. The guy comes from a long history of oil barons but ran away to Oregon to get a degree in environmental sustainability that is being funded by his mother out of spite after a messy divorce from his father. The nickname Tex can only be explained by a drunken night and the fact that *Okie* doesn't have the same ring to it.

"I don't see why you can't just live here with us." Julian pouts as he sits up and hops off the counter. "Your marriage is basically a piece of paper. Who cares if you two share a dorm? If Clover is anything like I remember, I doubt she even wants to breathe the same air as you."

"We have to play the part, chucklefuck. She's my wife." *Shit, that word.* "Besides, if I'm going to be married to Clover, I plan on using this opportunity to annoy the shit out of her." I slap Tex's knee as I stand up to head over to campus and check out my new living quarters, which I added on to my tuition at the last minute. I probably could have found someone to take my room at our town house, but I have no clue what the hell I've really gotten myself into and wouldn't mind the insurance policy. Besides, my mom's accountant pays anything that comes through with a Wexley logo on it without blinking an eye.

I scoop up the third key from the kitchen counter. "I'm out of here."

"Don't forget to carry your bride over the threshold," Julian calls after me.

"Fuck you very much!" I tell him.

Haystack Hall, named for the famous Haystack Rock off the coast just up Highway 9, is the oldest and most decrepit dorm on campus. It is one of two gender-neutral buildings, but most distinctly of all: It is simply *not* the housing assignment you receive when your family has an endowment. When Clover texted me to tell me where we had been assigned, I decided not to pull any strings and risk my mother finding out about this little *situation* any sooner than she needs to—which will hopefully be never, since Clover swears she will have housing lined up next semester and we can happily get divorced the moment we turn in our last finals.

I hover in the doorway of room 516. Behind me, the chaos of the hallway moves like a busy freeway.

Clover stands on a wooden chair in a pair of denim cutoff shorts, exposing her supple thighs and their shallow dimples. Her oversize hoodie skims the hem of her shorts as she drops her arms after failing in her attempt to hang a thin string of lights over the window on the left side of the room, which she seems to have established as hers. Because of course she wouldn't wait for my input. The girl is about as tactful as a bulldozer.

All my belongings are already unpacked thanks to the same moving company Julian hired. They unloaded all my furniture at the town house, but I slipped them a little cash to bring most of my other things here.

The elephant in the middle of the room is the two twin beds that have been bolted together to make a king-size bed. Shit. This is one thing I hadn't considered.

"I actually prefer the left side," I say.

The string of lights she is trying to hook over the side of the window slips from her grasp and with a frustrated groan, she spins around with those small hands on her hips, the ring I gave her sparkling just as brightly as it had two weeks ago when I last saw her at the courthouse.

"Then *maybe* you should've gotten here first," she says.

"Or *maybe* you could have had the decency to wait before you made decisions about our dorm room."

She only glowers at me in return.

"Need help with those lights?"

She huffs like a frustrated Pomeranian, blowing a strand of hair out of her face. "No. Yes. No."

"There he is! The groom!" chirps a sweet Midwestern voice from behind me. "I can't believe there are married couples on our floor. *So* cute."

"Sure," responds a deadpan voice. "Cute."

Clover steps down from the chair as two girls—both varying degrees of curvy—step in behind me. One wears a floral dress that is both virginal and slutty while the other is in bike shorts, Doc Martens, and an oversize T-shirt that says *eat the rich*. It doesn't take much guesswork to figure out which voice belongs to whom.

"Uh, Bennett," Clover says, "these are our neighbors from across the hall. Meet Daisy."

The girl in the dress gives a shy smile and I make a mental note to keep her far, far away from Julian, who never misses an opportunity to corrupt.

"And Briar Rose."

The one who looks like she stomps around involuntarily nods, her oversize and ornate septum ring glittering. "Actually, it's just Briar," she says. If I weren't suddenly a married man, I might ask how she feels about being mean to me for a night.

Clover flings a careless arm out, presenting me. "This is Bennett Graves. My . . . husband." She swallows the word like half-risen bile.

"Oh, right," Daisy says, "of Graves Coffee? I'd heard Wexley was a Graves family tradition."

"You know your trivia," I tell her.

"I love the new slogan you guys came out with a few years ago," Daisy says.

Briar almost smiles. "It's pretty good. Graves Coffee—wake the dead."

"That would be my mother's idea." Then, because I'm either committed to our sham marriage or just a prick, I sling an arm around Clover's waist and tuck her against my side so closely that the warmth of her flushed cheeks radiates through the fabric of my T-shirt.

She lets out a quiet yip, but tries to play it off as a giggle, which she fails at. Miserably.

The top of her head doesn't reach my chin, so I lean my cheek against her soft blond hair, inhaling the delicate scent of vanilla and amber. "How's dorm life so far?"

With a harrumph, Briar crosses her arms. "It's fine. Despite the fact that the building is old enough to be condemned and our narc of an RA made me get rid of my lava lamp. He said it was a fire hazard and I told him the whole goddamn building is a fire hazard."

"I love it," Daisy chimes in. "The building has so much character."

"That's generous of you," I tell her, and she just blinks in response. "Look at the three of you! All flowers of some sort. Like a lovely little garden."

Daisy beams, and I have a feeling she will be susceptible to the same magnetism my mother often calls on when I am her date to charity dinners. To my credit, I'm a real hit among older wealthy women who raise money from each other for fun in the name of causes like hedgehog rehabilitation and other things that don't involve actual poor people.

Briar grinds her teeth so hard that they could chip, and beside me Clover looks like she would like to do unspeakable things to me. Sadly, not in a kinky way.

"Clover is typically considered a weed," Briar says with a slight glower.

I might as well sign my own death certificate when I turn my head to kiss her on her forehead. "You'll always be my flower."

"Gross," Briar mutters.

Daisy practically swoons. "I'm dying to know how you two met. And married so young! How romantic."

Briar coughs "*pregnant*" into her fist.

Clover's mouth opens and closes as she searches for the right answer, her cheeks and neck burning into an angry shade of red.

"It's quite the story," I tell them. "But one we'll have to save for once we've unpacked. Right, baby?"

She pulls her head away so that my cheek loses its resting spot, and the soft line of her brow is furrowed with irritation. "Right, *darling*." Without wasting any time, Clover politely steers our neighbors out the door. "Well, so good to see you both. I'm sure we will have plenty of time to get to know each other."

Daisy spins around in the doorway. "Oh yes! At the dorm orientation tomorrow night? We'll see both of you, right?"

"Alas, I have a family commitment and won't be able to attend, but you'll definitely see my sweet Clover," I say as I lean forward conspiratorially. "In fact, she's a bit shy. Would you mind knocking on her door when the time comes so she has friends to go with?"

Daisy nods excitedly before sighing. "You are *such* a good husband." She shakes her head at Clover wistfully. "He's one of the good ones."

I turn to Clover, her hard gaze narrowed on me as I sweep a strand of hair behind her ear. "She's the one who makes me good."

"Darling," Clover says as she clings to my arm. "I forgot to tell you! Your mother called and said she didn't need your help tomorrow night after all, so we can get oriented *together*!"

My bicep flexes under her touch as my fist clenches. "Wonderful."

CHAPTER 3

Bennett

"I think the fuck not," I tell Clover.

"We have no other choice," she snaps back with a little stomp of her foot. Ah, there's the know-it-all brat I once knew. "The beds must be unbolted. We are not sleeping in the same bed."

"And you don't think that will look suspicious to people?"

"Plenty of married couples sleep in separate beds. And who would even be in our room anyway?" With her phone in hand, she crawls under the bed. "We have to separate these beds. Don't you have a toolbox?"

"Okay, first off: Sexist of you to assume that every man owns a toolbox. Second: I happen to have one out in my car. But I am not sleeping in a twin bed. And we are not sleeping in two beds."

There's a clunk under the bed and then an "Ow!"

"Fucking hell," I mutter as I get down and army crawl under from the other side.

"Oh, so you *are* helping now?" She's flat on her tummy and

inspecting the leg at the foot of the bed where the two wooden frames are conjoined.

"Definitely not. I just came down here to make sure you're not concussed because that would be very inconvenient for me as your husband."

She looks up at me, the phone lighting her face and a vicious response on the tip of her tongue, just as a firm knock sounds at our door. "Come in!" she yells.

The door opens and it occurs to me that the only visible thing at the moment is my feet sticking out the side of this bed.

"Hello?" The voice is distinctly low. "Everything okay under there?"

"This discussion is not over," Clover hisses before shimmying out.

"Feels over to me," I manage to respond with a grunt as I crawl back.

The guy at the door is a fucking giant. His shaggy black hair blends in with his worn black T-shirt and jeans, and I think it's fair to say he's never smiled a day in his life. He wears wire frame glasses that you'd get punched for in high school but must play really well with the college girls who want to get drunk and talk about their Myers-Briggs type. "I'm Dylan, the fifth-floor resident adviser." His lips hardly move as he speaks, making it clear he would rather be anywhere but here.

Me too, man.

I glance over to find Clover blushing and my chest puffs out like a fucking ape. I step up beside her as the dutiful husband I am pretending to be. "Bennett," I tell the RA. "And this is Clover."

Beside me, Clover audibly swallows, making it perfectly clear that she would climb this guy given the chance.

"Is there a problem with your bed?" Dylan asks.

Clover takes a step back and motions to her side made up with her comforter and sheets while my side is still bare. A far cry from the picture of a marital bed. "We were trying to disconnect the frames."

The expression on Dylan's face—and I use the term *expression* generously because the man is so mechanical in voice and movement—is puzzling. He checks his clipboard, his head tilted to the side. "I've got you two signed up for a married dorm."

Beside me, Clover's breath catches, and I am just a little pleased to be right that I've got her number when it comes to this guy.

"We were disconnecting them to reconnect them," I explain quickly. "The beds felt a little loose." I shake the foot of the bed, and of course the thing is firmer than the drop deadline for classes. "We just didn't want to wake up the whole floor with our newlywed escapades, you know?"

Clo makes a shabby attempt at playing her grimace off as a smile.

"No, actually, I don't know," he says. "But I can call maintenance out if you need me to."

Clover nods. "That would be totally—"

"Unnecessary," I finish for her.

Dylan shrugs, his gaze still bored. "Right. You both already signed off on the housing contract, but I'm leaving a hard copy here for you. The housing office is trying to keep tabs on all the non-trad students, so don't be surprised if they pop in from time to time."

He opens the door and some very loud music blares from down the hall. "My fucking eardrums," he mutters.

It's just the two of us again and the noise from the hallway dulls as the door shuts.

Clover stands with her arms crossed over her chest. "We are not sleeping in this bed together."

"Hate to break it to you, wifey, but I'm not sleeping on the floor."

Her cheeks flood with a delectable blush, and I wonder what other things I can do to make her rosy with color.

"We need some rules," Clover says, and then more to herself, "This is such a fucking joke." She plops down on her side of the bed and takes the notebook off her dresser. "As you know, I plan on resolving this little housing situation before the end of the semester, so we can just go ahead and schedule our divorce for the last day of finals if that works for you." With that said, she scratches *December 9th* across the top of the page.

"Fine," I tell her as I slump against my desk with my legs and arms crossed. "First rule: one bed. Even you can admit that there's no great way to explain two beds if we plan to keep this story going."

She looks over the bed with a forlorn expression and pushes up the sleeves of her sweatshirt to reveal the familiar smattering of freckles on her arms. "At least it's a big bed."

"And we'll need to get matching bedding at some point."

"It's very European to have two different duvets," she says, catching the way my brow arches before a defeated groan fills her chest. "Fine. But I have a rule of my own."

She begins to write and I stand up to watch over her shoulder. Her hair swings out in front of her face, and my fingers itch to tuck it behind her ear. Thankfully, she does it herself before I make an ass of myself.

No bringing hookups home.

She gives a pointed look, like that rule will be some sort of challenge for me especially.

Her opinion of me is so incredibly low, and it's unfortunately earned. "I would never do that, and I'm insulted by the fact that you think I would."

She has the decency to look guilty for just a moment and offers me the marker. “Well, what’s your next rule?”

“That’s it for now. Maybe the rules should be an ongoing sort of thing.”

“Excellent.” She makes a show of closing the notebook.

“All right, I’m going out to meet some friends at a party.”

She perks up at the word *party*, and before she can even get the question out, I’m shaking my head. After today, I need a drink and some romantic alone time in the shower to jack off in peace. Seeing as my privacy is currently compromised, I’m going to have to settle for a drink. There’s no way I can take Clover to a college party full of lecherous frat guys eager for a first-year to pounce on and still manage to have fun.

“It’s not like I need you to get into a party,” she says.

“No, just the good ones. Besides, you need your beauty sleep. You only have one first day of college.”

She rolls her eyes, but I can see the fight draining from her as the nerves over tomorrow begin to settle in.

“Don’t wait up,” I tell her with a wink.

Tonight, Julian took the lead on locating a party to kick off the semester, which explains why I am sitting in the middle of a crumbling three-story Victorian that smells like patchouli.

“I love theater majors,” Julian says as a guy I vaguely recognize as one of his spring semester hookups curls against him and nibbles at his ear.

He nods toward Tex, who is in the kitchen talking to a pixie-like girl with long, strawberry-blond waves that skim her lower back. She looks like she just walked out of a Renaissance festival.

"Girls love a shy guy," I tell him. "The whole Southern manners thing goes a long way too."

"It's pretty hot," Julian confirms.

The party is so low-key that it's more of a get-together, which is a nice change of pace after last year. There was a huge bash over at 1919 Hemphill tonight, which we were not invited to—no surprise there. We got a few other invites, including some from frat houses and one event co-hosted by a bunch of prelaw and marine biology majors. But the theater majors and art weirdos have some good music, decent weed, and a few kegs. Plus, any party hosted by this crowd is always one step away from turning into a poly compound, and that's entertaining at least.

"Incoming," Julian whispers.

But it's not enough warning to prepare me for the lanky beauty with brown curls who welcomes herself to the armrest of my chair and drapes her legs across my lap.

"Vanya," I say as she brushes a lock of hair off my forehead. "It's been a while."

She smirks, but her chocolate-brown eyes harden a little as she says, "Yeah, I think the last time I saw you, your pretty little bare ass was sneaking out of my room in the middle of the night."

"I had a final the next day," I tell her.

"That you were exempt from," she reminds me. "I would know. I was your Intro to Sociology TA, remember?"

I give her the boyish grin that has gotten me out of trouble many times. I slept around a lot last year, but Vanya was very intent on coaching me in and out of the classroom and I'm a better lay for it. She's finishing grad school this semester and then plans on doing her PhD dissertation on the rise and downfall of monogamy, which sounds hot if you're a guy looking to get his dick wet, but in reality means that every hookup ends with a joint (which she hogs) and a long lecture on how Western culture is the biggest killjoy of all time.

"How was your summer as an au pair?" I ask.

"Oh, fine." She sighs and leans her head on my shoulder. "Until the mother and father tried to sleep with me."

"Independently?" Julian asks, his interest piqued.

She grins. "At first, yes. But then . . . let's just say it eventually turned out to be a restorative marital experience."

Julian's eyes light up. "Speaking of—"

My gaze cuts to him before he can say another word. I actually think Vanya would be impressed by how Clover and I are using marriage to game the system, but she still works for the university and if all this goes up in smoke, I won't let it be my fault—and another reason for Clover to hate me.

He rolls his eyes and turns to the guy who is practically in his lap now. "Let's go find a surface to defile."

Vanya laughs and cards her hands through my hair again as she sinks down farther into my lap. "What about you?" she asks. "Any interest in kicking off the semester with a bang? Literally."

My dick twitches at her offer as I mindlessly play with the ring on my left hand.

Ah, shit. The ring on my left hand.

I don't know what the ethics of infidelity are when your real marriage is actually fake, but things with Clover are complicated as it is. I told her I wouldn't bring anyone back to our dorm, of course. But we never established any sort of rules around sleeping with other people.

Vanya is beautiful, and we have had very, very good sex in the past, which is why—despite my biological reaction—I am concerned to find that I don't feel like indulging.

It wouldn't be a good look, I decide. If and when people find out that we're married, sleeping with other people would discredit our marriage.

"I'll have to take a rain check." My hands curl around her waist and I lift her up just enough for me to stand and then place her in my recently vacated armchair. "But I guarantee there are plenty of people in this house who would love to be your mistake tonight."

She pouts and I give her a quick kiss on the forehead before saying a brief goodbye to Tex, who is happily receiving a full-on sermon from his little pixie about the importance of male contraception.

On my walk back to campus, there is a line of students waiting to rub the bronze statue of Crumpets the goat, Wexley's unofficial thirteenth founder, for good luck this semester. I feel a little bad that I didn't skip the party and bring Clover to participate in the tradition.

It seems wrong to be going to our ancient dorm with its communal bathrooms and shitty, shitty beds. Especially when I have a whole third of a town house and a plush mattress that costs more money than many of the cars in the student parking lot.

But for better or worse, I've always secretly enjoyed watching Clover get her way. And if helping her start college on time and finding some small sliver of redemption only costs me a marriage license, a stiff neck, and a bathing ritual that necessitates shower shoes, I suppose I can oblige.

CHAPTER 4

Clover

I wake up to a good-morning text from my mom and Bennett's leg slung over my hip. The wall of pillows I'd erected before I fell asleep has been shoved to the foot of the bed and my back is snug against his bare chest. Shallow breaths tickle the back of my neck, warm with the smell of scotch. He shifts closer to me and something . . . stiff is pressed against my ass.

Oh god.

The wall of pillows is no longer erect, but Bennett certainly is.

Okay, this is normal, I tell myself. Morning wood is biological, but that was why I built the Great Wall of Pillows.

"You have five seconds for your boner to sever contact with my ass," I announce.

But he doesn't even startle. All Bennett does in response is grumble into my ear and band his arm around my waist. "Your breath reeks," I tell him.

He nuzzles into my neck, sending a slight chill down my spine.

I'm going to get out of this bed and I'm going to kill him. I just have to decide if it's better or worse if I wait for him to become conscious. I push back against him and not so accidentally kick him in the shins as I pry myself free from the dead weight of his arm.

"Fuck," he yowls, as I practically fall out of the bed. "You have zero bedside manner."

I already have my notebook and pen in hand to scribble down the next rule. "No. Cuddling," I tell him, and then toss it onto the bed for him to see.

He grunts in response as I search through the pile of yet to be organized items on my desk to find my toiletry bag and knockoff Crocs—lovingly referred to by Marianne as frocs. Three years ago, I would have cut my own bangs before being caught dead in a pair, but they're just so comfortable to wear at the diner.

"What happened to the Great Wall of Pillows?" I ask.

"It got too hot with all the pillows." He rolls over to my side of the bed and burrows his face into the silk pillowcase I brought from home and have held on to for three years. Now it's going to have oils on it from his dumb face. "Mmm, smells nice."

"So, you then searched out my body heat?"

"Well, then I got cold." With great effort, he hurls his body upright and holds his head in his hands, elbows braced against his knees as he sits on the edge of the bed.

The hard lines of his back stretch as his spine curves into an arch and something pops. "Fuck, I slept like a rock."

"I know," I tell him. "That wasn't the only rock-like thing in bed this morning."

"That's just a natural response," he says, and when he stands up, I have to consciously avert my eyes to avoid his half-mast boner that is very much visible in his black boxer briefs. Or maybe that's just his starting line, and he's not hard at all. Oh god, I have got to stop thinking about his—

"Clo?" he asks. "You there? You look like you're concentrating hard enough to pop a blood vessel."

"I'm just—I'm just wondering why the hell you can't sleep in pajamas like a normal person. Do you have no sense of modesty?"

He shrugs. "What do I have to be modest about? We ran around in our underwear all the time when we were kids. Sometimes even buck-ass naked."

"Kids," I remind him.

"So just my underwear, then? That's what's got you so anxious." He shakes his fingers through his bed head, and my eyes wander to the familiar, faint scar bisecting his chest—which is defined in ways that I don't recall—from when he had open-heart surgery as a baby to correct a defect.

"It's not just your underwear. It's—" My hands flap senselessly. "Never mind. I guess I'm nervous about classes and this work-study program I signed up for. And I'm antsy about my Intro to Pottery class. My adviser bullied me into signing up for an elective."

"Work-study?" he asks. "Where are you working? How do you plan on having time for a job?"

I check the time on my phone as I run a brush through my hair. I should have done a trial walk over to my buildings yesterday. "Either I make time or I'm broke. I know that's a novel concept for you. And not that it's your business, but I'm just working a few night shifts as a library clerk. Plus, I'm picking up catering shifts when I can." Marianne's brother is the head waiter for the university's contracted catering company, and she said I can take a few shifts with her when they need extra bodies.

"The night shift? Catering?"

"Is that a problem?" I ask as I gather up the stack of clothing I'd set out last night while I had the room to myself. "Don't tell me you take issue with your wife working, Bennett."

He scoffs. "No, of course not. I just know that holding on to a scholarship is a full-time job." He rifles through the dresser on his side of the room and yanks on a white T-shirt. When he turns back to me, I notice the discreet H for Hermès embroidered on the pocket. His steady blue eyes watch me from across our bed, and he makes no effort to hide the way he takes in my bare legs and my chest. I'd yanked my bra off after he fell asleep and dropped it off the side of the bed. Which I totally forgot about until this very moment when I realize that the shape of my nipples is definitely visible.

I press the pile of clothes to my chest and begin to gather up the rest of my things. "How . . . how long does it take to walk over to Mariner Hall from here?"

A lazy smile curls along his lips. "A good twenty minutes unless you've figured out the campus buses."

"Fuck!" I don't have time to go wait for a stall in the bathrooms to change clothes and I'm also pretty sure it will look a little suspicious if I'm constantly leaving the room I share with my husband to get changed. I take the yellow lacy bra from the pile of clothes and pull it through the sleeve of my baggy sleep T-shirt.

Bennett stands there, watching me like I've just started walking around on my hands.

"Are you just going to stare?"

He bites down on his lower lip, dimples just barely present. "Yeah, if that's okay. Besides, you've seen me in my underwear."

"That was *your* doing," I remind him as I pull the straps of my bra over my shoulders and then shimmy out of my shorts. His eyes widen as they hit the ground and his nostrils flare when my panties follow.

The perk of barely skimming five foot one is that most T-shirts come down past the middle of my thighs. I am most definitely not Bennett's type, but if he's going to walk around our room with a boner the size of an elephant trunk, then I can at least take pleasure in watching him squirm.

"A matching set?" he asks, his brow hiked at my yellow lace panties as I pull them up my thighs.

"I like to match. Especially on the first day of school," I explain. "It makes me feel prepared and it's good luck."

"I, for one, am feeling very lucky, Clo." His gaze is hot and intent.

"*Clover.*" I make a spinning motion with my hand, and Bennett begrudgingly turns around so that I can put on my plaid dress. "Okay, it's safe to turn back around."

He still stands there in a T-shirt and boxer briefs, and I find myself asking, "Don't you have classes to get to?"

With far too much grace, he flops back down on the bed, lying on his side with his head propped up in his hand. "Class before ten in the morning is a rookie first-year move, my darling girl."

"Can we *not* with the pet names?" I pull on an oversize Stella McCartney cardigan that I copped from my mom. The thing about money is that it can't buy you fancy clothes when you're a plus size. You just sort of buy the best stuff you can find and occasionally stumble upon something like this cardigan that is meant to hang off waiflike models.

"No, I think we *will* with the pet names."

Hurriedly, I step into my untied combat boots before throwing my toothpaste and toothbrush in my bag. "You are insufferable. I'm adding pet names to the list when I get home."

"Have a good first day, my sweetheart! You are the sun and the moon!" he calls after me loud enough to elicit an *awwww* from Daisy, who is curling her hair across the hall with the door open.

"You two are so lucky to have each other," she croons.

I hit the down button on the elevator at least seven times and stride forward without looking up when the door opens on a ding.

"Excuse me!" says the human-shaped wall I've just walked into.

"I'm so sorry," I tell them as I stick my foot out to hold the door for them to exit.

"Clover? Clover Walsh?"

I look up, eyes still bleary with sleep, and I'm face-to-face with Madeline Linch, the assistant director of housing and the woman who first called to inform me I had lost my housing scholarship.

"Um, yeah. Hi, Miss Linch."

Madeline is a young but stern woman who is even more intimidating in person than she is in her no-nonsense headshot on the university website. When Bennett sent in his last-minute married housing application with me listed as his spouse, she called to congratulate me in the most non-congratulatory tone of all time and then proceeded to say *It seems that love has very fortuitous timing for you, doesn't it?* I was then given an earful about how she's happy that the university is offering these options for married students this semester, despite the concerns that the accommodations might be taken advantage of.

When I hung up the phone, I was visibly sweaty.

"I was actually just coming to check in on a few of our nontraditional students to pass along some information and see if their accommodations are sufficient."

"Oh!" The elevator door begins to ding, angry with me for holding it open for so long. "Yeah, of course. It's great. Quite the love nest." Why the *fuck* did I say that?

"Charming." Her voice is not charmed at all as she steps off the elevator. "I did want to mention that the student life center in partnership with the housing department has organized date night mixers for married couples living on campus." She hands me one of the papers she carries. "I'd like to meet your husband if I could—"

"He's sleeping!" I practically shout. I can't count on Bennett not to give us away. "He pulled an all-nighter."

"In preparation for his first day of classes?" she asks.

"My hubby is a real overachiever," I tell her, the smile brittle on my lips.

"Lucky you," she says, but her voice is flat. "Have a good first day, *Mrs.* Walsh. Or is it Mrs. Graves?"

"Still Walsh for now." I hold my painfully wide smile until the moment the doors close on my floor and I spend my entire walk to class muttering a chorus of *fuck*s.

CHAPTER 5

Clover

I make it to Mariner Hall for my Intro to World Lit class with two minutes to spare, which means the only seats left are in the front row. After Mom lost her job and I switched over to public school, I had no interest in building social circles. The only thing I spent my time building was my college application, taking as many honors and dual credit courses as possible, so I'm able to jump right over first-year English classes.

Even though it's only a year's difference, I feel like the youngest, most inexperienced person in this lecture hall. Because I am. Of course, sitting in the front row by myself like an eager little teacher's pet who is awestruck by her surroundings isn't helping anything.

But I've wanted to be here at Wexley for so long, and now it's finally a reality.

Haystack Hall may be the oldest dorm on campus, but Mariner is the oldest academic building, and according to the campus tour I took in the spring, the ceiling beams are rumored to be from a shipwreck found just below the bluff. It's the sort of place that makes you feel like you're in another time and another world, and it is one of the reasons I fell in love with Wexley.

The building has a large courtyard in the middle and the first time I visited here with Bennett and his mom, Sydney, during an alumni weekend, she told us a ghost story about the basement. Supposedly it's haunted by Beatrix Hallowell, one of Wexley's founders. The story goes that one day she walked into Mariner Hall and was never seen again. It was love at first ghost story for me.

After world lit, I have a break until pottery, which I am dreading. Growing up, I was around money. I had expensive things. We lived in a stunning guesthouse just behind the Graves family home. Mom drove nice cars thanks to her job as the live-in personal assistant to Sydney Graves. I went to a prestigious school. All those things cost money. Money that was never really ours.

So, I am here at Wexley University to get a degree that can make money. My own money.

I wish I had the brain for engineering or computer science. Both prelaw and premed seemed like a circle jerk of ego stroking, so those are out too. However, after living around Sydney Graves for most of my life, I learned that rich people are happy to make money with almost anyone. But they only trust a select few to handle that money, and that trust comes at a price.

When my adviser saw my stacked course schedule, she encouraged me to hold off on economics until next semester in favor of knocking out an elective. With my work schedule and other classes already firmed up, my options were limited to Intro to Theater and Pottery 1.

After taking advantage of my pricey meal plan and grabbing a sandwich at the cafeteria, I get to class early to claim a seat at the back of the room, which has rows of tall tables and stools. The class, housed on the third floor of Bachrach, fills in quickly when a herd of art majors file in looking exactly like . . . well, art majors.

Just before the professor—an older woman with long gray hair pulled back into an intricate braid—closes the door, a tall golden retriever of a boy steps inside and seats himself directly next to me. He is also very hot.

"You look as uncomfortable as I feel," he says.

"Oh, um, I sort of got forced into this class."

"Elective?"

I nod. "It's my first semester, and my adviser didn't make taking an elective feel very . . . elective."

Golden retriever boy grins, his chin dipping down as he laughs quietly. "Yeah, it's like they want us to be well rounded or something."

My stomach flutters at his easy charm. What can I say? I'm living with Bennett. The bar is low.

He is an overgrown Ken doll but with warm chestnut eyes instead of blue, a square jaw, and an open smile. The only things he has with him are a beat-up notebook and golf pencil. He is clearly the kind of guy who is completely unconcerned with making himself unnoticeable even as he strides into class nearly late on the first day. His stool is a little too close to mine, and normally I would find the manspreading and the constant brushing of his elbow invasive. But he's watching me with this loose smile that makes me feel like we're old friends, and the golf pencil *does* make me laugh.

"We should make some sort of pact," he says.

"What were you thinking?" I whisper as the professor begins to pull up the syllabus on her screen.

"You stop me from getting brainwashed into an art major, and I'll do the same for you."

"A united front," I say.

"Exactly." He grins and wags my hand up and down before giving me a sly little wink.

For the rest of the class, my tablemate mutters commentary under his breath, and I have to cover my mouth several times to hide my smile, especially when the pottery examples we are shown take a turn for the phallic.

After class, my neighbor steps in front of me and holds a hand out to help me up. Like everyone else in my life, he is tall. I can't really say how tall because when you're short, there is a single binary: eye level and definitely not eye level. But he's probably close to Bennett's height. "I'm Tate, by the way."

"Clover," I tell him.

"That's a good name," Tate says, and then his expression lights up. "Have I seen you at the Cannon Beach Country Club before?"

I opt for a noncommittal shrug. "Years ago, maybe."

He nods to himself. "I went to a boarding school back East, but I'm sure I saw you there during the summer or something."

Tate hands me his phone with a blank contact form open. "In case you're having a moment of weakness and need someone to talk you off a ledge before you change your major to performance art or comparative textiles." He has a smooth sort of confidence that flows so easily I don't even realize he's successfully asked for my number without even posing the question.

I fill in my name and number before passing his phone back, and his fingers wrap around mine, warm and firm, before the moment is gone.

He winks and then calls back to me as we part ways, "See you soon, Clover."

☘ ☘ ☘

After class, I find a missed call from my mom and decide to call her back.

"Hey, you," she says on the second ring. "I'm just walking back in from my lunch break but wanted to see how your first day was going."

"Well, I haven't failed anything yet."

"That's my girl!"

I snort and the very cool, hot girl passing by me looks at me like I'm contagious. "I'll let you get back to work," I say more quietly. "Nothing to report here."

"Okay, all right," she tells me. "I get it. You got college-girl shit to do, but I just wanted to—we didn't really talk about this before you left, but you know Benny is at Wexley, right?"

"Oh." Uh, yeah, if she only knew he was living in my dorm.

"I don't want you to be caught off guard is all."

I want to tell her. She would be upset . . . confused, even. I don't think she would be mad. But this will all be in the past the moment the semester is over. "Thanks."

We say our goodbyes and by the time I hang up, I'm nearly back to Haystack.

Even though Bennett sort of trapped me into going to the dorm orientation, I am a little bit excited. However, as I walk into the common room, I truly regret cornering Bennett into showing up because my brain conveniently forgot that we would be forced to keep this charade going in front of the entire floor. But I hold out hope that he will flake.

As promised, Daisy collects me from my room a few minutes before, and Briar drags her body behind us.

In the common room, there are three seats left: two together and one by itself. It feels weird to split up the two roommates, so I head off to sit by myself next to a crowd who are all dressed like

Adam Sandler and reek of weed. The room is filled with mismatched couches, a few random armchairs, and old wooden folding chairs that look like they survived World War II.

On the walls are things like Wexley felt pennants, informational posters, and a few framed photos of the school mascot over the years, the fighting bear. Directly above the older television—in a place of pride—is one piece of sketch paper tacked to the wall, edges curling, with an impressively hand-drawn and very muscular bear with *huge* balls. School spirit, it would seem, is alive and well.

Dylan the RA walks in looking like a brooding snack. He hops up on the counter and just waits for people to shut the hell up with this bored expression on his face. He's the kind of guy who can do that. Like when a teacher feels a class is getting rowdy and they stand at the front of the room with their arms crossed until each student one by one realizes they're all in trouble.

A hush rolls through the crowd, except for the guy behind me who is quoting lines from some old Will Ferrell movie. Someone swats the back of his head just as Bennett jogs in, his hair a little damp, wearing workout shorts and a black T-shirt with the sleeves cut off.

Every girl on the floor plus a few guys are practically drooling as he flashes a dimpled smile and a shy wave. Shy, my ass.

They're all crestfallen as he strolls across the circle to me and plants a kiss on my cheek.

The absolute rage I feel at the innocent touch burns. He's technically doing me a favor. At the cost of my pride, sure. But I still have to remind myself. *He is doing me a favor. He is doing me a favor.*

"We're all out of chairs," Dylan says. "You'll have to take the floor or stand against the wall."

"Sorry about that," I tell him with a sweet smile.

"You could always sit on my lap," he says with a wink before walking past me, his fingers grazing my shoulder before he posts up behind me. I can feel the heat of him at my back, but I refuse to turn around.

Dylan rolls his neck one way and then the other, making an audible crack. "All right, so let's make this quick. This is your common room. Keyword is *common*. Don't be a dick and make a mess of a space you have to share with sixty other people. As you can see, we have tables and couches. Kitchens are located on the first, fourth, and eighth floors. Please don't be the person who burns a bag of popcorn. The bulletin board on the far wall has info on student resources including the student health center, which generously provides us with a tub of unlimited condoms. You will find those on the counter behind me. Do not steal all the condoms at once. You are not having that much sex."

That gets a laugh out of everyone.

"Unless you're the newlyweds," calls some guy on the other side of the circle.

The room breaks into chatter. Many people already seem to know who we are, while others are surprised to hear that there's a married couple on the floor.

I sink into my chair a little and wish that I could melt into a puddle and slip through the cracks of the walnut-colored hardwood floor.

Bennett squeezes my shoulder. "Says the sad fuck who isn't getting laid."

There are a few *oooooh*s, and Dylan's baritone carries over the noise. "The Wexley dorms have a no-drug-and-alcohol policy. Based on the whiff I just got, someone is already breaking that rule." He shakes his head. "Listen, just smoke your weed anywhere but here. Laundry is in the basement. It's not haunted. It's just old. If you feel unsafe for any reason, unless you think the laundry room is haunted, my number is on the emergency evacuation instructions on the back of your door. I'm also in the room at the far end of the hallway with the hand-drawn mer-cat taped to the door."

Briar snorts. "So we should just look for the door with the wet pussy?"

Daisy rolls her eyes at her roommate's crass comment.

Dylan's expression becomes nearly deadly. "I'm sorry. Was that a joke?" he asks. "I don't do jokes."

"Fucking A," someone mutters, and Briar flips Dylan off when he turns away.

"All right, let's get this icebreaker over with so we can all get back to our lives," Dylan says.

A girl in head-to-toe Lululemon raises her hand. "My friends on the seventh floor got an activities calendar that their RA planned out for their floor. When should we expect ours? Also, I heard each dorm tries to steal the trident in front of the dean's office in the spring. Is that true?"

Dylan hops off the counter. "You want activities?"

The girl nods.

"What's your name?"

"Sara. No H," the girl says.

He claps his hands together. "Congratulations, Sara with no H. You are officially the floor five activities coordinator."

Sara with no H is at once confused and overjoyed.

Dylan then explains that our icebreaker is to find two other people we have something in common with that isn't a physical attribute. The moment he gives us the all clear to break the ice, I make an effort to disappear into the crowd and away from Bennett.

And then I realize that this exercise will require me to approach people. I used to never think about things like this when I was younger.

Ever. But I don't even raise my hand in class anymore, because it takes me too long to come up with the perfect answer. It's the same way when I order food or run to the grocery store for my mom.

I'm spinning around, searching for anyone who hasn't found their partners. Surely I can find something in common with most people. But then someone takes the hand dangling at my side and I'm pulled through the crowd by Daisy, who has Briar by the other hand.

"Found you!" says Daisy with a laugh.

"What do we have in common?" I ask.

Daisy winks. "Our names, silly! All flowers."

"Again, clovers are a weed," Briar says with her arms crossed.

"And aren't briars just thorny shrubs?" I ask her.

"Wasn't the whole purpose to break the ice with people we don't know?"

"I'm sorry." Daisy's voice takes on a distinctly take-no-shit-mom quality and I find myself impressed. "Would you rather me leave you to the wolves so that you have to make *another* friend?"

Briar rolls her eyes but doesn't budge.

"I tend to attract stray black cats," Daisy whispers.

Once everyone has found a group of three, we all introduce ourselves to the rest of the students and explain what we have in common.

The trios range from heartfelt to absolutely and desperately random. Three students dub themselves the Dead Mom Club. Another three have never been to the state of Ohio. Weird, but okay. Three are lactose intolerant. Three blondes are natural brunettes—they sound traumatized. Homecoming court members. Military brats. Bennett is paired off with a girl and a guy. All of whom dislike the taste of coffee.

I try not to smile. Poor little rich boy doesn't even enjoy the very thing his riches are sown from.

After the orientation, Daisy loops her arm through mine and I listen to her chatter about how her mom almost named her Dawn but changed her mind at the last minute, while Briar excuses herself to run some sort of errand that has to do with cheese.

When I get back to my room, Bennett is thankfully gone. I open the notebook with our rules and add two more.

No pet names.

PDA on as-needed basis only.

In the middle of the night, I wake up to pee, and when I open the door, a line of students has formed just outside Daisy and Briar's room. They smell like varying combinations of cigarettes, weed, and booze. The door swings open and one guy ducks out. I catch a glimpse of Briar sitting just inside the door in a short folding beach chair with a mini ironing board sitting low to the ground in front of her. She wears an apron, and her hair is pulled back into a tight braid.

Maybe I'm high.

I have to rub the sleep out of my eyes to ensure I'm actually seeing this. I feel like Alice after she fell down the rabbit hole. Along the wall is a line of four students, who look to be varying degrees of drunk or high.

She glances up to see me staring as she flips a grilled cheese on the board and then presses an iron down on top of it.

The next student walks in, and Briar motions for him to leave the door open. She puts the grilled cheese on a paper towel and hands it to him. "Ten bucks."

He hands her a ten and then drops two extra dollars into a paper cup that sits at the tip of the ironing board.

"I can't tell if this is real or not," I say, the words thick and sleepy on my tongue.

"Real," she says as she slathers two pieces of bread with mayo before adding three slices of cheese without looking up. "I spent twelve dollars on ingredients at the dollar store and I've already made over a hundred bucks tonight." She presses the iron down on the first side of the next sandwich. "You want one? No neighbor discounts. Sorry. I'm a small business. You get it."

I rub my eyes again and shake my head. "I—I have to pee."

She shrugs and I scurry down the hallway to the bathrooms.

When I return, two more students have joined her line.

"Last call," she says, her head poking out of the door. "I have enough for three more sandwiches."

The last girl in line groans and shuffles away.

"Clover," Briar says. "If Dylan or any other RA-shaped humans ask you if you saw me selling grilled cheese tonight, no you didn't, understand?"

She sounds sufficiently threatening and I'm too tired to push the point. I still don't fully know what the hell I'm seeing right now. "Understood."

I let myself back into our room, and Bennett, still mostly asleep, mutters, "Does it smell like grilled cheese in here?"

CHAPTER 6

Bennett

Surprisingly, sharing a living space with Clover feels normal when I'm not thinking too hard about it. Prior to the summer before junior year, I don't remember a time when Clover and her mom, Beth, didn't live at our primary family residence. Graves Coffee is headquartered in Portland, but we only have a penthouse there for when one of us is in town. The cliffs of Cannon Beach are home.

But before that came into our life, I spent the earliest months of my life in hospitals under constant monitoring. After I had a surgery to rectify my congenital heart defect and my parents were told I would lead a mostly normal life other than having a cardiologist for the rest of my life, my parents moved out to the Cannon Beach estate. They divorced when I was eighteen months old because it turns out when they had nothing left to fight against (whether it was my grandfather's disapproval, infertility, or my health issues), they figured out that they didn't actually like each other.

Now, my father, Brady, is happily living on alimony checks in

South Carolina with Priscilla, his second wife and a retired Dallas Cowboys cheerleader who is seven years and four days older than me. But he was never a real parent to me. Not in the way that Beth or my Grandpa Dean were.

Of the three adults in my life, though, Beth was the warmest, and it felt unfair that she was Clover's mom. Clover, who would squirm away from hugs and flush with embarrassment when her mom whistled at her choir concerts.

My mom has never been affectionate like that with me. Beth would always say that was just her way, but that didn't stop my mom from doting on Clover. Maybe I'm not the son she expected. Or maybe she just tried so hard to have me only to nearly lose me that it feels safer to keep me at a distance.

When I've woken up the last few mornings, it seems that my body has found some way to touch Clover regardless of how many pillows are between us when we fall asleep. I wonder if I am just subconsciously that fucking desperate to feel some kind of connection.

I'm pathetic.

Which is why I am avoiding going back to the dorm for a while in favor of drinking at the town house by myself while Tex and Julian are god knows where. I scroll through a dozen calendar invites from Whitney, my mom's latest assistant—they never stick around for more than six months. There are charity dinners, meetings in Portland she wants me to sit in on, and a few scheduled phone calls labeled *mother/son check-in*.

At least when Beth was still running the show, she never let me know that quality time with my mother was a window that had to be carved out of her calendar.

As kids, Clover and I spent time together in a de facto sense. We were a year apart. Our mothers' lives were more intertwined than most marriages. Clover attended the same schools I did. She was given as many Christmas and birthday presents as I was. When my mom and I went on vacations, Clover and Beth did too. It wasn't until I was fifteen that I realized that, for as much as Beth and Clover were treated like family, they were still just the help.

Still a little groggy and possibly tipsy from last night, I'm just beginning to wake up as Clover backs into our dorm and closes the door gently. She jumps the moment she sees that I am awake and very much trying to ignore the way wet droplets from her hair roll down her shoulders and then over the tops of her breasts only to be absorbed by the seam of her towel.

I would like to be a towel. That would be a good life.

"Oh!" she says with a gasp. "I thought you would still be asleep. Sorry, I just forgot my clothes—"

I throw a pillow over my face and with muffled speech say, "I'm not looking, I swear." Because I've already seen enough to be hard.

"Oh. Okay. Uh. I'll be quick."

My breath is hot against the pillow as the seconds tick by and I force myself to think of anything but how naked her body is under that towel.

"Okay," she says. "You're fine."

I remove the pillow and my heart stutters in my chest. Should I tell my cardiologist about this? Would Dr. Gladstone advise me to move out for the sake of my health?

When I open my eyes, I am not fine. Not at all.

Clover Rowan Walsh stands with her back to me in a pair of pale pink underwear as she pulls a soft, matching lace bra over her head.

She scrubs her hair with the towel and then tosses it behind her on the bed. The image of her yellow lace underwear dropping to the floor on the first day of classes is at the forefront of my mind. Does she really match every day? Does she expect other people to see what she's wearing under her clothes? My chest heats with rage at the thought of sharing this sight with anyone else.

My lips smack together as I search for words to explain to her that she is not actually dressed because it turns out I am very much qualified to be an expert witness on the topic.

"You don't have to look if my body makes you uncomfortable, but I just figure it didn't matter, since according to your logic we spent at least a quarter of our lives in swimsuits together."

As the resident authority on nudity, I would like the record to show that there is a substantial difference between what she wears under her little skirts and dresses and the swimsuits she used to tromp around in when we would chase after each other with water guns past Grandpa Dean's beehives and through the fields of clover he planted one year for her birthday.

"Besides, let's not forget how you just saunter around in boxer briefs," she says.

"That's my sleepwear," I clarify.

She tugs a loose but short dress on over her head and spins around to find me looking right at her. Her lips twitch, almost as if they are torn between a smile and a frown.

A knock at the door interrupts the thick silence, and she goes to answer while I put on a white undershirt, the closest thing in reach, and a pair of sweats, strategically positioning the situation below the belt.

"Hi," Clover chirps, her voice lifting in a soft question.

I pop my head around the door and see two women—older than

parents but not as old as grandparents—standing there in matching Wexley sweatshirts. They look like they like to go on cruises. (I've only been on private yachts, but I have a feeling that matching shirts play nicely on cruises.)

"Is it already parents' weekend?" I mutter. Thank god—and perhaps the matching sweatshirts—that blood is no longer rushing to my cock.

The shorter woman laughs in response, but the taller one just looks at me curiously.

"They're here, Greta," says the shorter one, who is holding a Tupperware container.

Clover puts on a polite smile. "I'm so sorry, but do we know each other?"

Greta, who seems to radiate calm, says, "Well, Sandra here thinks she knows everyone, but no, we don't know one another."

"Not yet!" Sandra stands there for a moment with an expectant expression on her face.

I can see Clover's brain working on overdrive as she tries to puzzle together what exactly is happening. "Oh," she finally says. "Did you want to come in?"

"Love to," Sandra sings as she sweeps right past us both, but then stops short, only for Greta to run into her back.

I jog over to the bed and do my best to pull the mismatched collection of sheets and blankets into something that could pass for a made bed.

Clover glances around for seating options. Her desk chair is piled high with clothes and my stuff is already unpacked, but disorganized. She holds her hand out to the bed. "Uh, you're welcome to sit if you—"

"Oh, no, no," Sandra says. "We're just popping in and out to introduce ourselves to the other married couple on the floor."

"Oh. Ohhhh," I say. "Right. I remember hearing we weren't the only ones."

Greta rocks forward on her toes. "The first Married Mixer is next week, and we're really hoping to see you both there. We thought we should come introduce ourselves first."

Married Mixer? What the hell is that? I spare a glance at Clover, but she waves her hand away slightly.

"We're both retired first responders." Sandra points to herself and then hitches a thumb over at Greta. "EMT. Firefighter."

"Did you two meet on the job?" Clover asks.

Sandra grins. "This one was on the scene when she tripped over a twig and broke her ankle."

"Funny how you fail to mention that I was running into a burning building," Greta tells her. "I was young and reckless, so I tried getting back to work immediately and this little fireball strapped me to a stretcher and threatened to make me talk about my feelings if I didn't stay put."

"And now we're here," Sandra continues. "Two old ladies back in school to pursue degrees in—"

"Marriage counseling," Greta supplies.

Oh god. They must be able to see right through us.

Sandra foists her Tupperware on me. "Skillet brownies," she says. "We made them in the common's kitchen on the fourth floor. Word to the wise: That stove could use a good cleaning and the burners tend to run a little hot."

"I thought the dorm kitchens were an urban legend," I tell her.

Clover rolls her eyes and cruelly takes the brownies from me as my stomach rumbles.

"Will we see you both next week?" Sandra asks as Greta begins to steer her toward the door.

Beside me, Clover silently stutters, and I manage to say some kind of version of *sounds good.*

The moment I close the door behind them, Clover plops down on the bed and peels the lid back on the brownies. She lies back with the container balanced on her chest while she bites into one thoughtfully and then purrs in response. "Oh shit, these are so good." She groans. "I'm going to be late for financial accounting."

"Did we just commit to a double date?" I ask as I bite into one myself, unable to control the pornographic moan it elicits.

"Nah," she says. "I'm sure no one will notice if we skip out."

CHAPTER 7

Clover

"I thought you said people wouldn't notice if we skipped," Bennett whispers as we're both bent over, tying the laces of our bowling shoes.

That was before Miss Linch emailed me personally to make sure we would be here.

He glances over to where the assistant director of housing sits behind a scorekeeper next to her boyfriend, a kindergarten teacher named Marshall who brought his own bowling shoes from home. The only way I can describe them is *orthopedic.*

"It'll be over before we know it," I tell him.

In the end, six other couples show up. We are spread out across two lanes.

Sandra and Greta claim us as their teammates no matter how many times I tell them that we have collectively bowled maybe two and a half times in our lives.

In our same lane is Miss Linch (who asks us to call her Madeline, but I can't bring myself to do it), Marshall, Blake, and Danielle. The latter are in their late twenties and have a seven-month-old daughter, so they live in the campus apartments, which are so far out of the way that they're technically in a different zip code. Blake seems to be very committed to competing, while Danielle is studying the baby monitor app on her phone like it's the season finale of *The Real Housewives of New Jersey*. (The best in the franchise, obviously. No, I will not be taking questions at this time.)

Marshall is first up and before he takes his ball (also brought from home), he dons a leather fingerless glove from his bowling bag.

"We're fucked," Bennett whispers. "The guy has invested in equipment."

Sandra claps a hand down on his knee as Greta slings an arm over her shoulder. "Intimidation tactic," she says. "My Greta throws a strike her uncle taught her called the One-Eyed Willy."

"He was a dirty old man," Greta says, "but his heart was in the right place."

I crack a smile until Miss Linch turns her attention on us. "I'm curious, Clover. How did you and Bennett meet?"

Shit. We hadn't really prepared for this question, which feels absurd, but honestly, we've known each other for so long that I didn't even consider it. That's okay. The best lie sounds like the truth. I'll just say we were childhood friends.

"We met in a haunted house," Bennett blurts.

There's no stopping the way my head snaps up at him and the absolute nonsense that's just come out of his mouth.

"You're up," Greta tells him.

He turns to me, no hint of apology in the crystal of his blue eyes, and then tucks a strand of hair that's fallen loose from my half-up bun. "You tell the story, baby. I love to hear you tell it."

The moment he stands, Sandra slides over to sit closer to me. "A haunted house? Now, that's a meet-cute I've never heard of."

"You listening to this, baby?" Blake asks as he motions to me with the neck of his beer bottle.

Danielle hums in response while not looking up from her phone, and I swear Miss Linch leans in like she's just caught me in her web.

"Uh, right, so a haunted house."

Bennett approaches the lane with his ball in tow, and with everyone facing me, he looks back over his shoulder and blows me a kiss.

A vulgar retort sits on the tip of my tongue, but I'm forced to smile and pull a story out of my ass, because even Danielle is paying attention now.

"It was a few weeks before Halloween and I went to a haunted house out in Cannon Beach with some of my friends. I don't like haunted houses," I explain, my cheeks warming up. "Because I hate surprises. They just really, really get under my skin." I emphasize each word just for Bennett. "But it was my friend's birthday."

Bennett steps back from the lane after missing every single pin and walks down to retrieve his ball. "What was that friend's name again?"

My eyes dart around searching for inspiration before landing on the beer bottle in Blake's hand. "Coors—ina."

"Ah, that's right. We haven't seen Coorsina since the wedding."

"She's one busy girl," I tell everyone.

"Didn't she start brewing her own beer?" he asks as the machine spits out his ball again.

I shake my head. "I don't recall. Anyway, the haunted house. We went inside and everything was so cheesy, but the jump scares were awful. Then . . . then this clown appeared out of nowhere—"

Bennett spins around, his brow pinched and jaw dropped open.

"I screamed right in his face. And I guess I must have startled him, because he screamed right back at me."

Sandra snorts. "Gave him a taste of his own medicine."

"Exactly!" My lips curl into a grin as I nod my head. "It was this high-pitched, girlish scream."

"I was in character," Bennett says as he makes his return, having knocked out four pins before his ball fell into the gutter. "She always leaves out this part. The clown was maniacal. His backstory was really interesting actually—"

Danielle gets up to take her turn, and I wrap my arm around Bennett's bicep, leaning my head there.

"Oh, darling, you're always so serious about your craft."

"Ben," Brady says, "can I call you Ben? Are you a man of the theater?"

"He is!" I answer for him.

"Oh, dude!" Marshall scoots to the edge of his seat. "I've been looking for an improv partner for months now."

"Do you hear that, honey?" I ask before turning back to our audience with big doe eyes. "He has such a hard time making friends."

Miss Linch doesn't really know what to make of all this. "So, he was a clown in a haunted house?" she asks.

"Yes," Bennett chimes in. "And then my fragile little bird choked on her piece of gum, so I immediately knew what to do." He turned to Sandra and Greta. "I take first aid very seriously."

Sandra is enthralled and Greta is charmed by this.

"If only more young people would," Greta tells him.

Bennett looks down at me and runs his knuckle along the apple of my cheek, and I suck in a breath. His finger is cool against my warm skin and it's a bit of a shock is all.

"I started by pounding her back," he says as he looks into my eyes with adoration, "but when that didn't work, I knew it was time for the Heimlich. It only took one try and that little piece of mint gum that had been lodged in her throat went flying and hit a little boy right in the eye."

I grit my teeth, holding my smile as I very quietly murmur, "You dick."

He turns to everyone else. "The child cried, and my sweet, generous girl went over to comfort him. She nearly died and all she could think of was someone else."

"Damn," says Blake as Danielle reclaims her seat beside him and Greta takes her turn.

"You two were destined for each other," Sandra says. "There's no other way around it. Just like me and Greta when she broke her ankle."

"We're young," Bennett continues, "but who am I to question fate?" He looks back to me, watching from beneath his thick, dark lashes, and then drags the pad of his thumb down the center of my lips.

The bowling alley is suddenly very quiet and all I can hear is the blood pumping in my veins. We might as well be alone.

His teeth dig into his bottom lip, and he looks . . . hungry. "No more chewing gum for my girl," he says just loudly enough for everyone else to hear, and then in a low tone meant for only me, he adds, "My wife."

Miss Linch claps her hands together once. "My goodness. What an unusual story."

"The best ones always are," says Blake, and I sense a slight bit of annoyance from Miss Linch in return.

"And how did each of you meet?" I ask, disentangling myself from Bennett.

Blake and Danielle glance at each other and say in unison, "Tinder."

When I stand up to take my turn, Bennett gives me a little pat on the butt. I shriek and everyone looks at me like I've just stepped on a spider with my bare feet.

I attempt to cover it up with a giggle as I take my ball and approach the line.

The last thing on earth I know anything about is bowling, but I stand there nonetheless to pretend I'm lining up my shot or something. Really, I just need this moment to settle my racing heart and attempt to have a single clearheaded thought.

This—the flirting, the banter, the pet names—it's all just Bennett taunting me. In certain moments, I'll admit, it's easy to forget that he is who he is and I tell myself that's normal. It feels nice to be touched and looked at lovingly, even though the person on the other end is telling a whole group of people that I spit a piece of gum into some poor kid's eye.

I retrieve my ball and Bennett gives me another swat on the butt. At least this time I don't shriek.

"For good luck," he says.

As I walk up to the line again, I make a decision. Bennett wants to push the envelope? He wants to absolutely torment me in the name of playing our roles?

Well, let's see what he does when I match his energy.

The bowling ball is heavy in my hands, and as I glance at the lane to my left and then to my right, I decide *to hell with it* and widen my stance before dipping into a deep squat and letting go.

Behind me, both teams fall silent and I think I can even feel some of them standing, inching closer for a better look.

The ball is steady and straight. I squeeze my eyes shut because I can't look.

The sound of pins falling echoes and then there's a sudden silence. I squint one eye open and watch as one last pin teeters back and forth before falling to the ground like its ill-fated brethren.

"Oh my god!" I scream. "Oh my god?" It comes out like a question because I am well and truly shocked. "Holy shit!"

I'm jumping up and down and pounding my fists in the air. Sandra and Greta stand to give me high fives as I squeal the whole way back to my seat.

"Now, that performance deserves a kiss," Sandra says.

"Good job, gorgeous," Bennett says as though he actually means it. "I know how shy you can be, though, so I'll let you collect on that kiss when we get home."

Someone sighs an *awwwww*.

"Actually," I tell him as I sit down on his lap, my legs crossed and my arms circling his neck, fingers lazily playing with the hair at the nape of his neck. "I think I'd like to cash that in right now."

I don't give him a second to prepare or protest before I go straight for his lips. My mouth is already parted, and his is as well because I've caught him so unaware. His tongue is cool from the ice water he's been drinking, and he tastes like spearmint and salt from the pretzel he'd been nibbling on.

I deepen the kiss, leaning farther into him and into the moment, my teeth tugging at his lip.

There's a wolf whistle somewhere around us, and his brain finally seems to click on because the arm that had hung by his side circles my waist. Fingers dig into the soft curves there and I pull back quickly and breathlessly before the roles are reversed and he's suddenly taken the lead in this little game of ours.

Panting, he looks down at me, and his tongue darts across his bottom lip where I nipped at him.

I turn back to the other couples. "I guess this means we have a real game going now, doesn't it?"

CHAPTER 8

Bennett

I can taste her tongue in my mouth for days.

When we returned from bowling, Clover hardly spoke to me. She slept on the farthest edge of the bed, and I followed her lead.

The list of rules grows and becomes increasingly specific.

- *No trash can sharing.* (I had been using the trash can on her side of the room to throw away my protein bar wrappers.)
- *No going to bed with wet hair.* (She'd accidentally gotten my pillow wet. It also made the smell of her unbearably strong as I tried to fall asleep. It was inconsiderate.)
- *No sharing water bottles.*
- *No sitting on the bed when there are index cards laid out in a certain order.*

Clover is gone most mornings before I'm up, but I've gotten in the habit of waking up early to jack off in a shower stall and then going back to bed.

Maybe I'm a sick fuck, but sometimes she makes this noise in the middle of the night. It's a soft whimper, and likely just a muted giggle or a failed attempt at talking in her sleep, but it's the kind of sound that sends a rush of blood straight to my groin. I tell myself it's biology and beg my brain to think of anything but her as I pump my hand up and down my dick. Every time I fail, the tailspin of self-disgust has me promising that next time, I won't touch myself at all as punishment. Then it's the next morning, and the pattern begins again.

On Fridays, Tex, Julian, and I have identical schedules. The three of us have business law in the afternoon and German 1 two hours later. It's not quite enough time for us to go back to the town house and hang out, and today we have a quiz to study for.

I haven't gone to the trouble of learning Clover's schedule, but last Friday she was gone, so I take my chances and offer up the dorm as a hangout space so we don't have to leave campus.

Julian wrinkles his nose as we step into the muggy, practically antique elevator. "Maybe we should have taken the stairs. Does this elevator shaft go to the pit of hell?"

Tex rolls his eyes and hits the doors' close button.

We make it to our floor with a dramatic jolt, and Julian darts out as soon as the doors open, then clings to the walls dramatically.

"You expecting visitors?" Tex asks, motioning to the four girls gathered at the door to my and Clover's dorm room.

I shake my head. "Probably Clover's—"

"Guten tag, ladies!" Julian calls to them from up ahead.

And then I recognize them as the giggling girls from our German class who sit behind us.

Julian turns back to us, shrugging innocently. "I thought we needed a study group."

"Really?" I ask Tex quietly. "So, he chose the four hot first-years behind us—one of whom said she was inspired by Heidi Klum to learn German."

"Julian only convinced us to take German so we could have a fully immersive experience at a Berlin sex club one day. I don't think we're exactly academics here, Ben." He nudges me with his elbow. "Hey, the tall, shy one looks like Cortana from *Halo*. I call dibs."

"You're supposed to be on my side," I remind him as he saunters toward them.

After I let us all into our room, I hurriedly make my side of the bed. Clover's is already made, of course.

"No need to tidy up for us," says one girl, who I recall being named Felicity, as she wanders over to the other side of the room and pokes around a few of Clover's cosmetics.

"Hey, could you leave that stuff alone?" I ask her, feeling suddenly protective over Clover's things.

"Touchy, touchy," she whispers as she unceremoniously drops some sort of small metal spray bottle.

The look on my face must be enough to silence the other three, because they all cluster and cower at the end of the bed.

"Uh, sorry," I say in an attempt to be less of an asshole. "We don't really have enough room for a large group like this. We should go to the common—"

Julian flings himself across the bed. "*Or* we could have a cuddle puddle!"

Felicity stretches along the head of the bed in what I think is supposed to be a seductive pose.

"We *are* already here," Tex says, eyeing his Cortana look-alike.

I sit on the foot of the bed with one leg hiked up while Julian uses Felicity as his own personal pillow. Tex sits on Clover's side of the bed opposite me. The Cortana look-alike, who I learn is named

Gabby, sits between us while the other two girls lie across the middle. Reagan is on my side while Zara is over by Tex.

There are so many of us on the one bed that it's impossible not to touch.

Reagan glances over to me with a charming little smile. "Do you mind?" she asks as she slings her legs over my thigh.

And normally I wouldn't. In fact, I don't. She's cute, but whatever speck of morals I have says this doesn't feel right.

"Of course he doesn't," Julian says.

Like always, he manages to ignore the violent glare I point in his direction.

Tex, who spent a few summers in the German countryside with his uncle when he was a kid, manages to lead some semblance of a review, but with the way Felicity and Julian are eye fucking and the others are giggling, I barely string together how to introduce myself and ask a few basic questions.

After forty-five minutes or so, Zara is using my lap as a pillow while Gabby plays with her hair and Reagan is still using me as a footrest.

It is the exact worst moment for Clover to walk in, wearing a beat-up flannel shirt speckled with wet clay, cutoff jean shorts, tights, Wellies, and one earbud in her ear.

"Wifey is home!" sings Julian.

"Oh shit," mutters Tex.

Felicity picks her head up. "Did you say *wifey*?"

Clover, at first, looks deeply embarrassed and hurt. Her pillows have been tossed to the ground. The books and makeup on her desk have obviously been moved, and it's then that I notice Felicity is wearing a bubblegum–pink beanie that I recognize as a Christmas present from my mom a few years ago.

Seeing Clover like this takes me back to one of the most reprehensible days of my life. The memory is clear. I can see Clover earnest and hopeful as she waited for a person who didn't exist.

I hate it. I hate seeing her like this. I would literally do anything for her not to look like this again.

But then her expression quickly turns to outrage. Those full lips purse as she throws her tote bag to the ground and crosses her arms, nostrils flaring. And the guilt I was drowning in just moments ago begins to recede. Her embarrassment and hurt feelings? Those, I cannot handle. But her anger? I could feast on it.

"Should I go ahead and add no unauthorized visitors to our rules?" she asks.

"Hubby's in trouble," Julian points out rather unhelpfully.

I stand up and Gabby's head hits the mattress as Zara fumbles a little.

"You're *married*?" one of them asks.

"Oh my god," says another. "I was wondering why this bed was so huge."

"So fucking weird," one of them—I think Felicity—mumbles.

"No," I tell Clover. Even though I feel guilty and awful, I still find it in me to bristle at her attitude. "I don't think that's a rule I plan on adhering to. But luckily, we were just about to head out, darling."

The girls are quick to evacuate the bed and Tex leads the way, giving Clover a polite nod.

Clover yanks the beanie off Felicity's head as she walks past her, and Julian lingers for just a moment before giving Clover a hug.

With a discontented sigh, Clover returns the embrace, her anger deflating just enough to indulge in this reunion. "You look good," she whispers.

"Oh, I know," he says. "Don't be too hard on him. I'm the one who invited them all."

"Yes, and I'm sure you also had them throw their bodies all over my bed."

"Actually, he did," I say, but am ignored.

Julian gives her a kiss on the cheek before joining the others, and the moment we are alone, Clover prickles like a porcupine.

"I swear to god, if I find any of their loose hairs on that bed, I will murder you in your sleep and I'll wake you up halfway through so that the last thing you see is my face."

"It's my room too," I remind her. "Considering I'm the one paying for it."

Her shoulders slope. That was an asshole thing to say, but it's true.

"Whatever," I say, and begin to step past her.

"I'm picking up as many extra shifts as I can to cover next semester's dorm fees, so you'll have your life back before you know it."

"It wouldn't hurt to come up with a backup plan," I tell her. "Maybe look into community college."

"That's none of your business," she says bitterly.

"It is when you're using me to game the system."

She lifts her hand to her face and swipes it across her cheek.

Now I've made her cry. *Fuck.*

She turns her body away from me and it's such a stark difference from her warming my lap just last week that I can't believe these two instances can even coexist in the same universe.

"Get out." When she doesn't immediately hear me move, she says it again more loudly. "Get. Out."

So, I do.

That night, after class, I go to the town house with Tex and Julian. I'm tempted to stay the night, but I guess I have to go back eventually, so I decide to get it over with.

I'm about to walk into our building when I get a text from Vanya inviting me to a party.

I stand in front of Haystack Hall and count to the fifth floor. I'm not sure which room is ours exactly, but every window in the right area is still lit up, and I think I can make out Clover's fairy lights from here.

I should go upstairs so we can talk and at least come to some sort of truce.

But the invitation in my phone doesn't come with any guilt or need for conversation, so I turn around and send up a flare to Tex and Julian.

The girl upstairs, waiting with her light still on, already has plenty of opinions about me. It's easier to just let them be true.

CHAPTER 9

Clover

Sure enough, there is one single strand of auburn hair on my bed. Gross. At least it's on Bennett's side. I pick the hair up using a pair of tweezers and drop it into *his* trash can.

After I got back from pottery, I skipped the TA-led college financial-accounting tutoring group because I had a catering shift with Marianne. There was some sort of afternoon tea hosted by the dean with goats from a local farm in honor of Crumpets the goat, and she said it would be a simple event and a good time to train me. I picked up on it all quickly enough, and despite the tragic uniform of unflattering black pleated pants, matching vest, tux shirt, and bow tie, it was fine. I wanted to literally crush teacups with my bare hands, but it was fine. And the goats were smelly, but cute.

"You okay over there?" Marianne asked.

"No, but I can't get into it without losing my temper and inadvertently fucking up something my first day on the job."

I was already miserable enough from the required shoes. The

female waiters are forced to wear these hideous pumps that aren't even comfortable, which violates every law of footwear. All shoes should ideally be comfortable, but they can't be both ugly and painful. And yet . . . Oh! And as I left for the night, Marianne's brother informed me that the cost of my uniform would be deducted from my first check. Pyramid scheme bullshit if you ask me.

After my shift, I ran back to the dorm and changed before stopping for a quick bowl of cereal in the dining hall and showing up for my shift at the library.

My feet were killing me and my irritability was off the charts, so when they asked for one student worker to volunteer to go home at eleven instead of one in the morning in order to rectify some sort of payroll overage, I jumped at the chance and would have probably stepped over a dead body if I had to. Financially, it was a bad decision, but that would have to be future Clover's problem.

Now, at fifteen past eleven, I'm lying in my bed with my feet up against the headboard in the hopes that the blood will drain down my legs and I won't be able to feel the throbbing in my toes.

There's a sequence of knocks at my door that creates an almost sunny tune. "Sorry!" an upside-down Daisy calls as she lets herself in. "The door was cracked. But oh good! You're here!"

"Physically, yes," I tell her. "Got out of work early."

"Perfect," she says. "I need a wing woman."

"I'm not really wing woman material," I tell her in the hopes that she will see that my current form is comparable to a cicada exoskeleton.

Undeterred, she plops down on Bennett's side of the bed so that she's beside me. "You can't be worse than Briar," she says. "We went to a party last week and she left after an hour to go home and set up her black-market grilled cheese stand."

"Wow. So that's a real thing, huh? I saw her the other night and honestly thought I was hallucinating. I admire the hustle."

She nods. "Very real. And she's definitely using my iron. She said it was a business investment and that I would get my money back when her profit margins were—gosh, I don't even know." She waves her hand around. "I just ordered another one online."

"Sounds like you really won the roommate lottery," I tell her with obvious sarcasm.

Daisy smiles. "It could be way worse. Some girl on the third floor joined some group called Boxwatch. Apparently, like, sixty people get together every Wednesday at three in the morning and stare at a box in the quad. Now this girl won't let anyone on her floor throw out or recycle boxes."

"To watch a box?"

She shrugs. "Paul, the guy two doors down . . . his roommate has a scrapbook of his favorite autopsies. He's majoring in forensic science, so I guess it's not that weird, but next to his bed he keeps a mouse, which is also named Paul, in a jar full of formaldehyde. The roommate swears it's a coincidence, but I don't know."

I laugh and silently decide that at this point I would take the creepy roommate over my own husband. "Okay, you win. So when do you need a wing woman?" I ask.

"Um . . . right about now?" Daisy says as though it's an apology. "Honestly, an hour ago, but as soon as you can be ready will do just fine. I was invited to a party by a hockey player from my speech class. I hate to objectify someone, but he is what most women would refer to as pantie-dropping."

"Oh god, I can't tonight," I tell her. "I'm exhausted and Bennett and I are—"

"In a fight," she says. "I know. Most of the floor heard you screaming at him to get out."

"Was I really screaming?" I ask.

"Loud enough for the reclusive Dylan to stick his head out of his door."

"Christ," I mutter.

"Don't worry. He must have decided no one was in danger of being murdered, because he immediately retreated to his hidey-hole." She yanks on my hand. "So come on. You need a drink and I'll call us a car so we won't even have to hoof it."

I rub the heels of my palms into my eyes.

I should do this. I should go out and do college things. Daisy is nice. I have no friends and I do not want to be here if and when Bennett comes home. I'm a few weeks into the semester, and I have hardly had any experiences that could be classified as distinctly college.

"Fine, fine, fine," I tell her. "But I can't promise how late I'll stay."

True to her word, Daisy orders us a car, and we are caught in a minor traffic jam when we get stuck behind a herd of students walking to the football stadium for some late-night pep rally.

The party is ear-splittingly loud, but it does the trick of making my brain quiet.

Daisy's hockey player is huge, burly, and very objectifiable in his navy blue hoodie that reads GRAY IVY—Wexley's unofficial nickname—in tall white letters. I hang out with them for a drink while she sits on the counter as he creeps closer and closer between her thighs and she becomes increasingly giggly.

When he goes for a beer, I lean over to her. "Are you good if I roam for a bit?"

"I am so, so good," she says as she watches him pop the top on a glass bottle with his bare hands. "He has good hands, right?"

"Sure," I say, even though I can't really distinguish anything other than that they are huge.

I polish off my drink and grab two cans of some sort of spiked seltzer before heading out to the backyard.

In high school, I went to a handful of parties, but I never lasted very long and usually showed up because I'd been casually invited, only to find that the person who invited me was preoccupied and had probably just extended the invitation to be polite. It was easier not to make friends, because I could live with never attempting, but a failed attempt would play over and over again in the middle of the night.

String lights hang over the backyard. It's still loud and there are people dancing near the firepit, but simply being outside diffuses the noise. I settle on the top of a picnic table since all the stumps by the fire are full, and I'm kicking myself for not bringing a jacket. It's that time of year when a sunny day is still warm and summer-like, but the moment the sky goes dark, everything is damp and chilly.

I don't drink often, so once I finish off my first hard seltzer, I am feeling sufficiently buzzed.

"I didn't take you for a hockey groupie. What do you call yourselves again? Puck bunnies?"

I peer over my shoulder. A bottle of beer hovers at Tate's lips, and with an easy smile, he helps himself to the empty spot beside me.

"Definitely not a puck bunny," I tell him. "Whatever the hell that is. I'm here as a wing woman. Honestly, I don't even know whose party this is."

"Sort of just an ice-sports-in-general party, I think." He motions with his beer. "I think the house is mostly hockey players, though. It would at least explain why the place smells like a jockstrap."

"What are you doing here, then?" I ask. "Or are you a puck bunny as well?"

A dry laugh rumbles in his chest as he leans over, bumping shoulders with me. "No, no. Hockey players aren't my type, but I do enjoy betting on their little games."

Like most other people at Wexley, Tate has money to lose. He's shared a pottery worktable with me since the start of the semester, and just this afternoon we put the finishing touches on our air-dry mugs. Between trying to one up each other with vulgarly shaped clay, I've learned that he's prelaw and wants to specialize in patents. He's on the lacrosse team, too, which isn't in season until the spring, and his mom has been married four times. She's engaged to tech-bro husband number five. Her cat, Pepper, has six toes on each paw, is famous on TikTok, and has recently signed with a pet talent manager. They have a summerhouse in Cannon Beach, so the likelihood that we have actually seen each other before is high.

I shiver through a sip of my drink, and he takes off his fleece zip-up and throws it over my shoulders.

"Thanks," I tell him, something in my stomach sparking, and pull my arms through the sleeves. I might be curvy, but Tate is tall, so the jacket is plenty big and covers my legs at least a little. It's so silly, but a guy giving you his jacket is the kind of thing I thought only happened in books or movies and it is impossible not to be charmed by the small act of chivalry.

He points to the people dancing on the other side of the firepit. "Dance with me." It's not a question, but it's not a demand. "It'll warm you up without going inside and subjecting yourself to the stink of jockstrap."

Tate is already standing and pulling my hand to help me step down from the table.

The music isn't the kind I would normally dance to even if I could dance. It's a little slow and folksy and the couples who are dancing are swaying dangerously close with their arms wrapped around each other. It feels a little intimate, and my muscles tense with uncertainty.

Tate gives me a spin as we join the small cluster and a genuinely surprised laugh slips out of me like a hiccup as he pulls me back to him, the warmth of the fire welcoming me.

He holds one of my hands to his chest, and the other rests at his waist while he softly rubs up and down my back with his free hand.

"I feel like I need to spin you around a few times just to get you nice and toasty."

"I think that would make me feel like a rotisserie chicken."

He looks down at me from under his pale lashes. "You're weird, but you're fucking funny."

"Is that good?" I ask.

He winks. "Very good."

We dance for a little while, mostly in a comfortable silence interrupted by a few pieces of clever commentary from him. Again, it's the sort of romantic moment that I didn't really let myself imagine much past the age of fifteen. That was the year that the dream of happily ever after burst, and I realized that no one actually gets that kind of fairy talc. They just pretend they do.

Eventually he asks about my family.

"My mom works the front desk at the ER," I tell him. "Over in Cannon Beach."

"And your dad?"

I think for a moment. I don't freely offer up information about my dad very often, because I don't have much to share. He was a surfer, driving up and down the coast in a van full of guys. Honestly, Bennett's Grandpa Dean was more of a male parental figure in my life than my own father.

Now, I don't even have that. We had heard that Grandpa Dean passed away last summer. It was a private funeral, and Mom didn't feel comfortable reaching out beyond a condolences card, which meant I never got to say goodbye in any real way. All the grouchy old man cared about in his retirement were his beehives and following tennis. But when I went through my stage of being deathly scared of thunder and lightning, he would let me sit curled up behind him in his rocking chair while he watched the storm with Bennett. I felt safe without being left out.

God, we were a little Frankenstein of a family, but at least if Bennett's mistakes and lies hadn't led to our lives imploding, things would be how they used to be. Even if they were never perfect. And I would have had a chance to say goodbye to Grandpa Dean.

"I never knew him," I finally tell Tate, my gaze lost in a dark corner of the yard over his shoulder. "My dad died in a car accident a few years after I was born."

Tate gives my hand a gentle squeeze, and I glance up at him before laying my head against his chest. His fingers stroke up and down my back. "That fucking sucks," he says.

I hum and give a little shrug. "There's no missing what you never had."

"Well, if that's true, I think I'm going to be disappointed the next time I have to spend a Friday night doing anything but dancing with a pretty girl with a bizarre sense of humor."

I smile up at him to hide the flush of pink staining my cheeks.

We sway for a while longer until Tate spins me out again, and this time when he reels me back in, my back is to his chest, and this feels even more intimate than before.

He leans down so that his words tickle my ear when he says, "I think we have an audience."

When I look up, I see him glaring at me furiously from the other side of the firepit.

My husband.

CHAPTER 10

Clover

Bennett is sharing a small log with a beautiful girl with brown curly hair. She's even more stunning than the four that were sprawled across my bed just this afternoon.

The girl, the definition of lean and strong, is whispering in his ear, but he is watching me with unflinching concentration, his jaw working.

Tate's hands drop to my hips, and we're still swaying, but now his body curves to mine as he drops a soft kiss to my neck.

If I weren't so consumed by the angry bastard across from me, I might have taken a moment to enjoy the warmth of his lips and the fact that a guy this hot and funny and charming is coiled around me like a snake.

Dancing flames frame Bennett as he stands and says something brief to the girl beside him. His gaze narrows on me for a moment before he storms off around the side of the house.

I reach up and cup the back of Tate's neck to pull him down to me just in time for Bennett to glance back and see. I expect to find a hard, angry expression on his face, but what I see is harder to read. Hurt? Pain? That can't be right.

"I'll be right back," I whisper to Tate.

"Sure," he says. "Don't go disappearing on me, pixie."

Without Tate's body heat and the proximity to the fire, an immediate chill hits me. I grab my empty drink from where I left it beside Tate's and toss it in a recycling bin on the side of the house.

Now, I'm angry. He wants to stomp off with hurt feelings after I walked into our room this afternoon to find four girls hanging all over him *on our bed*? I don't think so.

In the front yard, Bennett is pacing up and down the sidewalk, and the moment I see him, I hate myself for following him out here. It reeks of desperation, and an old ache that I've worked so hard to bury begins to resurface.

I spin around to go back, take three steps toward the backyard, and then turn around again, reinvigorated with rage as I march toward him.

This is a ridiculous waste of time.

What am I even doing?

I double back again before throwing up my arms in frustrated indecision.

"I didn't mean to interrupt you." His voice drawls as he watches me with his arms crossed now, leaning up against a random car, seemingly amused that I am at war with myself.

"Where the hell do you get off stomping around and pouting like this?" I ask as I subconsciously move closer to him.

"I don't know," he says, like this interaction is the most boring thing he can imagine. "Maybe I thought you might have the decency to not grind all over a piece of shit like that while we're legally married."

"Need I remind you that you literally had four girls in our bed this afternoon?"

"Julian!" he snaps. "*Julian* brought four girls into our room."

"Well, you seemed pretty comfortable with them."

He claws his hands down his face, muffling a noise that is half groan, half growl. "You have great taste, by the way," he says. "Tate? That guy is basically a fucking predator." The second the word is out, his mouth snaps shut.

"A *predator*, really? You mean someone who takes advantage of another person in a vulnerable state? Hmm, that sounds so familiar."

Bennett pushes himself off the car and comes to meet me so that I'm toe-to-toe with him and am forced to tilt my head back to see him. "That is not the same fucking thing and you know it," he says. "Forget about the fact that guy is trash. You want to blow up this whole little married act? Go ahead. See if I give a fuck. This was all your doing. You think Wexley is going to punish me? You think they want to risk losing a private donor like my mother on top of the corporate dollars she funnels into this place? Besides, I'm not the one taking advantage of this situation. You are! So maybe you should think about that next time you want to let a guy like Tate hang all over you for everyone to witness."

A feverish heat spreads through my core as his focus darts from my eyes to my lips, his frame hulking over mine. I want to bite him. I want him to get close enough for a kiss and then I want to sink my teeth into his lip until he bleeds. I want him to hurt.

His hand comes up to my face, inches from my cheek, and I refuse to pull away. This thing between us is a game of chicken and I will not be the one to flinch right now. He's been so brazen with me in public, but when it's just us—I refuse to be the one to move first.

"Clover?"

I stumble back a little and see that Tate is just a few feet away.

"Everything okay here?" he asks, and holds a hand out for me like a lifeline as he lifts his chin toward Bennett.

"Tate," mutters Bennett.

"Good to see you, man," he says, and it is quite clear that *good* is the last thing he means. "I was about to head out if I can give you a ride, Clo."

"Her name is Clover," Bennett bites back.

"Clo is fine coming from friends." I take a step back from Bennett without breaking eye contact. The adrenaline slowly leaves my body as I wrap my arms around my middle and pull Tate's jacket tighter. "That would be great. Let me check on my friend inside."

Against my better judgment, I leave the two of them outside while I head in to hunt down Daisy, who is cuddled up on a sofa with her hockey player.

She moves to stand up, but I wave her back as I lean down and yell in her ear over the music. "I'm going to head out, but only if you're okay."

"I'm fine," she says. "Text me when you get back?"

"Of course," I tell her. "Have fun."

As I'm walking back outside, my body collides with another, and Bennett is gripping my shoulders. "Where's your friend? Who'd you come with? Daisy? Briar?" he asks.

"Daisy. She's fine," I tell him. "She's staying. I'm leaving."

He shakes his head vehemently. "No. No way. You cannot go with him alone."

"I'm a big girl," I tell him. "But thank you for your sudden concern."

"I know you think I'm a monster, but that guy is a pig, okay? He isn't safe."

I can't stop from rolling my eyes. "Do you ever wonder how many people warn their friends to stay away from you?"

Bennett flinches, but I'm not done.

"Safe or not, he's more than a coward who plays people like a fucking piano."

He shakes his head slightly, still holding my shoulders, chest heaving. I can see the words piling up on his tongue. The pulse in his throat is thrumming. He is so close to me that I can see the flecks of green in his blue eyes and I dare him to try to explain himself. To come up with an excuse for the damage he caused me. For how he broke me when I still believed in good things.

Stupidly, I glance down to his lips and I'm left wondering what would have happened just a moment ago if Tate hadn't interrupted us. An inexplicable, irrational part of me wants to trace the bottom curve of his lip.

However, the miracle of common sense forces me to look back up into his eyes and see the absolute torment there. I am so angry at him for daring to be the wounded one in this scenario.

Bennett remains silent as I push past him and out the front door. I don't bother to apologize when my shoulder collides with his arm.

Tate is waiting for me. "Everything okay with you guys?"

"Just an old family friend," I tell him. "Proving over and over again that he hasn't changed."

"Yeah, I know Bennett. We've run in the same circles before. Thinks he's the center of the universe and that every other person is basically an NPC."

"That's exactly it."

He walks me to his car with an arm around my shoulder.

"You want to grab a late dinner?" he asks once he's behind the wheel of his Range Rover.

"Is it okay if you just take me back to the dorm?" I wait for the moment when he will do something to prove Bennett right, but it never comes. And I'm not surprised.

"Of course," he tells me, and then flicks my seat heater on for me. "Let's get you back to campus."

We drive back and he pulls up as close to the dorms as he can get. "I can walk you up," he says as he reaches for his seat belt.

"Oh, I'm fine, but thank you. Here." I start to take off his fleece.

"Keep it," Tate says. "I don't want you to get cold walking inside."

"Thanks," I tell him. "For the fleece and for a nice time."

"Of course. See you on Monday, Clo."

When I go inside, Briar's door is open and she has a line of at least nine people and a tip jar full of singles. I let her know that Daisy is safe and with her hockey player and she gives me a nod while accepting a digital payment on her phone.

Our room is dark and empty as I change into my sleep shorts and T-shirt.

I curl up under the blankets with the fleece on. Despite my absolute exhaustion, sleep is impossible. Old memories that suddenly feel as fresh as yesterday play on a loop in my head.

When the door finally opens, I stay as still as possible while Bennett undresses and gets into bed.

It's only when the room goes quiet that my growling stomach gives me away. Normally, I would apologize, but not tonight.

He gets up and leaves the room, and I sit up, wondering if I should follow him. Was my stomach that offensive? Is he going to sleep on a couch in the common room? God, that's not really going to send the message of happily married, is it?

As I'm still debating what the hell I should do, the door swings open again. Lit in moonlight, Bennett is shirtless, wearing only a pair of joggers and carrying two paper plates.

He turns on the small reading lamp next to his bed and hands me a grilled cheese with an iron imprinted on the bread.

"They're not bad," he says. "I bought one from her last week. I think she uses a garlic mayonnaise."

As I glance down at my plate, I decide that I'm not too proud to call a temporary truce in the name of grilled cheese.

He's right about them being good. Or maybe I'm that hungry. The cheese is the perfect degree of molten and the bread is crisp on the outside and soft on the inside.

After we're both finished, Bennett turns off his light and I slide back down in bed, curled up on my side with my back to him.

I wish I had some kind of white noise app, because the only sound there is to concentrate on is the pattern of his breathing.

"I'm not going to see anyone else this semester. And I haven't been, just so you know," he says into the darkness. "It's too risky and . . . it's too complicated."

Our bed feels so cold in comparison to the warmth of Tate's body and the fire earlier tonight. It's been so long since I let myself open up to someone. It seems unfair that once it finally happens, it's simply not the right time. "Okay," I tell him. "Tate is just a friend."

"Not what it looked like tonight," he spits back, and then adds, "Sorry. I, um, I know this afternoon wasn't a good look either."

"Yeah." It's one word, and right now it's all I'm willing to give him.

"Vanya is just a friend," he says. "The girl you saw me with tonight."

"Oh, really? Not what it looked like," I say, parroting his words back to him.

"Well, she wasn't always, but she is now. And we were never anything serious anyway."

"Okay." I don't give him anything else because I'm scared he'll hear the relief in my voice.

I force my eyes to close and come up with a word. And then I think of a word that starts with the last letter of the first word. I do it again and again. It's an attempt to tire my brain out, and by the fifth word it's starting to work. Sleep skirts the edges of my mind and laps over me like a wave.

"You should come out to see Grandpa Dean's hives sometime," Bennett says. At least I think he does. "Vance, the groundskeeper, helps me keep them going."

Vaguely, I hear myself make some sort of affirmative sound.

Then as I'm in the fragile space between awake and asleep—between dreams and reality—I hear four words that could very well be my imagination.

"I was jealous tonight."

CHAPTER 11

Bennett

Grilled cheese turns out to be the truest mender of fences. Well, as much as the fence between Clover and me can be mended.

The next few weeks are . . . polite. I go home for my birthday. Tex and Julian join me and my mom for dinner at the Cannon Beach Country Club. Tex helps me winterize Grandpa Dean's beehives in advance of a cold front. I go into Portland with my mom twice and she casually floats the idea of me moving into the penthouse after graduation to take a more hands-on role at the company. I say sure, because I have no useful skills other than being the only full-blood Graves heir to take over the operation.

There's Julian, whose mother is my mom's stepsister, but she's happy to take her monthly draw and spend her time microdosing psychedelics and handcrafting soaps and candles that are sold (but barely sell) in seaside boutiques at an astronomical price. And it appears Julian will be following in her footsteps—at least in spirit.

The peaceful balance Clover and I have maintained at the dorm is nice, but I think I'm starting to miss Clover being angry with me, which is probably not what my therapist from high school would refer to as emotionally healthy.

It's all fine. Everything is fine. She goes to her classes. I go to mine. She works at the library and then other times she comes home in her catering uniform smelling like cocktail sauce. It says more about me than her, I know, but I hate that she's working. And not just one, but two jobs. I hate that she has to work so hard to scrape by.

I find myself doing little things that mean nothing, really, and are probably the result of sheer boredom since I'm not attending parties or chasing tail like I did last year. I replenish her granola bars without her noticing. When I see that her phone charger is fraying, I swap it out for an identical one. The melatonin gummies she takes at night run low, so I buy another bottle and refill hers, because the label is peeling on her bottle and she would notice if the whole thing was brand new. They are small, cowardly acts of kindness that I do to assuage my guilt over a history that will never change.

A history that started when Clover and I were still in diapers.

The story goes that soon after my father moved out, Mom was at the grocery store by herself with me and I was screaming my head off. She was looking for baby food. I was the pickiest eater, but carrot puree was always a sure bet.

She says everyone who came down the aisle looked at her like she was the world's worst mother.

And then came Beth with long blond hair and rosy cheeks, a giggling Clover strapped to her chest. She stopped in front of me and held Clover's chubby hand up to wave at me, and the tears just . . . stopped.

Our sleep-deprived mothers became fast friends and when Mom learned how little money Beth made cleaning rooms at the Cliffside

Inn, she asked her to move into the guesthouse and hired her as a live-in assistant.

Beth managed to navigate the line between employee and best friend, and my mother would always say they were platonic soulmates and that they could never go back to life without each other.

Clover and I were inseparable from that day in the baby aisle until she was ten and I was twelve. Mom insisted that Clover and I go to the same schools. She argued that it was easier, especially when she was on business trips, and that Beth should consider it one of her employee benefits. We were practically family anyway.

Clover was in fifth grade at our elementary school, Bradford Academy, a smaller private school a few towns north. And I was going into sixth grade, which meant I would attend Calvin Prep, a hybrid boarding and day school for grades six through twelve. I still lived at home, but I was suddenly in a pool of peers whose parents had the kind of status that could compete with the Graves family name. Even at the age of twelve, it was very apparent that "friends" were simply future networking opportunities, and as the son of Sydney Graves, I was a hot commodity.

I found myself in a crowd of people that I didn't particularly like. They were cruel, but I quickly learned that the best way to protect yourself from getting bullied was to be a bully.

Over the course of that school year, I began to resent Clover for being a living reminder of all the ways I had changed. She knew too much about me. She knew that I sighed every time Beth gave me a hug and that I was secretly scared of bees but could never tell Grandpa Dean. She knew that I didn't like people to know who my mom was because what if that was the only reason they liked me? She knew too much.

When Clover started at Calvin Prep the following year, she

would try to talk to me about how I was acting different. How I was being a dick. It pained me, but I ignored her and so did my friends.

Sometimes I would hear our mothers discussing the sudden divide between us late at night while they shared a bottle of wine. They chalked it up to puberty. Beth was always saying not to push anything between us and that this was normal. Forcing us together would make it worse.

After a few months, Clover stopped trying. Over the next few years, she would make the occasional friend—usually a kid who stayed for a couple months before changing schools.

I wouldn't have admitted it at the time, but I lived for summer. Because it was a reprieve. Things bounced back a little, like a rubber band returning to its shape. Our moms would take us on trips. We were never the same Clover and Bennett, but there was always a ceasefire and sometimes things even felt normal.

Sometime around when Clover started ninth grade, everyone at school found out that Beth was my mother's assistant. That word was all wrong for what she meant to us and how important—how integral—she and Clover were to our everyday lives. But Clover went from the quiet thicker girl to having a target on her back, because now they knew she wasn't one of us.

That April, Clover turned fifteen and was granted the keys to the social media castle by her mom. After school, she would speed through her homework and spend the evenings scrolling on her phone.

I was painfully jealous. All I wanted was to know what she was looking at. What meme or video had her laughing under her breath. But I had no right to know what made her smile on that little screen of hers.

One night, a few weeks before the end of the school year, one of my text threads with some of my friends—if you could call them that—started blowing up.

Val, a vicious girl who could stab you in the back with her eyes closed, sent out a link.

My stomach dropped the moment the page loaded.

It was Clover. A selfie in a patch of clover with the bigger house just behind her and a bee buzzing at the edge of the frame. The ground was fresh with rain, but the sun had just broken through the clouds and she was squinting into the light with a laughing smile on her lips. The caption simply said: home.

VAL

What a fucking fraud. I can't believe she's posting Bennett's house and trying to pass it off as hers.

She lives in that little pool house, right, Bennett? It's barely the size of an apartment. Honestly, she has no idea how lucky she is that your mom pays for her to go to CP.

The responses were immediate and furious. Not even because Clover had done anything so wrong, but because no one wanted Val to believe they thought she was anything other than right. And no one had the guts to cross her.

I eventually turned off the notifications on the thread as I scrolled and studied the handful of photos that Clover had posted. My thumb hovered, nearly liking a photo of her with a book open on top of her face. Beneath, the caption said: osmosis.

Then I remembered that I was Bennett, and she was Clover.

I started to imagine it was me who she was giggling over every time she looked at her phone. Over the next week, I brushed the thought aside, determined not to even entertain the idea. But I would fall asleep with my phone in my hand, wondering what it might be like if she and I could just start with a clean slate. What it might be like if I were someone else entirely.

It was six days before I gave in and created a fake profile. I had never done it before, but Val and her friends were always making secondary profiles for snooping on people who had blocked them or doing recon on crushes.

And that's how Josh happened. Josh went to Cannon Beach High School. He was going into eleventh grade. He liked sketching, because it was something I was okay at enough to do and post. He used to play basketball, but had quit last year to concentrate on art, because that felt like the kind of fantasy normal teens could have. He had a mutt named Lucy and two younger brothers. His parents were stupidly in love.

JOSH

hey

The message sat for a week before I got a response.

CLOVER

hi unless you're an old creep or a bot

JOSH

Ha. neither. You?

CLOVER

not that I'm aware of

that would be bizarre. To be a bot and not know it.

JOSH

or to be an old creep and not know it

CLOVER

JOSH

you live in CB?

CLOVER

that's a question an old creep would ask

but yeah. U?

JOSH

born and raised. How have I never seen you?

CLOVER

I go to private school

JOSH

the lowly public school kids are missing out on your company

CLOVER

Trust me. I'd rather attend any other school than the one I do.

We talked every day for hours and hours and well into the summer. We shared secrets and talked about big things that felt nebulous, like why the hell do we even exist and how are we supposed to know what we want to do with our lives.

I couldn't stop flirting simply because I finally could. I couldn't stop hinting at how beautiful she was and speculating about how she could possibly be single.

She asked for pictures, and I sent her some random guy I found online. He was good-looking enough but no one I felt threatened by. I was Josh in so many ways. I told her so many truths that it became easy to convince myself that this was just a white lie. It was just a name. And a picture. And a backstory. But I had a hard time with the idea of her falling for anyone who didn't look like the real me.

When she broached the topic of meeting, I told her I was gone for the summer and that my family rented our house out every year to out-of-towners.

She believed the lie . . . and so did I.

CHAPTER 12

Bennett

"Tex, you look dapper as hell," I tell him.

"And what about me?" Julian asks.

Tex kicks one cowboy boot–clad foot out. "The boots *do* give me an unfair advantage," he admits.

The three of us are huddled around a cocktail table in the Founders Hall on the first floor of Bellcliff. My mother had to cancel at the last minute and asked me to step in as her table's host for the alumni fundraising dinner. When I made grumbling noises in response, she sweetened the deal by telling me I could bring Julian and Tex. She did make it clear, however, that we were to be on our best behavior and that she needed me to woo an alumnus she had invited herself.

Lacey Rosen, a twenty-nine-year-old alum, had launched her own skincare line by the age of twenty-six that is now carried in major department stores across the world. And my mother is fascinated by her. Mom has been eager to get into the beauty business for a while now, but Lacey grew her company without investors and has been elusive in the past about being courted by the Graves Corporation.

I had already blown my mom off earlier this week when she tried to get me to sit in on a virtual board meeting. She bought the excuse that I was tired, but in actuality, Clover wanted to watch *The Wolf of Wall Street* so she would get all the references one of her professors kept making to it, but her laptop dies quickly and easily overheats. I bought a projector and screen, which I'd been planning to do anyway. We kept our distance as we lay on our stomachs and shared half a package of Twizzlers. She fell asleep for the last forty minutes, but she got the gist of it. (The gist being when Matthew McConaughey pounds his chest and does his grunting song.) I woke her up and she clumsily pulled her bra (dark blue) off through the arm holes of her dress and then went back to sleep. It was worth missing the meeting.

I spend the reception hour watching the door for Lacey Rosen while Tex and Julian make attempts at charming older men and women. They're both the kind of people who parents love, so they play well with this crowd.

Eventually, we're ushered into the Silent Six Alumni Parlor, which is only open to non-alumni once a year for this dinner and houses the six sculptures representing the six silent founders of Wexley. According to Wexley history, the school had thirteen founders. Twelve of them were shunned professors and philosophers who migrated west to reimagine education on their own terms. Six of the twelve were silent founders because they were such controversial outcasts in the world of academia. And the thirteenth founder was none other than Crumpets the goat, who was also the first dean on record.

(However, the drunken version of the story says the silent six wanted to remain anonymous because they thought the plans for the school that unfolded on the train journey west were an elaborate joke and were embarrassed to find that the other six were completely serious.)

The long, narrow room houses six sculptures to represent the silent six: a spiral shell, a closed eye, an open eye, a broken compass, a single lit candle, and an open book. The parlor exists so that Wexley alumni will always have a home on campus, and in the fall, it is a sort of speakeasy for a few hours before every home football game. As an undergrad—albeit a flaky one—I am willing to admit that seeing this place before I've graduated is stirring up a bit of school spirit.

Lacey appears just as the reception is ending, and I wonder if she sat in her car until the very last minute because she looks like she would rather be anywhere but here.

I intercept her and introduce myself. "My mother sends her apologies," I explain.

Lacey's hair is long and blond, skimming her waist, and her structured white strapless dress is subtly luxurious. I expect to be a punching bag for her comments about being stood up by my mother, but instead she only looks me up and down and tucks her arm through mine so that I can escort her.

"I should warn you: I'm a mediocre replacement for my mother."

"Are you going to make me talk business or can we just get drunk on free champagne?"

"No business," I promise her.

She pats my forearm. "Correct answer."

We find our table just off the side of the stage. Beside me Lacey is seated next to a senator and on my other side is an honest-to-god rocket scientist. I would catch their names were it not for the sudden scent of vanilla and amber as our server reaches over me to place a napkin on my lap.

The familiar ring on her left hand winks beneath the chandelier overhead, and my fingers are wrapping around Clover's wrist before I can stop myself.

The whole table is staring at me for manhandling our waitress, including Lacey, who was in the middle of a debate with Julian about a Mormon mom influencer they are both fascinated by.

Julian saves me from any further awkwardness. "Clover, what are you doing here?" he asks in that easy tension-slicing voice.

I turn and look up at her. She's in her uniform and her hair is pulled back into a smooth bun that doesn't suit her.

I haven't really seen much of her in the last forty-eight hours, but she looks drained. Her normally rosy cheeks are colorless and her under eyes carry deep-set purplish bags.

Julian is rambling about how Clover is one of our oldest friends, but I'm having a hard time looking away and stomaching the fact that she's supposed to be serving us tonight when she looks like she's about to fall asleep on her feet. Or honestly, that she's waiting on us at all.

"Are you okay?" I ask softly.

"Fine," she says, lips pressed into a thin line, before moving on and helping the senator with his napkin.

I am not at all coy about watching her, because I get a covert text from Tex telling me so. Beside me, Lacey clicks her tongue, and I can't blame her. She has officially dropped off the face of the earth as far as I'm concerned.

We make it through our second course when I notice the pitcher of water trembling in Clover's hand. A few moments later, she clears our plates and when she's halfway back to the service door, she trips on absolutely nothing and a few plates clatter to the floor. A vaguely familiar woman rushes over to help her and they're both gone before most people even have a chance to turn around and check out the commotion.

"I'll be right back," I say, interrupting Lacey saying something about supply chains.

I feel Tex and Julian watching me as I step through the swinging service door into utter pandemonium.

"On your left!" someone shouts, and I duck to avoid decapitation by a tray full of third-course salads.

I search frantically for her familiar blond hair, but the kitchen and staging area are packed with cooks in white and servers in black. I'm tugged by my bicep out of the action and down a linoleum hallway by the woman I recognized earlier, and it suddenly clicks.

"You were our witness," I say. "Marianne, right?"

She flashes a grin over her shoulder. "That would be me."

"I never forget a pretty face."

She laughs. "Oh, you're good. No wonder Miss Legs for Days out there was so smitten by you."

I start to protest, but my voice trails off when she leads me into a small women's bathroom where Clover is sitting on the floor, propped up against the wall, head in her hands.

"I'll be right out," she calls miserably.

"You have to take her home," Marianne tells me. "I told her to not even come in at all, but it will be a surprise to absolutely no one that she refused to listen."

"I can't afford to miss any shifts," she whines, still not having looked up to see me here. "How is it possible to be sweaty *and* freezing at the same time?"

Marianne gives me a conspiratorial look and motions for me to take over.

"Clo," I say as I drop down into a squat in front of her. "You don't look great, kiddo."

She groans and lifts her head before rolling it back against the wall. "What are you doing here? I'm not a kiddo. Go back to your fancy dinner with all those really hot, smart people."

"They weren't all smart," I tell her.

She nods. "You're right. Julian was there."

The corner of my mouth quirks up. "Come on. We're going back to the dorm." I'm already building the excuse I'll have to sell my mom, especially because I'm starting to think she missed the dinner on purpose in the hopes that Lacey would take to me.

"But—"

"But you won't have a job if you puke all over your table."

"Joke's on you," she says. "I haven't been able to keep anything down since last night. I have nothing left to puke."

Marianne laughs. "The girl loves to have the last word."

"I'm very aware," I tell her.

We both help her stand, and I walk her outside and thank Marianne for her help.

"Text me," she calls after us. "I'll cover your tables."

"I hate you," Clover moans in return. "Thank you for momming me."

Marianne smiles before heading back in.

"I'm gonna sit you down on this bench while I grab the car, okay?"

She slumps down on the engraved concrete slab and wraps her arms around her waist.

"Hot or cold?" I ask.

"Both," she huffs.

I shuck off my jacket and lay it next to her. "In case you need it."

The fact that she doesn't fight me tells me she's sicker than she's letting on.

CHAPTER 13

Bennett

The lot I parked in isn't far, but is too far for Clover in this state. A few minutes later and I'm pulling up to find a *Weekend at Bernie's* situation with Clover slumped over and my jacket pulled to her chin.

"Up you go," I tell her as I wrap her arms around my neck. My Highlander is a little too tall for her, so I help her in by her waist and buckle her in.

My hands linger for a moment on her, because something in my brain just quiets when I touch her.

I park in the fire lane and walk her inside. I try to give her space at first, because I don't want her to think I'm taking advantage of the situation, but I stay close behind her and we eventually make it to our room.

She kicks her shoes off and tumbles into bed without removing her uniform. When I come around to see if I can convince her to get a little more comfortable, her eyes are closed, framed by furrowed brows, and her lips are curved into an exaggerated frown. She looks like a grumpy old man. Adorably so.

"What?" she demands after I let a laugh slip.

"You just—you look so angry when you sleep. You always have."

She huffs and pulls the blankets up even farther. "Don't make fun of me."

"Not making fun, I promise. Just glad to see some things haven't changed."

"My mom says I'm going to give myself premature wrinkles."

I perch on the edge of her bed so that she's curled around me, and I pull the blanket back a little. "Let's at least get this bow tie off," I tell her.

With her eyes closed, she makes a half-hearted attempt at unhooking the bow tie, but her fingers still a few times as she falls asleep before stirring slightly and trying again.

There's this ferocious urge inside me to take care of her. Suddenly, Munchausen by proxy makes just a tiny bit of sense, because I like that she needs me right now.

I am a broken piece of shit.

"Let me." Gently, I push her hand away and she tilts her chin up to give me access. I unclip the hook and pull the cheap bow tie free, undoing the first two buttons of her shirt while I'm at it.

She starts in on the buttons of her vest, but I take over for her, careful not to touch anything I shouldn't and trying so damn hard not to imagine what she's wearing underneath and if it's a matching set. By the time I'm done, I have only accidentally grazed her breast once and she's fast asleep. I figure that I'll leave her be for a little while before I try to convince her to put on some pajamas.

After turning off all the lights except for my small reading lamp, I go across the hall and give Daisy and Briar's door a knock.

Briar opens the door a moment later, her eyes wide and frantic. She's wearing an apron with iron-on letters across the chest that spell out SAY CHEESE.

"Nice," I tell her, and point to the apron.

"I've been working on branding," she says with a dry smirk.

"Ah. You guys have a thermometer? Clover is pretty sick."

She turns around and sifts through a few drawers on her side and then Daisy's side. "I wouldn't be surprised if Daisy has, like, some sort of aesthetically pleasing first aid kit around here somewhere, but she's out with her hockey player right now. Let me run down the hall and poke the bear to see if he has one."

"The bear?"

"Our crabby-ass RA."

"No offense," I say. "But crabby seems to be your vibe."

"I prefer a good chaos puppy. Creates a healthy balance." She tosses her apron on to her bed and makes her way down the hall. "I'm pretty sure Dylan's only kink is following rules."

I can't decide if it would be a good or bad idea to put Briar and Julian in the same room.

When I go back to check on Clover, she's turned toward my side of the bed, sleeping fitfully with that same frown and furrowed brow.

After unknotting my own bow tie, I sit down beside her and smooth my thumb over her worried brows. Her forehead is warm to the touch, and Briar returns just in time with the thermometer.

"Thanks for poking the bear," I tell her.

"He was singing 'Build Me Up Buttercup' to himself when I knocked, so I'm sure it's a very busy night for him." Briar takes a quick glance at the Clover-shaped lump on the bed. "Let me know if you need anything else."

"Thanks," I say. "That's nice of you."

"I know," she snarls at me. "Please don't tell anyone."

I hold a hand over my heart. "I would never." Quietly, I return to our room. "Okay, sweet girl," I say, and Clover's frown deepens.

I smooth her hair back. I shouldn't touch her so freely, but it feels wrong not to comfort her in some way. It just so happens that it comforts me in return.

The summer she was nine and I was ten, our moms sent us off to camp for a week. I use the word *camp* loosely because this place catered to the wealthy. The dorms were more like luxury log cabins and the activities ranged from equestrian sports to sailing to fencing. Clover was incredibly homesick and hated being separated from me in the girls' dorm. One afternoon, she was stung by a swarm of bees. She wasn't allergic, but it was painful. She had one sting on her lip and a few on her arms and legs.

I snuck into the girls' dorm during afternoon activities with popsicles and a few *Goosebumps* books I'd found at the lending library next to the cafeteria. We ate the popsicles, melted syrup running down our wrists, while I read her *Night of the Living Dummy*. She fell asleep somewhere around the third chapter and turned on her side toward me with her arm draped over my lap. I stayed there all afternoon tracing patterns up and down her skin, careful to not disturb the angry welts.

That wasn't the first time or the last time that I sat with Clover while she wasn't feeling well or was upset. So, this current situation is nothing new. Touching her like this feels so normal. Nothing like the frenzied show we put on in public, but also more deliberate than when I wake up with my arm wrapped around her.

"Clo," I whisper. "I need to get your temperature."

She moans in response but lifts her head to me. It's like the moment someone gave her permission to give in to her body and let herself be sick, her will crumbled.

With my thumb, I pull down on her lower lip and slide the thermometer inside. "Lift your tongue for me." She does so and I wait for the beep.

The digital numbers light up and read 102 degrees.

"I'm fine," she says, and pulls the blanket over her mouth so I can't check her again.

"Clo, I think you should let me take you to an urgent care clinic. That's pretty high."

She shakes her head and then flings the blankets off. "It's so hot."

Then, before I can stop her, she's unbuttoned her pants and is shimmying them down her hips.

I'm ashamed to say I take an inventory of the little black boy shorts she's wearing underneath and the way her adorable tummy curves at the waistline.

She kicks her feet, knotting the pants around her ankles, and huffs. "Off," she moans.

"Okay, okay," I tell her, and help untwist the pants before draping them over her desk chair. I dig around in my desk for any kind of medicine and come up with a small travel bottle of Tylenol. After giving her two and encouraging her to drink as much water as she can handle, I say, "I'm going to check your temperature again in thirty minutes and if it's still this high, we're going to urgent care."

"I can go to the student health center tomorrow," she mumbles. "But no urgent care. It's too expensive."

Fuck. I hadn't even thought of that. Or honestly even realized that they were expensive, but it doesn't matter. "Don't worry about how much it costs."

"No. No way."

I don't fight her, because it's not like she could stop me.

"Get some rest," I tell her as I set a timer for thirty minutes.

I scroll through a few texts from the guys after I didn't return to our table.

JULIAN

Uh, were you abducted?

Sweetie. Your father and I just want to know you're safe.

TEX

seriously tho where did you go? This chick is asking for you.

JULIAN

This definitely has to do with Clover.

Please say you're not texting back because you're reaping those marital benefits.

You owe me, btw. The level of bland small talk I was subjected to likely caused a brain tumor. The minute you left Lacey decided that you were the only interesting person at this thing and she's been watching herself in the reverse camera of her phone for 30 min

Tex went home with a 34 year old mommy

TEX

Lindsay is not a mother.

JULIAN

A mommy is different from a mother

TEX

We're just laying in bed talking

JULIAN

is talking code for something else?

Tex?

!!!!!!!!!!!

Sorry for disappearing, I type. The time stamp on the last message was twenty minutes ago.

BENNETT

Clover wasn't feeling well

JULIAN

It's fine. Except they had a 2 drink max at dinner. Do you know how many people asked me what I was majoring in?

BENNETT

Do YOU even know what you're majoring in?

JULIAN

I just declared my major actually. Early childhood ed

BENNETT

Wasn't that girl you were talking to last Friday doing a teaching practicum at the elementary school?

JULIAN

I was inspired.

TEX

Inspired by the two days he spent with his head between her legs.

JULIAN

As the only living queer person in the Graves family tree, it's my duty to uphold the stereotype of slutty bisexual.

BENNETT

Heavy is the head that wears the crown.

J, I might need you to run to a pharmacy for me

JULIAN

At your service. I'm already in bed wearing my overnight collagen mask, so please know that it will be a sacrifice

BENNETT

noted

CHAPTER 14

Clover

"Open up," Bennett says two minutes after he last took my temperature.

"You just did this." My throat is sandpaper.

"Actually, it was forty-five minutes ago. I gave you an extra fifteen minutes."

I open my mouth and hold the thermometer between my lips. "Do you want a prize for that?" My eyes are still closed and my words are a garbled mess.

"Still at a hundred and two and still a smart ass."

He keeps talking about doctors and spending money however he pleases, but I'm drifting back to sleep and I think I use his sleeve to wipe a bit of sweat from my forehead. But that can't be true. That would be mortifying and disgusting.

The next time I hear anything is Bennett on the phone with someone.

"I'm calling on behalf of my wife." There's a firm, nonnegotiable quality to his voice.

My wife. That sounds . . . nice. It's nice to belong to someone.

"Still at a hundred and two," he says. "No, no nausea currently. But she did say she hasn't been able to keep food down."

I shush him. I want it to be quiet again and I'm cold and my hands are grabbing for blankets they can't find. Then I'm enveloped in warmth, and I huddle my head underneath so that his words become more muffled.

The last thing I hear him say is: "What should I do to break the fever if it goes up? And you'll do a house call if that doesn't work?"

That sounds expensive.

I reach for something warm and hug myself to it. Something cool presses to my forehead and even though I'm cold, my face feels warm.

Bennett's voice wakes me again, though he's trying to be quiet. "The prescription is under her name. Get some over-the-counter stuff too. I don't know. Just ask the pharmacist. Literally buy everything he tells you to. She really doesn't want to go—I know. She still feels warm."

"I need tampons," I croak and my voice is louder than I mean for it to be. It's a sudden thought that I can't stop myself from saying. I don't need them now, but I will in a few days.

"Is there a certain kind, Clo?"

I picture the logo on the box in my head and that feels good enough.

Light washes over me as the door opens and closes. There are two voices and some bickering. I open my eyes and begin to sit up. "I'm thirsty."

Bennett and Julian turn around and look surprised to see me alert.

I slump back against the pillows and accidentally hit my head on the wooden headboard. "Fuck," I moan.

Bennett is there, gently lifting my head and putting another pillow behind me. "Good girl," he says. "I need you to take one of these before you fall back asleep."

I nod as he turns the cap on an orange pill bottle. "I can't have amoxicillin," I tell him.

"I know," he says in a soothing voice that feels like a pat on the head. "Our moms made us memorize each other's allergies before we went on that trip with my dad to Ontario, remember?"

I do, vaguely. They didn't trust his dad to know the important details, I think.

The pill takes two tries to swallow because my throat is so dry, but once it's down, the water feels so good. I gulp until there's nothing left.

"Eat a cracker for me," he says. "It's the buttery ones you like."

He laughs softly and I think I'm frowning again.

"What are we supposed to do with all this shit?" he asks.

"You told me to be thorough." I think it's Julian.

"That bitch loves shopping," I mumble.

The next time I wake up, I am dizzy and hot and everything feels too close and too much.

I sit up and manage to swing my legs over the edge of the bed.

"Clo?" Bennett asks somewhere behind me, but now *he's* the sleepy one.

"I'm going to take a shower," I announce.

I use the wall facing my side of the bed to stand up, but my legs feel a little like jelly.

The room is suddenly brighter.

"Not the big light," I tell him as I squint against the harshness of the overhead light.

He's at my side with an arm around my waist. "Let's save the shower for when you're feeling a little better."

"I need it now. It's too hot." And it is. I want the feeling of a cold drink of water, but all over my body.

I move toward the door and use the bed to steady myself.

"So fucking stubborn," he mutters.

Some drawers open and close behind me.

The hallway is quiet and still until he runs up beside me with his arms full.

"You know you don't have pants on, right?" he asks.

"They were in the way."

The bathroom is gender neutral, so the showers are little stalls with doors instead of curtains.

Bennett leaves me to sit on a bench while he runs into the first free stall with some of my things.

He comes back out and helps me up. "I'll wait just out here."

I nod and close the door behind me. The shower is already going and I reach my fingers out to find that it's nice and cool but not freezing.

It takes some wrestling, but I'm out of my shirt a few moments later. The effort makes me dizzy and I step into the shower's spray with my underwear and bra still on. My legs are tired of being legs, so I let them take a break and plop myself onto the wet tile, taking down some bottles in the process.

Whatever. It's fine.

My head isn't even resting against the tile when the door cracks open.

"Are you okay?" His voice is nervous. "Did you fall?"

"I'm too tired," I tell him. "I just need to close my eyes for a minute."

"No. No way am I letting you fall asleep in the shower. Let's go back to the dorm."

"Will you wash my hair?" In a distant part of my brain, I know that I would normally rather sit here by myself for hours than ask him for help, but I don't have it in me to be embarrassed for my future self. I'm also imagining the feeling of my mother washing my hair when I was a little girl and her fingers working into my scalp. I think it's the only thing that will fix me right now.

At first, I don't think he heard me, but then he asks, "Are you sure you want me to come in there?"

The cold water feels so good, but my skin is still sticky from all the sweat. "Yes."

He enters carefully and I open my eyes all the way to see he's still in his suit pants and tux shirt, which I guess he fell asleep in. He strips out of his pants and shirt and steps right into the shower wearing a white undershirt and black boxer briefs. "Do you want to sit down or stand up?"

"You're going to get wet."

"That's typically what happens in showers."

"And boning," I tell him. "I hear people boning in here all the time."

He grunts out a laugh. "Up or down?"

"Down."

"Okay," he says. "Let's scoot you closer to the spray."

He helps me slide forward, and then he sits behind me and my body happily sinks against him.

"You make a really good armchair," I tell him. "I know you don't have to work because you're rich, but you could be an armchair."

"Armchair for hire," he says.

A small wiggling thought in my brain is telling me that I shouldn't feel so cozy against him, but I'm tired and the water feels good and with him there, my body doesn't have to make any effort to support itself.

He leans back a little so the water isn't directly on me when he begins to massage shampoo into my hair and I let out a low moan.

"Bet you never thought you'd do something to get that sound out of me."

He scoffs and then guides me closer to the water, his hand shielding my eyes from the soap. "You have no idea what I'm capable of, Clover Rowan Walsh."

"Does that statement come with a warranty?" I ask. "Orgasm guaranteed or your money back."

"Satisfaction guaranteed." Behind me, he groans softly and his hips shift, like he's trying to create space, but there is nowhere else for him to go.

My head lolls and I smile. I think I could live with this. With someone bathing me every day.

There's something stiff at the base of my spine and I tilt my head farther back so I can see him. "You have an erection," I pronounce.

"I'm holding a pretty, barely clothed girl in the shower. I'm sorry." He sounds genuine and a little uneasy, his bravado having worn off.

"I'm flattered." Again, embarrassment is a problem for Future Clover.

The stall is infused with vanilla and amber the moment he opens my conditioner. "Only use a little bit on my ends," I tell him. "It's almost gone and I'm going to have to switch to the cheap stuff."

My ridiculously expensive conditioner is probably one of the things I miss most. I didn't even realize it was expensive because it was always just there and part of the household shopping list. For the last two years, Mom has splurged on it for Christmas, and I do my best to make it last, only using it every few showers and applying it sparingly when I do.

"It smells like you," he says.

"I've used it since I was in sixth grade, but now it's just a treat."

I relax into him and slip in and out of consciousness as he applies the conditioner and then rubs some body wash into my legs and arms before rinsing me off completely.

When the shower turns off, he helps me to stand and I lean my back into his chest. His shirt is soaked through completely, and I feel his nose in my hair.

"That felt so good," I tell him. "I could kiss you."

His laugh sounds uncomfortable this time as he rubs a fresh towel up and down my limbs and in my hair.

For a moment, he leaves me to stand on my own and spreads my clean clothes out.

"I'm going to turn around while you change," he says.

I shrug and immediately begin to unhook my bra.

He spins around so fast that he practically crashes into the wall.

I find my favorite sleep shorts, a Calvin Prep Fall Festival T-shirt, and fresh underwear waiting for me, so I toss my wet clothes on top of his discarded shirt and pants.

Bennett sits me on the bench outside while he gets changed, and when he comes out, he's carrying our laundry and wearing nothing but tux pants slung low on his hips.

In our room, he changes and I definitely do not accidentally open one eye to see his butt, because that would be creepy. (It has dimples like his cheeks. The ones on his face.)

He gives me another glass of water and sits behind me again so he can brush my hair. He even remembers my leave-in conditioner.

Just as I'm falling asleep, he feeds me the thermometer again, and this time when it beeps, I hear him make a satisfied sound.

"Thank you for taking care of me," I whisper.

"Thanks for letting me." One of his fingers brushes over my forehead.

Only because you have a cute butt, I think to myself.

I fall asleep and I dream of his arrogant laugh and a light kiss on the forehead. As far as dreams go, it's not too bad.

CHAPTER 15

Clover

I'm in and out of it for another three days. When Bennett isn't in class, he's in our room, watching movies with me and forcing me to eat and stay hydrated.

On the fourth morning, I wake up clearheaded and feeling much less corpse-like. Beside my closet is a shrine of period products that I hadn't noticed before. Huh.

Bennett walks in carrying some shopping bags while I'm investigating a menstrual cup.

"What is all this?" I ask as he sets the bags on the bed. He's wearing dark jeans and a blue Oxford shirt with enough buttons undone to be considered slutty. His scar and the divot in his chest are visible and I quickly avert my gaze back to the feminine-hygiene-product drive happening in our dorm room.

"You asked for tampons the other night."

"I did?" Oh, yes, I vaguely remember. "I did. But I just needed one box."

"Yeah, we weren't sure what exactly that meant. Like, one box per day or . . . ?"

"This is more than just tampons," I tell him.

"Julian panicked. So he just bought one of everything."

A smile flickered on my lips. "Right, well, we should put these out in the common room for whoever wants some and then donate the rest. And Bennett?"

"Yeah?"

"Out of curiosity, how many times a day do you think a person changes their tampon?"

His eyes bug out a little, and he is completely perplexed. "I don't know? Fourteen?"

I pat him on the shoulder and his eyes, full of warmth, follow the movement. "Not quite. What's in the bags?"

He shakes out the bags to reveal brand-new linen sheets in a soft dove gray, and a feather duvet plus four fluffy pillows. "We can keep the wall of pillows, of course," he says. "But I just figured the room looked a little out of place. And if you don't like it, we can—"

I stand up on tiptoe and use his shoulder to balance while I give him a light kiss on the cheek.

His whole body goes rigid, and I immediately step back.

"Sorry," I say. "I just wanted to thank you for taking care of me and now this."

A hand drifts to his cheek briefly and he nods. "I'm going to run to the gym, but I'll get these laundered so we can—"

"I know how to use a washing machine," I tell him. "It's the least I can do."

The apples of his cheeks have a pink tinge as he clears his throat and throws a few things in a bag. "I'll see you later, then. Glad to see you're feeling better." He lingers in the doorway for a moment with an air of regret.

"Have fun at the gym."

"Just doing what I can to maintain this cute butt," he says with a smirk.

He's gone before I can offer up any kind of retort about how it's ungentlemanly of him to even bring up anything I said while I was deliriously ill, so I just hold my pillow to my face and let it swallow my muffled scream.

After I get the duvet and the sheets started in two different machines, I sit on top of a recently used dryer, which is a warm relief in the damp basement of Haystack Hall.

I answer a few texts from my mom and nibble on the corner of my pencil as I consider the roughed-out concepts I sketched for my pottery midterm. Even though Tate and I still make fun of the art majors in a good-hearted sort of way, I'm finding that I actually enjoy letting my brain shut off as I focus on the sole purpose of creating something out of nothing.

"Mind if I join you?"

When I glance up, Daisy is in the doorway with an overflowing basket of laundry, cheeks flushed and eyes puffy.

"Come on in," I tell her. "In fact, the dryer next to me is still warm if you want. If I close my eyes I can pretend that I'm in a really nice car with a seat heater."

She sighs and begins to throw things into the machine. "That's perfect. I'm on my period and if I could just numb my uterus with heat, that would be ideal."

"Preach, baby."

After she drops her coins in the machine and adds detergent, she hops up next to me. Daisy is taller than me, and her upper body is narrow with small, perky boobs. Her hips, though, are magnificent. I've been attracted to a few girls in the past, and Daisy's hips make me understand the phrase *biological imperative*, because I don't even have the right equipment and even *I* want to get her pregnant.

She sighs again, and this time it's a little more tortured, reminding me so much of when we were little and Bennett would pout, dragging his feet until someone finally asked him what was going on.

"Is something wrong?" I oblige her. "You seem a little upset."

As if on cue, she tosses her book to the side and swivels to face me. "My hockey player won't sleep with me until I agree to be his girlfriend." The words practically steamroll out of her.

"And that's a problem?" I don't know Daisy very well, but she screams relationship material.

"Uh, yes. A *huge* problem." She jumps down from the dryer and then shuts the door to the room. "I'm a virgin," she whispers. "Like in every way. I've done some hot making out, and I gave half a hand job once, but that's basically it."

"Only half?" It's not the point, obviously, but that's a story I want to hear.

She leans on the machine next to me with her head in her hands. "Yes! It was the hockey player, actually. His name is Aaron, by the way. Anyway, things were going great. I practiced over the summer with cooking oil on a cucumber. I didn't mean to, but I was just in the kitchen and then—whatever. I was in the middle of, you know, and—is it weird that I felt powerful when I was . . . holding it?" She pauses and I realize she's waiting for a response. "I mean, you're married, so obviously you're getting the most action out of anyone else on our floor."

"Oh! Right, yeah. I guess I hadn't thought of it that way."

"Stop me if this is TMI, but is Bennett, like"—she holds her hands up, creating different circumference sizes with her fingers.

"Um, it's not like a two-hand situation or anything, but yeah, he's . . . average, I guess." Except I have no fucking clue. The closest I have to a clue is the time his boner was poking into my ass after our first night here and then only vague memories of a boner when we—oh shit, I made him take a shower with me. I knew that happened, but this is the first time since waking up from my fugue state that I've actually let myself consider what a bad idea that was. No wonder he looked like he'd just made a horrible mistake earlier this morning.

"Okay, good to know. I just didn't know what to expect and anyway . . . Things are going great. And then I tell him, maybe this whole part could be a warm-up for the main event—you know, sex. And that I've never done that before."

"Right, right. That seems . . . normal. And he said no?"

"No! He said *be my girlfriend.* And I laughed. Well, it was more like a flirtatious giggle. And then he literally removed my hand and told me that he couldn't let me have sex for the first time if it wasn't with someone I cared about. He wanted it to be *special.*" She says the word like she's allergic to it. "I don't need it to be special. I just need it to be over!

"I guess I could have just said I would be his girlfriend and then broken up with him, but that felt wrong, so I just said we didn't want the same things and to call me if he changed his mind. Then—this might be the worst part. He patted me on the head, like I'm his little cousin or something, and said he knew I was a nice girl."

"Oof! A real knife to the gut."

"I know! Anyway, now I have to start all over again. You'd think it wouldn't be this hard to just find a college guy to screw."

One of my washing machines beeps, and I scoot off the dryer to change it out. "Well, Daisy, I don't know you very well, but there is something . . . respectable about you. So maybe guys are picking up on that vibe."

Her lips turn into a devastating frown. "I know. I'm such an effing lady. Anyway, Briar told me that your darling hubby was in an absolute tizzy when you were sick. She heard him pacing up and down the hallway on a call with a doctor and said that he basically had an entire pharmacy delivered. That boy loves you something fierce."

"I'm pretty lucky," I say, but my voice is flat.

"Trouble in paradise?" She perks up a little and I can't blame her, because misery truly does love company.

"Oh, um . . ." God, I wish I had someone to talk to about this, but I'm also not sure about letting anyone in on our secret. "We just . . . we have a sort of past. I mean, of course we do. But this is something that happened between us a few years ago and it ended up causing a rift between us and our mothers. We were all very close. Like, vacations and holidays together."

"But he came back to you and swept you off your feet?" she asks wistfully.

"Yeah, sort of like that. And every time I think that maybe I'm over it, the whole ordeal feels like this big shadow I can't let go of."

"Wow. This is so *West Side Story*. Very Montagues and Capulets coded."

"You make it sound so romantic." God, if she only knew.

"Because it is!"

"Says the girl who just wants to have sex and get it over with."

She rolls her eyes. "This is different. This is *forever*. I'm not really an expert on healthy relationships, but you've both overcome so much to be together. All that's standing in the way now is your ability and willingness to forgive each other. One thing my dad says that is actually true is that forgiveness is a choice."

Daisy can pack a punch. My god. But there's something to what she's saying, isn't there? Forgiveness *is* a choice. And I've never even considered making the active choice to forgive Bennett. What might it be like if I just tried? "Goddamn, remind me not to ask for your advice unless I really need it."

She smiles. "I get it from my mom. Tough love with a soft touch."

We spend the next hour or so chattering back and forth while I tinker with my pottery sketchbook and she color-codes some notes. She lived in Vegas with her family. Her parents are divorced. She has a complicated relationship with her dad. When she orders ice cream, she asks for a cup of sprinkles on the side and dips every spoonful. I tell her about working at the diner and how essentially my only friend is a twenty-nine-year-old single mother. I also explain that we used to be more well-off in a sense and she divulges that her dad has Money with a capital M, and she should feel guilty about spending it because his job is rather unsavory, but she doesn't.

By the time all my stuff is dry, I find myself wishing that I had more laundry to do.

"Let's hang out sometime," Daisy says, and it occurs to me that I don't need laundry as an excuse to spend time with her.

"That'd be great. Though I don't think Briar is my biggest fan."

She snorts. "Briar is no one's biggest fan, but she's a softy deep down. And trust me, if she doesn't want to hang out, she won't bother keeping it a secret. Besides, she's an awful wing woman."

I give her a chivalrous bow. "I would happily be your wing woman again sometime."

CHAPTER 16

Bennett

I think I knew I was officially fucked the minute I decided to leave the alumni dinner to drive her home. That was the moment when this became too real for me.

And now I've had too much time to think over the last few days as I sat in bed with her. For the first half of the semester, I had somehow convinced myself that I agreed to marry her out of guilt and sometimes even out of spite. But the truth of it all has slowly risen to the surface.

When she asked to marry me, I was angry because it was everything I wanted except that it wasn't real. And now that I have her in my bed every morning and every night, I'm just desperate to soak this all in for as long as she will let me. So yeah, I'm fucked.

As I'm about to walk into the Osei Health and Fitness Center, my phone rings. I almost swipe out of the screen when I see it's my mom FaceTiming me.

I duck under the awning and out of the rain to answer.

"So, he answers his phone," she says. My mother is in a salon chair, her deep brown bob separated into foils. She's calling from her laptop; based on the way her eyes travel across the screen, she's currently reading something in a different window.

"Hey, sorry," I tell her. "I was under the weather and—"

"Yes, it must have come on quickly. Lacey said you seemed to be fine and then you just disappeared."

"Is that why you're calling?" I ask.

She sighs and her eyes focus on me. "No, actually, I was calling because Whitney said you declined her calendar invite to join me in New York this weekend."

"Yeah, I've got some studying to do." And I don't want to leave Clover for that long.

She eyes me wearily and sees straight through my bullshit.

"You know," she says, "taking over responsibilities little by little will be much easier than suddenly and all at once."

I give her a silent stare and she shakes her head, rolling her eyes. "I'm sure whatever debauchery you're planning on getting up to will be much more fun than a mother/son bonding trip."

"A bonding trip?" I laugh dryly. "Is that what you call business trips now?"

"Oh, Benny, you know there's always time for business and pleasure. We could see a show and go for steak and fries at that little French place you like and—" She stops herself when she sees that I'm unconvinced. "Okay, okay, I tried."

"I'll see you when you get back, though."

"I hear that Clover is at Wexley this year."

My spine stiffens at her mention. "Is she?"

She frowns slightly as her stylist tells her it's time to rinse. "I know you're off campus, but I just . . . I didn't want you to be caught off guard if you saw her—"

"I'm fine, Mom," I tell her, my throat bobbing with the truth. "But thanks."

After a quick goodbye, I walk inside and drop my gym bag off.

"There he is!" calls Julian as I head toward my friends. "I was starting to think you were going to no-show on us."

Tex hooks up the barbell on the rack above him and sits up, straddling a bench press. "He lives."

I leave my phone on the padded mat next to the rowing machine before setting the tension to my preference. "It was a busy week."

"Don't play coy with me, young man," Julian says as he drops down backward into the machine next to me and uses the front half as a backrest and the seat as a footrest.

"You rowing reverse cowgirl today?" I ask.

Julian's eyelids flutter as he relaxes. "You know I don't sweat unless under duress."

Tex takes up with the hand weights in front of us. "He's just here pretending to spot me so he can wear the new workout clothes he bought."

Julian motions to his purposefully tattered and cropped black hoodie and sweatpants. "It's Balenciaga." Tex mumbles something about consumerism, but Julian just smiles like he's being flirted with. "And that's not the only reason. I'm also looking for a muscle mommy or daddy to take me home and toss me around a little."

"Any luck?" I ask.

"No, but I've heard that the women's lacrosse team had a leak in their workout facility, so I'm hopeful that they'll end up here in the peasant gym. Did Clover throw herself at you for nursing her back to health?"

"That's not why I did it," I tell him, my tone defensive.

As he watches us in the mirror, Tex starts in on his bicep curls.

When we first met him last fall, the guy was borderline scrawny. Over the last year, though, Tex bulked up and he went from shy and awkward to strong and certain. "She feeling any better?"

"Yeah, she seems to be back to herself this morning."

Tex and Julian share a look in the mirror.

"What?" I'm not enjoying their whole silent-communication thing.

"You just seemed very worried for her is all," says Julian.

"Of course I was."

Tex nods slowly.

I pull the handle toward me with a grunt. "What are you two trying to say?"

Julian shrugs. "Well, based on our observations, you've been celibate since you two got married—"

"That's just being respectful."

"So, the marriage is fake, but the infidelity would be real?" Tex asks, getting right to the point.

I shrug because if I open my mouth, I'll say something ridiculous, like that our marriage is far from fake to me.

The two of them share another look and Tex gives a short nod.

"Our official diagnosis is that you have a crush on your wife," Julian informs me.

"You're down bad, son," Tex confirms.

My silence lasts for a minute too long, but it's all the confirmation they need, and fuck it, they're right.

Julian's eyes go wide. "You two aren't playing house anymore, are you? This ish is the real deal!"

I shake my head, but I know I've been caught. "I don't hate waking up to her every morning, okay? And she said I have a cute butt. But it doesn't matter. Even if she does want me, she could never forgive me. Every time we fight or every time she looks at someone else, I'll wonder if she's thinking about what a piece of shit I really am." I look to Tex, and then to Julian.

"I might have filled dear Tex in on the whole catfishing debacle," Julian tells me. "Sorry."

"No, I think I'd rather you did. Better than reliving it myself."

Tex drops his weights into the rack and turns around. "I know you're not that guy anymore, man, but damn, I can't blame her for holding on to that kind of damage."

I yank the rowing bar so hard the whole machine rattles. "Thanks." I definitely do not mean it.

"She might surprise you, though," he continues.

Not in my fucking dreams. Even if Clover could ever forgive me, I could never bring myself to accept. I don't deserve that. "Doubtful," I say. "We'll sign the divorce papers after finals. That'll give her enough time to get her housing situation figured out, and then she'll find some other guy who didn't totally fuck her over."

"I did see her walking out of the art building with Tate the other day," Julian says quietly, almost like he's admitting it against his will.

"Yeah, I saw her at a party with him earlier in the semester."

"Tate Farris?" Tex asks over his shoulder.

I nod. "I reacted . . . poorly."

His expression darkens and he curls his bicep with enough force that I wonder if he's picturing Tate's neck snapping in the crook of his elbow.

Last year, Tate lived down the hall from me and Julian. He slept in the dorms as a formality but spent most of his time at 1919 Hemphill, which is essentially a frat house for a fraternity that you can't just decide to join. The house is owned by the Carmichaels, an old Wexley family. They bought the place back in the sixties for their twins to live in while they were in school. The boys invited their closest, wealthiest friends to join them and the house immediately became iconic for its exclusive and oftentimes lewd parties.

As the first male Graves in my family to attend Wexley in decades, and with one of Tate's former stepfathers being a Carmichael, me, Julian, and sometimes Tex got into the habit of escaping there as well. It was a relief to be out of the dorms. There was plenty of alcohol, drugs, and willing sexual participants.

Tex and Julian stopped going after we heard a rumor about a scoreboard in the basement, which lists each of the residents with a number beside their name of how many first-years they've hooked up with. You had to be escorted down to the basement by a resident, which is why it was just a rumor. It didn't help that both Tex and Julian found Tate to be a dick.

I asked Tate about the scoreboard, but he swore it was nothing more than a story.

I was invited to move into the house for the following fall semester. I said yes, which triggered a huge fight between me and Julian.

I stopped sleeping in our dorm altogether and started crashing at 1919 Hemphill.

Then one night I walked in on something I wasn't supposed to see. But thank fuck I did.

She was a freshman and he was a junior. Nothing had happened yet from what I could tell, but she was so out of it that she couldn't even tell me her name. Why sleep with someone who is that comatose when you're in a house full of people who just want to get laid? You couldn't walk in a straight line without finding somewhere to put your dick.

I was furious with the guy in question and Tate, too, because he hardly seemed to care, but most of all, I was pissed at myself. I'd fucked up all over again.

I got the girl into my car and was able to get into her phone to call a few friends she'd recently texted.

I went back the next morning and snuck into the basement while everyone else was still asleep. As real as the bones in my body, there it was. The scoreboard. I got into it with Tate when he threatened to sue me for backing out of my rental agreement. I told him to fucking try.

Beside me, Julian crosses his arms, dropping all the sarcasm and playfulness. "You can't let him near Clover."

"I know. Trust me, I know." I've gotta change the subject before I throw a dumbbell through a window. It's not just the thought of her with Tate. It's the thought of her with *anyone*. I can still feel her body relaxing into me as I kneaded the shampoo into her scalp. The smell of that conditioner, too. Fuck, I've already bought six more bottles online, because I can't tolerate the thought of her running out. I would have never done anything with her in that moment, but being in the shower with her even while I was still clothed had me so painfully hard. Maybe I really am no different than shitbags like Tate.

Tex watches me in the reflection of the mirror with his jaw set. At least if I do something rash, I can count on these two to help me hide the body.

After a few more reps, I try to lighten the mood for my own sake. "Did you know girls only use a couple tampons a day?"

"No way." Julian shakes his head. "I for sure thought it was at least a box a day."

"They should be changed every four to six hours," Tex tells us with certainty. "To avoid toxic shock syndrome."

I duck down to wipe my forehead with the sleeve of my shirt. "That sounds like a garage band from Portland."

CHAPTER 17

WEXLEY

Bennett

Clover switches her shift at the library so we can attend the next Married Mixer. We missed the last two because I was with my mom and then Clover was sick.

"Have you gone to one of these Midnight Yells before?" she asks as we head to the meeting point. Sandra and Greta are strolling a few feet ahead of us, huddled together against the late-night chill. They'd both joked about being out past their bedtime.

"I've been a few times," I tell her. "One time when I was little, actually, I came to Midnight Yell the night before a game with my mom."

"Did you?" she asks through a shiver. "I wonder where me and my mom were."

"I don't know. It might have been when your mom was dating that mechanic."

"Oh my god," she says. "Your mom hated him. She used to call him a Mario Brother."

"It was the accent and the mustache," he says. "And yeah, I think she was just always a little scared that your mom might meet someone and move out."

"Such a Scorpio. It probably would've been doomed, but I used to wonder if they would just end up together one day. For some reason my mom still likes men." She glances at me. "No offense."

"None taken. We are scummy trolls."

When we walk up to the student union where the group is meeting, Clover reaches for my hand, her fingers leaving the warmth of her parka pocket. "Here," I say, and pull her hand into my fleece-lined pocket.

She moans. "So warm."

The group has grown significantly, so Miss Linch has everyone fill out name tags before we walk over to Rook Stadium.

Clover leans her head on my arm as Sandra and Greta come up beside us.

"All right," Greta says. "Bennett, you're an upperclassman. Is this just a late-night pep rally?"

"Sort of," I tell them. "The football team, cheerleading team, band, and the drill team—they all gather in front of the stadium at midnight before a home game. That part is like a pep rally, but it's also to practice the chants that will happen in the home stands for tomorrow's game."

"See, we did this all backward, honey," Sandra says to Greta like she's won some sort of argument. "No wonder we had no clue what the heck everyone was doing during the game last month."

Clover laughs softly and looks up at me, and my gut clenches at the reality that this will be over in less than two months and that we will never be middle-aged and bickering like Greta and Sandra.

"The best part," I tell them, my gaze intent on Clover, "is at the end of Midnight Yell when they turn all the lights off for a few seconds. You're supposed to kiss your date or hold up a lighter or a phone so that people without dates can shoot their shot with a stranger."

"That's so romantic," Sandra says. "I swear, some days being a student here makes me feel older than dirt." She pauses with a glance over to her wife. "But then I'm so thankful to have moments like these with my Greta because we weren't lucky like the two of you. We didn't find each other until much later on, did we?"

Greta drops a kiss on Sandra's forehead. "Better late than never."

Clover lays her head back against me and the contact sends a rush of relief through me.

The outside of the stadium is already full of students with chattering teeth. The ground is soft from the endless rain today, but the clouds have cleared enough for the moonlight to reflect off the high points of Clover's face: the tip of her nose, her cheekbones.

We stop at a hot chocolate stand, and I order a cup for each of us. She glances around as bodies begin to close in, swaying on the tips of her toes as she tries to find a gap in the crowd to see up ahead.

I tug her hand close and keep her tucked against my side as I navigate through the crowd.

"Excuse us, excuse us," she says over and over again.

"Here we go," I tell her as we reach a small stone half wall that breaks up the entrance to the stadium for crowd control, I assume.

"Where—"

I step in front of her, my hands on her waist, and begin to hoist her up.

"Bennett, what the fuck? You're going to hurt yourself."

I roll my eyes and she makes a puffy little *hmph* as I sit her down on the wall and step between her legs under the guise that it is noisy and we need to be close to hear each other.

"You can't lift me like that," she scolds me from above. "You're going to throw your back out or something. I'm too—"

I hold my pointer finger over her lips. "Don't do that," I tell her. "Don't tell me you're too big or I'm going to hurt myself. If I couldn't lift you up, I wouldn't. When have you ever known me to do something I didn't want to do?"

She wraps her fingers around my wrist and pulls my hand down, but doesn't let go.

My heart falters, and if my cardiologist heard the rhythm in his stethoscope, he'd probably send me in for an EKG.

"Our wedding?" she asks.

I shake my head. "Try again."

Her lips part on a protest, but the crowd swells as the cheerleading teams storm the temporary stage at the gates of the stadium.

So I turn around and lean against the wall with Clover at my back.

Her chest expels a sigh, her ribs meeting my spine, and then she drapes her arms over my shoulders, her cheek against my ear.

"Linch has eyes on us," she whispers, but I can't find the woman in the crowd.

"Best to play the part," I tell her.

The next forty-five minutes are an adrenaline shot of school spirit. We cheer for football players we've never heard of. There are spinning flags. The marching band lets loose, dropping their normal precision and uniformity.

When it's time to learn the yells, Clover whispers them back to herself rather than shouting along with everyone else. She stays draped over me and neither of us seems to feel as cold as we should.

It's one of the rare moments that I actually appreciate how many different life forms live on one campus and how, miraculously, there is room for us all. There is room for the cheerleader and the band nerd and the retired lesbian couple and the sardonic girl majoring in finance so that she can master the one thing that has always eluded her: money.

As Midnight Yell comes to an end, the starting quarterback, whose name is Brad or Brandon or Bryan or something, counts down to the blackout.

"Ten!"

Clover stays right where she is.

"Nine!"

Her breath is hot on my ear.

"Eight!"

Her heart is pounding at my back.

"Seven!"

Mine matches her pace.

"Six!"

I turn around.

"Five!"

Her watery blue eyes skip down to my lips and then back to meet my gaze.

"Four!"

My fingers skim along her jawline until I'm cradling her neck, my thumb smoothing circles over her cheekbone.

"Three!"

Her eyes flutter.

"Two!"

Her chins dips.

"One!"

We're cloaked in darkness for a split second before cell phone lights pop up sporadically.

Unlike at the bowling alley, it's me who leans in first. Her lips part, inviting me in, and my tongue tastes her mouth. I kiss her fully and take advantage of the moment.

A better person might keep it tame, but I don't know any other way to kiss Clover Walsh than the way I have dreamed of kissing her for years. Maybe since I was thirteen. Or honestly, much earlier than that.

It's so, so loud, but I think she moans into my mouth, and I have to press my groin into the wall to check myself before I'm walking around campus with a boner over a simple kiss.

My other arm coils around her waist, and I can feel the moment coming to a close, but I greedily soak up every second.

Her lips are soft and she tastes like chocolate and whipped cream.

The lights flicker back on and Clover's smile is glowing, her nose red, and white clouds of cold air mingle between us. "That was convincing, right?"

"Very," I tell her, my voice hoarse.

CHAPTER 18

Clover

The Beverly Cleary Archival Library is the most iconic building on campus. Outside of the shrine of a football field (for a very mediocre team), the gratuitous pictures of both the men's and women's rowing teams, and the Bellcliff building with its clock tower and observatory, the library is the star of every Wexley pamphlet and the home page of the university's website.

The carpets are a deep, rich red and each of the nine stories is open all the way to the glass dome roof at the center. On sunny days it showers the whole building in light, and on the rainy days it brings the moody Pacific Northwest weather inside without the threat of being cold and wet.

Each floor is bridged together with iron railings and dainty walkways that I find myself walking across while holding my breath. The building sits at the highest point on campus and the top floors stretch above the tree line, giving way to a view of the ocean on one side and mountains on the other.

I work three five-hour shifts every Monday, Wednesday, and Friday from eight o'clock in the evening until one in the morning.

On Monday night, my shift manager, a grad student named Rashid, sits me down in front of a computer for a training seminar about harassment in the workplace. It's dry but very straightforward, and only requires me to tap through each screen.

After I clock out, I make the trek back to my dorm and I suddenly hear someone rush up behind me. Before I have time to decide if I'm running or standing my ground, a heavy arm is slung over my shoulders.

The lamp lighting the path ahead casts a warm glow on Tate's cheeks as he beams down at me. "I thought that was you! What are you doing right now? Where are you going? I've hardly seen you outside of class."

I hold a hand over a tear-inducing yawn. "So many questions at once. I'm heading back to my dorm and yeah, I've been working a lot," I tell him after the yawn passes. *Also, I'm technically married and told my husband I wouldn't date anyone until we're divorced, even though you're hot and nice.*

"Come out with me. We've got some time before last call."

"Okay, first, I can't get into bars yet," I tell him. "And second, it's a Monday night. What are you doing on campus this late at night? You don't live here, do you?"

"No to living on campus, and I was studying in the library. I remembered you saying you worked the first half of the overnight shift, so I stuck around for a while and looked for you. Started to wonder if you were just trying to throw me off your scent until I saw you walking out the main doors."

Another yawn presses hard against my chest, and I partially swallow it back. "They had me doing a training tonight and I'm about to fall asleep on my feet."

"Well, at least let me walk you home."

He removes his arm from my shoulder and instead holds it out for me as he tucks my hand into the crook of his elbow. It feels wrong, especially when my brain does the inevitable and circles back to Midnight Yell with Bennett and how we spent the rainy weekend in bed watching movies in between studying sprints so I could cram for my financial-accounting test and finish my Intro to Professionalism essay. I only left once on Sunday morning to work a brunch and when I came back, Bennett was waiting for me right where I left him. The whole time I was gone, I felt restless with a pang in my chest. I need more space from him. Because every time I have some breathing room, I remember that he is only doing all this to absolve himself.

As we walk, Tate chatters about his friends, people I've never met who sound like they should probably hydrate more and have Breathalyzers in their cars.

"Clover Walsh, I guess I'll let you flake this time, but on Saturday night"—he fishes around in the front pocket of his jeans and hands me a small square card. "You're going to go to this address and show this."

"What is this for? Some kind of clandestine cult gathering?" I can't help but feel giddy. I have never been the girl who's invited places. "Can I bring friends to the cult meeting?" Not that I really have any just yet. Well, except Daisy. And maybe Briar, but the jury's out on that one.

"*Girl*friends," he says with a wink.

I roll my eyes. "You're a dog."

He flashes a crooked grin and hooks a finger under my chin, tilting my face up to his. "I make no apologies. Woof, woof."

My stomach swoops and I'm suddenly a little breathless. Under the weight of his attention, I simply nod.

On Thursday morning, just as I've mustered up the courage to knock at Briar and Daisy's room, the door swings open and Daisy jumps back, her hair wrapped around a silk foam curling rod and mouth tape shaped like lips firmly in place. "Mm-hmm!" She rolls her eyes and then peels back the tape. "Sorry, forgot about the tape. What I meant to say was: Oh hi!"

"Hi." I wave, and I can feel myself retreating already. She's been nice to me, and we sort of bonded the other week in the laundry room, but are we actually friends?

Behind her, a hand shoots up in the air from beneath a pile of blankets, one choice finger in the air.

"Hi, Briar."

"It's too early," Briar snaps back.

"Ignore her. She was up late making grilled cheese," Daisy says conspiratorially. "She doesn't bite."

Briar sits up in bed. Her long red hair is in a nest on the top of her head that is held together by a scrunchie and sheer will. "Just come in before Larissa gets any ideas."

Daisy pulls me in by the wrist and shuts the door behind me. "Larissa down at the end of the hall is obsessed with birth charts. After she did Briar's, she decided that they're cosmically linked or something."

Briar pulls a pillow over her head with a groan. "The only thing I want to link is my fist with her face."

"You're violent in the mornings," I tell her.

Daisy smiles and pats a papasan chair with a fur cushion for me to sit in. "Oh, that's an all-day thing." She opens a baby-blue mini fridge. "Can I offer you a cold-pressed juice? A jade roller?"

"Uh . . ."

"Say yes," Briar says as she emerges from the pillow. "I don't know what they put in that juice, but it's the nectar of heaven."

I nod, and Daisy presses a glass bottle into my open hand and a jade roller into my other.

"I was invited to a party," I tell them and then take a sip of the dark red juice, rolling the cool jade under my eyes. "Oh shit, that is great."

"Told you," Briar says as she holds her hand out for a juice of her own. "Turns out having a rich roommate is great."

"I'm not rich," Daisy clarifies. "Just comfortable."

Briar snorts. "Well, it takes a lot of money to be this comfortable."

Daisy smiles as she sits on her bed with her legs crossed. She wears matching silk pajamas with little chocolate-covered strawberries all over them. "You were saying something about a party?"

"Right. Yes!" I set my drink down on the dresser between their beds and pull the square card Tate gave me from the pocket of my sleep shorts. One side simply reads "1919 Hemphill" and the other has a QR code.

Daisy gasps. "You were invited to a party at 1919 Hemphill?"

Briar snatches the card out of my hand and immediately scans the code. "You have been invited to an exclusive party hosted by the residents of 1919 Hemphill," she reads. "If you've received this card, your cover charge has been waived. Party dress codes are strictly adhered to and this Saturday is an ABC party. Guests are required to wear *anything but clothes*."

Daisy turns to me with wide, pleading eyes. "We have to go!"

Okay, this is easier than I thought it would be. One girl down.

"This sounds like a breeding ground for date rape," Briar says.

"Point taken. Which is why I was hoping you would both come with me," I say. "Safety in numbers, right?"

"I thought it would at least be the spring semester before I got invited to a party at 1919 Hemphill," Daisy says.

"Dreams really do come true," I tell her. "I guess this is a big deal, then?"

Daisy nods like a possessed bobblehead. "A super rich family owns the place and guys live there by invitation only. And when I say rich, I mean, like, enough money to buy elections and own private planes."

Bennett definitely falls into that category of rich. God, I hope he's not going Saturday. Things between us have been too easy lately, and I need just one night to remind myself that there is life after this silly little marriage is dissolved. I need to remember that I will be okay.

Briar is unimpressed. "No can do. It's a Saturday night. I can't just close up shop."

Over the last few weeks, Briar's grilled cheese pop-up has become the thing of legends. She even has add-ons now like pickles, pesto, and jalapeños. The other night when I got home, I heard some girls walking down the hall, discussing a supposed secret menu. With the dining halls closing at ten and nonexistent food delivery options after midnight, Briar's business is booming, and Bennett has become one of her most loyal customers. (Which I have greatly benefited from.)

"Just one night," Daisy begs her roommate. "Aren't you a little bit curious?"

Briar is silent in response.

Daisy is quick to crumble. "Fine. You can extend your grilled cheese hours until three. But weekends only!"

Briar thinks on that for a minute. "Deal."

"The weekends are turning out to be in high demand," Daisy explains.

"And I can't make the sandwiches in the hall because running a business out of your dorm is frowned upon," Briar says nonchalantly.

"I wouldn't say *frowned upon*," Daisy says. "It's a blatant violation of the housing contract."

Briar pouts. "And our stick-up-his-ass RA has it in for me."

Daisy winces. "Maybe if you didn't call him that to his face . . ."

"I don't say things behind a person's back that I won't say to their face," Briar calmly explains. "And he started it when he made me get rid of my lava lamp. Fire hazard, my ass."

"I need to start crafting," Daisy says as she begins to furiously tap out a to-do list on her phone. "Oh! Is Bennett coming?"

I glance down at the ring on my finger. "Uh, no. I think I need a girls' night."

"Well, at least that's one less costume to make." Daisy chews on her lower lip, lost in thought. "Now, we just have to figure out a theme."

CHAPTER 19

Clover

Daisy chauffeurs us around in her cherry-red Mini Cooper Club. We end up going to three different stores to stock up on all the supplies we'll need.

We're all plus size in one way or another, which makes it easier to trust that Daisy won't do me dirty with whatever outfit she puts me in. I'm short, but full of curves—including some that aren't entirely even. Daisy is all ass with a nipped-in waist, while Briar is tall and soft like a Botticelli—a sharp contrast to her prickly personality.

We stop for burrito bowls at a local place called BOB (Bowl Only Burritos), and the girl behind the counter with pink hair practically pries the debit card from my fingers because I'm so averse to spending money on food when I have to pay for a campus meal plan regardless. However, she is so smitten with Briar that she gives us free chips and guac, so that does ease the pain of an eleven-dollar bowl of beans and rice. When she asks if I'd like a fountain drink, I ask for a cup of water and she gives me a soda cup anyway before winking at Briar.

"You should get her number," I tell Briar once we sit down.

"Not my type," she says.

"Oh, I'm sorry. I just—"

"No, no," she continues. "The girl is cute, but *no one* is my type right now. At least not for the next four years. In reality, *way* too many people are my type. That girl for instance is a big yes, but so are the two guys in the kitchen. I just . . . I'm constantly one step away from being the fourth corner in a polycule, and three significant others require a lot of emotional labor." She sighs and sets her fork down. "I only have four years to graduate and that's it. I'm on a timetable."

"It's doable," I tell her. "But what's with the strict timeline?"

"My grandparents. My dad is estranged, so I hardly know them, but they set aside a college fund for me that I could access if and only if I attended Wexley, their alma mater. I'm allotted four years of tuition because they're scandalized by the idea that a four-year degree could take longer than four years. It drove my dad batshit when their lawyer contacted us and he found out that there was all this money just sitting there—money that we could have really used and the only thing it's good for is my education."

"Sounds like a smart use of funds to me," I tell her.

"Concur," Daisy says as she politely shields her mouth as she's eating.

Briar sips on her cherry Coke. "Yeah, well, I was originally waitlisted, so I took last year off school and assumed I didn't have a shot in hell until I got the acceptance letter a week before move-in day. Anyway, Daisy's turn to jump in on this little sharing session."

"My dad is a pastor," she says shyly. "Just outside Vegas."

"No offense," I tell her. "I'm a scholarship kid myself, but isn't this place a little rich for a pastor's salary?"

Briar laughs. "Not if your dad is shelling the gospel like a used-car salesman on live TV every Sunday morning."

"Oh," I manage to say. *That* kind of pastor.

Daisy frowns.

"Can I please tell her the best part?" Briar pleads.

Daisy sighs, but nods.

"Daddy and Stepmommy have been led to believe that our sweet Daisy is attending Wexley's seminary school, but she's actually majoring in losing her virginity ASAP."

I smack Daisy on the arm. "Hell yeah, girl."

She grins down at her burrito bowl. "Thanks. They're going to be so pissed when they find out I didn't even apply to seminary school. My mom told me to, and I quote: Take their cursed money and run."

Briar nods solemnly. "Sound advice."

Daisy directs her attention to me. "What about you?"

"Nothing special here. Scholarship kid."

"How about the married-at-eighteen part?" she asks, her eyebrows waggling. "What's the story there?"

"Oh, that. Well, we just . . . we've known each other forever and . . ." God, I really should have thought of some sort of backstory for Bennett and me to agree on that doesn't involve a haunted house. "He asked after my senior prom," I say, looking for any details I can feed them, even if they're not true. Behind them is a poster of a churro. "He put the ring on a churro. And I said yes. He was always there when we were growing up, and I didn't want that to ever change." I make a mental note to fill Bennett in on the churro plot device in this version of our engagement story.

Daisy's lips tremble. "That's so sweet. If it's right, it's right. Why wait?"

"Oh, I don't know. Maybe because marriage is a sham," Briar says, but then relents. "But you two do make a pretty cute couple."

It turns out that Daisy is an artiste; foil is her canvas, and thanks to her dad's credit card, we have plenty of it.

"I'm concerned about the lack of pockets," Briar says as she sizes the three of us up in the narrow mirror hanging on the back of their dorm room door.

She throws back a glug of some absolutely vile cotton candy rum she scored off a guy a few floors down who ordered a grilled cheese last night before he realized he'd lost his wallet.

I take a little spin and eye myself from the back before taking a swig of the cotton-candy-flavored poison. My throat rebels against the awful decision, but I manage to keep it down. "I think our bras are the best we're going to do in terms of storage." We all mutually decided that underwear and bras are a must and if we aren't admitted because of that, then so be it. Going commando and sitting on surfaces at a college party feels like an invitation for things that I'd rather my vagina didn't come into contact with.

"We look like burritos," Briar says.

"I think what you mean is hot aliens," Daisy points out. "Or cheerleaders from the future."

She's not wrong. Daisy has crafted us skirts that even have a few pleats over our left thighs. We each have a different style crop top to accommodate our varying sizes of boobs. I'm in a bra top that has been molded to my actual balconette bra. Daisy is in a tube top, and Briar is in a sports bra–like top that is structurally sound enough that I'm starting to think Daisy could double major in fashion design *and* engineering if she really wanted to.

"Okay, I just need to grab the card to get us in and then we're ready to go," I say after we all pass around the bottle once more.

I dart across the hall to my room, immediately go over to my desk, and begin to dig through my purse for the essentials.

"Let me guess. An ABC party."

With a start, I drop my bag on the floor, the contents spilling everywhere. "What the hell?"

Bennett sits on the bed in black sweatpants and no shirt, his legs crossed and a thick textbook draped across his torso. I didn't even notice him. "Sorry, didn't mean to startle you." His voice is low and agitated, eyes roaming over my ridiculous outfit.

I attempt to squat down and pick up the contents of my purse, but I freeze upon hearing the sound of foil ripping. "Shit."

He tosses his book to the side and hops up. "Let me help."

I watch as he grabs my purse—a vintage Celine bag his mom gave me from her personal collection—and begins to grab my lip balm and tampons and—"Oh, I need that!"

He holds the card for the party between his fingers, clicking his tongue, and turns it over before pocketing it. "No, you don't."

"Ha, ha. Funny," I tell him. "Come on. Give it here." He ducks out of the way before I can reach into his pocket. "I'm going to a party tonight and I need that to get in."

"You are not going to a party at 1919 Hemphill," he says plainly.

I pause, confused and taken aback. "Don't be a dick. I gotta go. Briar and Daisy are waiting on me. I'll be back later. Maybe we can watch a movie."

He picks up the rest of my stuff and hands me my purse, sans card.

When he turns around to return to his book, I stomp my foot and reach for a paperback on my desk, launching it at the back of his head and missing by an embarrassing margin. "What the hell, Bennett?"

He practically growls in response and whirls around. "What the fuck?"

"Listen, living together has finally become manageable. Easy, even! And I'm thankful for that. But when, over the course of our long history together, have I ever led you to believe that you could tell me what I can and cannot do?"

It's like he's that smug high school boy all over again. "I guess this is me cashing in my one-time token, then, because you're not going to 1919 Hemphill. It's a bunch of pompous-ass rich boys and they treat every person who walks through their door like they're disposable."

"Oh, so you're jealous that you didn't make the pompous-ass cut? Is that it? Give me the card back, Bennett. Now."

"No." He crosses his arms, and I have to look away before I start thinking about what the veins that stretch across his biceps do to my brain. "I'm not about to let you become just another notch on their first-year body count scoreboard. Which is a real thing, by the way."

I can't help but roll my eyes at the absolute cliché of it all. Even if this little scoreboard is real, I'm not dumb enough to end up on it. "I'm pretty sure you forfeited your right to have an opinion about what college parties I choose to go to years ago. It doesn't even matter. I can just text my friend who gave it to me and get another one."

"Your friend, huh? Don't tell me you're talking about Tate. I wasn't kidding when I said that guy is not safe." I don't know what the deal is with him and Tate, but I'm not about to let him make me a chess piece in their little dispute.

I hold my lips tight for a moment, and then say, "You told me not to tell you. This is me not telling you."

He closes his eyes for a moment on a deep inhale and then exhales through his nose. "Will you at least share your location with me? Because that's the only way I'm about to give this card back to you."

The whine that leaves my mouth is the single brattiest noise I have ever heard in my life, but I need that card and it feels like an innocent enough ask. "Fine," I tell him as I unlock my phone and add him behind Mom and Marianne as the third person on the short list of people who can track my phone.

His phone pings in response and after accepting the request, he reaches into his pocket for the card. "Here. Just be careful, and for fuck's sake, keep your phone on you at all times."

Of course, he makes no effort to move or come closer, so I'm forced to walk around his side of the bed until we're only a breath apart.

I yank the card out of his hand with enough force to rip it, and he practically snarls at me, his gaze hungry as his eyes travel the length of my body.

I'm tempted to tell him that there is one way he could make me stay, but I'm worried I might actually mean it.

Before I flirt a little too close to the sun, I stomp out the door to where Daisy and Briar are waiting for me.

"Lovers' quarrel?" asks Briar.

"It's not anything that I'm going to let ruin my night."

Daisy squeals and claps her hands together. "To the slutty college party we go!"

CHAPTER 20

Clover

1919 Hemphill is a four-story Victorian just a few blocks away from campus near the center of town. Even if I didn't know where it was, I could find it simply by following the trail of shivering college students wearing anything but clothes.

"I thought *our* outfits were pretty scandalous," Daisy shouts as a few girls walk by dressed in bikinis made of McDonald's Happy Meal boxes. They're followed by girls wearing the Wexley seal as pasties and paper bags from the bookstore as miniskirts.

A small group of guys who are obviously trolling for something to do are walking toward us in the ultimate PNW bro uniform of khakis and Patagonia vests. They stare at us in confused silence.

"What are you looking at?" snaps Daisy.

Briar lets out a loud *meow* at Daisy's surprise sauciness.

"I'll tell you what you're looking at: three hot bitches who are invited to a very exclusive party. What do you see, Briar?" Daisy asks.

"Virgins who can't drive!" she shouts, quoting *Clueless*.

I snort, clutching my side, the act of walking suddenly becoming very complicated.

"Whatever," one of them mutters.

We finish our cotton candy booze on our walk. The buzz is alive and well and I am feeling *good*. As we approach the house, I notice flower boxes on the front windowsill. "Oh! Hang on a sec," I call as I skip to the window and swipe some dirt aside before planting my phone among the pansies.

"College guys with landscaped flower beds?" Daisy asks. "I'm impressed."

"It's so their mommies and daddies can make the house pretty on the outside and probably ignore the absolute debauchery on the inside," Briar tells us, her tongue stumbling over the word *debauchery*.

I pat the soil where my phone is sticking out like a budding flower stem. "I'll be back for you," I whisper. "You'll be safe here."

Daisy's head drops down over my shoulder, her chin hooked there as she giggles. "Is there a good reason why you're burying your phone in dirt?"

"A very good reason," I confirm.

I lead the charge with the card held above my head as we walk to the front of the house where a line is accumulating. Not only does the card get us out of the cover charge, but it also helps us skip the line when a guy wearing nothing but a moving box—and I mean *nothing*—waves us through.

We take a self-guided tour through the house and find that the main floor rooms are divided by activity. The living room is for lounging and lazy making out that is likely the prequel to something more. The formal dining room is home to a very intense beer pong tournament. The kitchen is drinks central. There are also about forty Taco Bell tacos and a few half-eaten pizzas up for grabs. The patio is reserved for recreational drug use. And the formal sitting area is where the DJ and a writhing sea of bodies can be found. It is every college movie I have ever seen and I am giddy, which might have more to do with my dwindling sobriety.

We find ourselves with cans of spiked sparkling water and Briar, the most bullish of us in such a large crowd, leads us through limbs and torsos with our hands locked together like a pre-K class on a field trip until we find a small alcove near a speaker. Our hands are marked with X's to show we're under twenty-one, but we have encountered zero resistance from the guys policing the coolers full of booze.

"It didn't occur to me that when you party with rich kids, all the booze is free," Briar says in an uncharacteristically cheerful tone.

"Every bar is an open bar," I shout back at her. "The oyster is your world!"

After a few minutes of us clinging to the walls, a girl wearing scraps of an IKEA shopping tote stops by with a plastic bag of sealed lime green shots. "GHB-free shots for the ladies? Three dollars each!"

"You're an angel," I tell her.

"And an entrepreneur," Briar says with admiration.

Daisy hands her a twenty and scoops up six shots. "Keep the change, baby!"

IKEA bag girl taps her nose. "I am but a humble woman-owned small business," she announces. "Just because the booze is free doesn't mean it's clean. No unsealed beverages for you ladies. Understand?"

"Yes, Mommy," I tell her.

She gives us each a kiss on the cheek and is off to the next group of girls like the safe party fairy she is.

"Cheers?" Daisy asks as she passes around the lime-green liquid-filled shot glasses that bear a striking resemblance to communion cups.

"Are we each taking two right now?" I ask.

Briar laughs. "I didn't come here to pace myself!"

I shrug and peel back the plastic seal on one of the cups before holding it out for a toast.

"Does this make us an official friend group?" Daisy asks. "We need a text thread."

Briar shrugs. "My general policy is no new friends, and I'm pretty opposed to group activities."

"You would have to have friends in the first place in order for that to be your policy," Daisy tells her sweetly.

"You are vicious," Briar says with a great deal of respect.

Daisy bounces up and down. "This is so *Sisterhood of the Traveling Pants* coded. Or—or, like, the three best friends in *Mamma Mia!*"

"I mean, we legit could share pants," I tell them. "I've never had friends I could potentially share clothes with."

Daisy slaps me on the shoulder, her jaw unhinged in shock. "Oh my god! Me neither."

Briar scoffs. "Well, I guess I could say the same, but I can't imagine wanting to wear either of your cutesy-ass clothes."

"Awww," I croon, and rest my head against her shoulder. "I'm always the grumpy friend, but you've really set the bar so high."

"Don't be too nice to me," she warns. "It'll make me horny and confused."

I reach up to pat her head affectionately.

With the second shot working its magic, I am a new woman who suddenly has the confidence to dance. "Do you guys like to dance?" I ask. "I feel like I would be so good at dancing."

Daisy grinds against me a little. "You read my mind."

She drags us toward the formal sitting room where the couches and leather wingback armchairs have been pushed to the sides. A crush of hardly clothed people are bouncing around and in many cases dry humping to "Dancing Queen" by ABBA and then "Espresso" by Sabrina Carpenter.

Daisy ends up squashed between us and she throws her arms in the air. "Slutty dance sandwich!"

A taller guy in a very tiny loincloth made out of condoms still in their wrappers settles in behind Briar and the look on her face tells me everything I need to know.

"How do you feel about virgins?" Daisy asks.

I slap my hand over her mouth and she licks my palm. "She's kidding."

The guy doesn't budge, so Briar very plainly yells, "We're not looking for a fourth and even if we were, it wouldn't be you, buddy."

"She called you *buddy*!" I shout at him. "What a burn!"

Briar laughs, taken aback, like she finds me both confusing and surprising. "You know what? Hell yeah!"

His face screws up in confusion before he disappears into the crowd that is awash with light from the blue strip lights that have been adhered to the ornate crown molding. Whoever's mom hired the landscaper is probably also responsible for the interior decor, and I have a feeling she would not approve of tape on her walls.

"You sure about not needing a fourth?" someone behind me asks. "I am the ideal candidate."

I spin around to tell this next guy to back off and stumble into Tate's chest, my palms resting on each of his very naked pectorals.

"Whoa there." He catches me by the waist and pulls me closer into a lingering hug.

"Hey, *buddy*," Daisy says with a snort, "she's married!"

"Settle down, kitty," he says. "I'm a friend. You don't have to make up a fake husband to keep me away. I'm the one who invited you three here anyway."

Daisy hiccups and then giggles to herself.

He takes inventory of the three of us. "And I'm guessing the person manning the coolers did not take the X's on your hands into consideration."

"It would be rude not to offer your guests beverages," I explain with his arms still around my waist.

"No, actually, it would be a *liability* to offer," he corrects. "In fact, you guys should just stay here and sleep it off. We have a few spare rooms at the moment. You don't want to get hassled by the campus police on your walk back."

Before I can kindly decline, Daisy yanks my hand up so that my ring is right in his face. "Married, remember? We've got to get this little lady home to her old man at the end of the night or else she'll turn into a pumpkin."

"Oh shit! You were serious." Tate looks down at me like I'm an absolute stranger and also a very interesting challenge. My cheeks warm as I remember how close we got at that hockey party earlier this semester. Since then, we've flirted in pottery class (when I usually take off my ring), but nothing has progressed beyond that, so it didn't feel necessary to tell him about Bennett.

He unfurls one arm from around my waist but still holds me tight with the other. "This husband of yours lets you out of his sight?" he asks. "I sure as hell wouldn't."

"She's an independent woman," Briar explains. "And they got into a fight."

I glare at her for spilling more details. Why couldn't I just keep flirting with Tate for the semester and then maybe we could reconnect in January when I didn't have to worry about the moral dilemma of cheating on my fake husband who I have a complicated history with and also enjoy kissing?

"Ahhh, well, you should take me up on my offer to stay the night," Tate says. "That would teach him a lesson."

Briar leans forward and whispers loudly in Tate's ear. "I could be swayed. I feel like there's a real market here for grilled cheese sandwiches. Do you have any spare ironing boards?"

"I have no idea what you're talking about, but I'm sure I could find you an ironing board," Tate replies.

Daisy hiccups again, but this time it turns into a burp. "I don't feel so great," she says, and covers her mouth with one hand.

She trips over her own feet as she moves to the edge of the room.

"Not in the vase!" Tate calls. "It's an antique!"

But it's too late. Daisy is already hunched over the oversize oriental-style vase with gold trim, retching.

"It's okay," Briar calls to Daisy as she comes up to rub circles along her back. "Let it all out."

"Or don't," Tate says.

"I'm sorry," I tell him as my head falls against his chest, and the way his hips press into my backside feels nice. Maybe we *should* just stay here. It's late anyway.

His body is moving to the music, and the fingers around my waist spread until they're brushing the underside of my foil-covered breast.

"We should go," Briar calls from where she's helping Daisy.

"I think we need to build up our party tolerance," I tell Tate.

His voice is low and his breath tickles against my neck as he whispers, "Don't you want to stay, Clover? That beautiful little head of yours is always spinning. Always thinking. Doesn't it feel nice to just shut it off for a little while?"

I let myself fully lean against him and a tired moan slips past my lips.

Fingers are tracing up along the length of my neck, warm breaths lingering.

And then I'm being tugged away by my wrist.

"Time to go," Briar says with me on one side and Daisy on the other. "As much as I would love to turn this place into a grilled cheese franchise."

"You guys go!" I tell them. "Tate's a friend. I'll be fine."

Briar eyes me and then Tate warily, but behind her Daisy gags and then burps.

"Really!" I tell her. "Plus, Bennett knows where I am!"

"Fine. Please text us when you're ready to leave. I'll send Bennett to pick you up."

"Sounds good!" I shout as I let Tate pull me deeper into the crowd and my body melts into his just like it did that night next to the firepit. My skin feels warm and tingly all over.

Briar uses her lengthy figure and commanding presence to part the crowd as she hauls Daisy along like a little duckling.

CHAPTER 21

Bennett

Once Clover leaves, I can't make it through a full page of reading without tossing my textbook across the bed. I watch the little dot on my phone move across campus and into the surrounding neighborhood. Then the movement stops, and I zoom in to see that her location is just in front of 1919 Hemphill.

"She's fucking fine," I mutter to myself before turning my phone face down on the bed. She has Briar with her and that girl is a Rottweiler.

I pace for about an hour, the textbook in hand, as I find myself reading the same paragraphs over and over.

When I check my phone again, her dot hasn't moved. I wouldn't find this weird except that it never moves. At all.

The decision is already made. I'm too impatient to wait for the elevator and run down the four flights, taking the steps two at a time and peeling out of the student parking lot. I'd rather Clover hate me for the rest of the semester than for her to end up as just another body on their disgusting scoreboard.

I follow the route she took to the house and slam on my brakes at an intersection when a girl in a foil skirt spins out in front of me followed by a tall and slightly irritated redhead.

Immediately, I roll down my window and yell out to them. "Hey! Daisy! Briar!"

Daisy skips over to my window and her whole face lights up when she sees it's me. "See, Briar! I told you he would come for her."

"Come for who?" I ask, the blood in my veins pumping twice as hard. "Clover? Where is she?"

Daisy gives me a far-off smile before clasping my cheeks with both hands and kissing me on the forehead. "It's cold!" she declares, and then opens the door to my back seat and lets herself in.

Briar strolls over to the window too slowly.

"Where is she?" I ask. "You just left her there?"

"We were literally on our way home and I was going to tell you to go pick her up. Chill, okay? She was fine. Just a little tipsy."

"Get in the damn car," I say, and hit my forehead against the steering wheel. "Isn't there some kind of girl code that says not to ditch a girl at a party?"

Briar slides into the back seat beside Daisy. "Obviously, but the girl code doesn't really have a decision tree that explains what to do when one friend is happily dancing at a party and the other is puking in an antique vase."

I grab a plastic bag I stuffed under my seat the other day and pass it to Daisy. "Here." I look in the rearview mirror at Briar. "You're just going to sit in the back seat while I drive you both around like an Uber?"

"That's the idea," she says. "Better get to driving if you want that five-star rating, *buddy*."

Daisy laughs like that's the funniest thing she's ever heard.

The two of them were only about a mile out from the house when I picked them up. I'd bet that Clover has been alone for thirty minutes or so.

I didn't want to bring Tate up earlier tonight since he was the source of our explosive fight earlier this semester, but I guarantee that once he saw us fighting outside that house party, he decided that she would be on his hit list.

The guy is a patient fucker. He did this last year too. He sets the trap early in the semester and does some harmless flirting. He gets in a girl's head and then he invites them to the house, and no one passes up the chance for an invite to 1919 Hemphill. The girls with cards get marked with X's and most assume it's to denote partygoers under the age of twenty-one. It's a fair assumption because most of the girls who get a card are first-years.

"Show me your hands," I say to Briar and Daisy.

Briar holds hers up and Daisy flings her body on top of the center console to show off her hands. Both girls are decorated with black X's.

"Shit," I mutter.

Each guy has their own color. Tate's is black.

"Stay in the car," I tell them as we turn down Hemphill.

"Yes, Dad," Daisy says, and slumps against the back seat with her lids half closed.

I slam on the brakes in front of the house and don't bother to check if I've parked legally. My phone is outstretched in my hand like a metal detector as I call Clover on speaker phone.

After a few seconds, a muffled ringtone leads me to a flower box under one of the windows where Clover's phone is sticking out upside down. Once I yank it out of the soil, I feel a little thrill at the fact that I am listed as husband 😩. I do take offense to the fact that my photo is a picture of Joffrey from *Game of Thrones*.

I know the layout of the place, as well as most of the guys who live here. There are the Rocco twins. Tate "Shitbag" Farris. One of the Garcia brothers and not the smart one. And then a few others who moved in this year that I have yet to meet.

It's late. Nearly three. People are starting to pour out of the house, and there's no one at the door to stop me. As if they could.

I make a lap around the first floor and then a nauseating thought occurs to me. What if Clover is in the basement?

The door leading downstairs is just off the kitchen. The smell hits me as soon as I take the first step. Weed and sex.

The basement of 1919 Hemphill is known as the Den of Misdeeds. It is also home to the legendary scoreboard. In a logical sense, I know that what Clover does with her body is none of my business. Maybe I wish it was my business or maybe it's archaic or maybe I'm just a bad person, but I can't stand the thought of anyone else's hands on her, especially Tate's. I can't stand the thought of her down here in this basement with the kind of guys who always get exactly what they want.

It's dark and hazy. An old Wexley Bears baseball scoreboard rests against the main wall, and where the innings would be listed are six names, two of which I don't recognize. Beneath each name is a number, and Tate seems to be in the lead.

There are people on couches in half stages of undress. The Garcia kid watches two drunk girls wrapped in caution tape make out with a hand gripping his crotch, and just beyond him is Tate with a girl straddling his lap while another is passed out beside them both. I'm relieved to see that the girl's hair is long, dark, and curly.

"Hey," he says upon noticing me, the girl in his lap lazily licking at his neck. "Bennett Andrew Graves. I thought you were too good for 1919 Hemphill these days."

"I'm looking for someone who came here tonight."

"Lots of people in and out this evening," he tells me as he bats the girl's hand away from his chest. "Got a name? A picture?"

"You know who I'm here for. Clover. Where is she?"

The way his grin turns wolfish makes my stomach drop.

My hands clench into fists at my side. "You fucking shitbag. Has anyone ever told you how punchable your face is?" I ask him as I take a few steps closer. "Where is she?"

"Clover? She's a real sweet one," he tells me. "I'd never had a fat chick before and she's pretty cute."

I lunge toward him, and the girl on his lap clumsily slithers off just in time for me to gather his collar in my fist and yank him toward me.

He grins down at my left hand. "I thought her yappy little friend was kidding about the marriage thing. But look at you. A married man. I gotta admit, I'm shocked. You keep her on a pretty long leash, don't you?"

I let go of his shirt with enough force to throw him back against the sofa. Tossing him around should make me feel better, but it does nothing to stop the anxiety clawing up my throat.

Tate makes a move to stand up, but I'm too close and towering over him. If I put a hand on him again, I can't promise I won't do something that will require legal representation. He leans back into the couch with his arms spread out across the tops of the cushions. "Does your little wifey know that you've slept around on campus so many times your dick might as well be communal property?"

He's trying to bait me, but I'm not falling for it. "I swear to god, if you touched her, I will ruin you. Don't think I won't. The kind of money I have to play with makes your mother's Silicon Valley divorce settlements look like pocket change. Now, where is she?"

He rolls his eyes. "Upstairs in my room."

I leave him there and race up the steps, dodging a few lazy drunk bodies on the ground floor, and then up the dramatic staircase at the center of the house. Tate's room is the third on the left and when I open the door, I find Clover sleeping on her stomach. Her foil outfit is in poor shape and it's hard to say if that's from wear or from Tate's grubby-ass hands.

She's wearing a pink set with little red cherries, and because I have absolute perversion for her, I can't help but catalog that fact.

"Chill out, man," Tate says from behind me. "She passed out up here like thirty minutes ago. I was going to let her sleep it off for a while."

I turn on him and slam his body against the wall just outside his door with my forearm pressing into his neck.

He tries to roll his eyes, but he can hardly mask his panic as he sputters, his cheeks turning red, and so I push even harder into his throat. "We danced," he coughs out. "Probably would have gotten further if I'd had more time with her."

"That won't be happening again." I pin him with a grunt, the back of his head cracking against the wall, before letting him fall. "How did you meet her?"

He rings a hand around his neck while he catches his breath. "We have pottery together."

"Not anymore. Drop the class. Get into another section. I don't fucking care."

"Yeah, not gonna happen."

"Listen, you fucking piece of shit, I'm sure you plan on applying for the Bailey & Parsons prelaw internship next summer."

He says nothing, which tells me all I need to know. The Bailey & Parsons internship is the ultimate get for Wexley prelaw students, and the Graves family also keeps them on retainer. "Should I call Bailey or Parsons?" I ask, holding my phone up. "I have both of them right here in my contacts. Or you know what? I could just wait to see them at my mother's New Year's Eve party."

His lips purse, and he's unable to hide that he's seething.

"You think I'm bluffing?" I ask. "Try me. I would fucking love that."

He gives the faintest of nods, and I leave him there while I go back into his room and slam the door shut behind me.

CHAPTER 22

Bennett

I sit down at the edge of the bed with one arm braced on Clover's other side as I brush a hand gently up and down her spine. "Hey, Clo. Time for us to go." She stretches and moans and then buries her head into her arm. "Clover," I try again. I just need to know that she is okay. I need her to be okay.

She rolls over with an adorable huff as her vision seems to focus. "Bennett," she says as if she's caught me being naughty. "Did you follow me here?" She giggles. "You did! Didn't you?"

"I wanted to make sure you're all right and you obviously aren't."

She gasps a little, the apples of her cheeks ruddy. "You're jealous!"

I shake my head and help her up into a sitting position, but the air is sucked from my lungs when she swings a leg over my lap.

She loses her balance a little, so I hold her waist to steady her.

Those wide blue eyes stare down at me, the same color of blue as a receding wave, her lids heavy and languid. She drapes her arms over my shoulders and scoots up my lap. My body burns in response.

Fuck, fuck, fuck.

The foil is mostly gone and she is in nothing more than her matching set. The friction on my lap is sparking a physical reaction that I can't seem to stop. If I were standing, my knees would buckle. Tate could open that door right now and find what I suspect to be true: that I am no different than him.

She chuffs as her head rolls back, her neck exposed, and I can't contain my laugh. "I'm trying to be sexy and you're making fun of me," she purrs, her lips in a dramatic frown.

I smooth her disheveled hair back and shake my head. "At least it's to your face." A breathy little sigh causes her lips to puff out, and I want to do very bad things to her mouth. *God, those lips.* "And trust me. You're plenty sexy."

Her smile is pleased and smug all at once with her mouth parted just so. "I wasn't going to hook up with him, you know. That's why he left me up here."

"I should have gotten here sooner." I don't want to argue with her right now, but I don't think Tate left her up here indefinitely. I'm sure he was saving her for later.

Her fingers dance along the hairline at the back of my neck, and I begrudgingly remove my hands from her waist and clench the sheets at my sides to stop from touching her. I want to. I really fucking want to. But she doesn't want that. Not really. She's drunk and—

"Can you keep a secret?" she whispers into my ear, her tongue swiping along my lobe as she grips my hair, pulling my head back. "I'm horny." It comes out like a whine and I want to reward her and punish her and do completely reprehensible things to her.

Her tongue licks a stripe up my neck.

The moan that escapes me is helpless and pathetic. "Clo," I rasp as she bites and sucks and settles herself right against my erection, which appeared in no time at all.

"Did you come here to save me?" she whispers again.

"I didn't want anyone to take advantage of you," I manage to say.

"What if I want you to take advantage of me? Does that change anything?"

My hands are on her waist now and I'm trying to push her back. I'm *trying* to do the right thing. For once in my goddamn life, I'm trying to do right by her. "You can't ask me shit like that. I'm not a good person."

She's not fazed by that admission in the least as she kisses and nibbles along my jawline. Her teeth bite down on my bottom lip and tug.

"When I danced with him tonight, I pretended that his hands were yours." Her hips roll forward and her mouth finds mine again with soft, hot kisses. I part my lips, beckoning her to continue, and her tongue darts into my mouth. I lose all sense of control.

In a matter of seconds, I have one hand in her hair, and the other cradling her ass as she mewls into my mouth. She pulls away for a moment, and her head rolls back as I rock up into her, encouraging her to chase her satisfaction. So many of my dreams have brought me to this exact moment: us still clothed and her grinding against me, chasing whatever friction she can find.

I lick and suck along her collarbone like a starved man because I am. The only thing keeping us from each other is the small barrier of clothing between us, and I'm so tempted to slide my hand down farther to see if she's ready for me.

A giggle bubbles up in her throat, and suddenly I'm having a moment of déjà vu and I can't stop my brain from showing me the blurred memories of my endless drunk hookups last year that were only temporary remedies in my constant effort to forget Clover and how much I—

"Stop," I whisper. "Clo." My voice is firmer now. "We have to stop. Come on."

I pull her hands away from where they are on my neck and chest, and she pouts down at me.

"We *can't*," I tell her. "I don't want us to do something either of us will regret."

Her brow creases with hurt as she stands up and stumbles back away from me, her arms wrapped self-consciously around her.

"Hey," I say softly. "I just—you're drunk."

"It's fine," she spits. "I wouldn't want you to do anything you'd regret."

Fuck, now she's pissed and I'm still just as hard. All she has to do is push back once—maybe twice more—and I'm likely to let go of whatever scraps of morals I have for just a taste of her.

I stand up, because I've hurt her more than enough in this lifetime and I'd rather spend the rest of my life wondering about the taste of her, the feel of her, than hurt her again. I hope that telling myself that over and over will make it true. I pull my thermal off over my head and hand it to her, leaving me in my undershirt.

She shakes her head. "I don't need it."

"The goose bumps on your arms say otherwise."

Like an insolent child, she stomps over toward the door, but I step in front of her. I might be a piece of shit who just put my hands all over a drunk girl while I was stone-cold sober, but I refuse to let all those clowns downstairs see her like this.

She sizes me up and must decide that it's not worth the fight, because she yanks the shirt away from me and tugs it on over her head.

I move out of her way, and she flings the door open before tearing down the stairs and out the front door.

Tate is sitting on the porch, sipping a beer. He's smart enough to keep his mouth shut, but when he sees me following a very unhappy Clover, he raises his bottle with a self-satisfied smirk.

She crams into the back seat with Daisy and Briar, who are both chanting, "French fries! French fries! French fries!"

Daisy leans forward and pats my shoulder like I'm her noble steed. "Uber man, bring us to the french fries!"

I glance up at the rearview mirror to see that Clover's ego has slightly recovered as she soothes Briar about her lost Saturday night revenue.

"To the french fries," I grumble.

CHAPTER 23

Bennett

I head off toward Sports Ball, one of the only places in town that might still be serving food at this hour.

When we get there, I go in and return with four take-out containers of fries. Once Briar inspects my bounty, she sends me back in for extra ketchup and some mayonnaise.

The girls plow through the fries like muscle heads pounding protein powder and by the time I turn into the student parking lot, I have a back seat full of drunk first-years wrapped in foil and sleeping like babies.

The term *herding cats* has never been so true as it is when I direct them inside.

Upstairs, I make sure Briar and Daisy are settled in their room while Clover gets changed and into bed.

"Water and Tylenol," I tell her as I walk around to her side of the bed. "Come on."

"You have to stop taking care of me. It's not fair," she says.

"It's your first semester of college. What kind of husband would I be if I didn't help minimize your hangover? Now, open up."

She obeys with her tongue outstretched and I place two pills there. Before I can pull my hand back, she closes her mouth around my finger and sucks for a moment before letting go.

"Flirt," I whisper. Yeah, that image is going straight to the spank bank.

She shrugs and drinks down half a bottle of water. Once again, she sticks her tongue out to prove she's followed instruction before settling back into bed, curled on her side.

After she lies down, I head to the showers with a change of clothes. With the spray pulsing over the back of my neck, I press my forehead against the wall of the shower and feel like I can breathe for the first time in hours. Clover is okay. She is safe.

But fuck if I don't see her the moment I close my eyes. Her clit rubbing against the head of my dick. The wet spot she left on my sweatpants. Her lips closing around my finger.

It only takes a handful of pumps before I've painted the tile with my release.

When I return, our usual wall of pillows is scattered at the end of the bed. I pull back the covers to see that Clover is wearing gray boy shorts with a thick, masculine-style band around the waist. Her ribbed white tank top is cropped, the seam rolled up just below those gorgeous tits.

I'm already getting hard again. There is nothing to separate us when Clover shifts closer to me and nestles her head in my lap.

"I am a very bad person," I whisper, like that will somehow absolve me. Because if I were a better person, I would reposition her so that she has pillows to cuddle instead of me. But this moment is too much like ones I had allowed myself to only briefly imagine that day when we said *I do*.

She gives a contented sigh as I stroke her hair. At one point, her arm is draped across my thighs, painfully close to my balls that feel too heavy.

I pray for exhaustion, but sleep takes her fucking time and memories of the past start piling up one right after the other.

Sometimes I wish I could talk to Clover as freely as I did when we were just two profile pictures on a screen. It felt simple even though it was anything but.

My foray into catfishing started falling apart when Clover and Beth went to Texas to visit Beth's older brother and his family two weeks before we were supposed to go back to school.

I'd managed to avoid my Calvin Prep friends for the summer, but they were getting harder and harder to put off, so I figured this was a good time to get them off my back. A group of us spent a few days in and out of each other's houses, skimming off family liquor cabinets and getting high.

I had passed out one night on a lounge chair next to Val's pool and she held up my phone to my face because Clover had sent me a steady stream of messages, telling me all about how weird her uncle's kids were and how the whole family was obsessed with God and guns.

When I woke up a while later, Val was still scrolling through messages and laughing with everyone else rounded up behind her.

I was frozen with fear. They had found out that Clover was my weakness. They knew the things I'd told her. Surely, anyone who read those messages could see what I knew to be true even if I could hardly admit it to myself. Surely, they could see that I was in love with the girl everyone ridiculed and called *the help* behind her back.

But then Val turned to me, a wicked grin on her face. "Bennett, this is fucking genius. I can't believe you've spent the whole summer catfishing this poor little fat ass." She tossed the phone back to me.

My heart stammered in my chest, sweat gathering on my forehead. It felt like swallowing nails, but that didn't stop me from saying, "Yeah. So fucking gullible, but at least she's entertaining."

"I'm surprised she hasn't sent you any nudes yet," someone said.

Val shook her head. "No, no, you don't want to get caught with actual pictures. That's asking for trouble."

"Totally," I said. Just the thought of Clover being vulnerable like that made me want to puke.

Everyone began to disperse and returned to their chosen vices.

Val stood and then leaned down to me, giving me a playful slap on the cheek. "Couldn't let you have all the fun, though, Benny. If you thought those messages were entertaining, just you wait. The grand finale I just cooked up is going to make you jizz your pants it's so good."

I laughed, but it came out nervous and breathless.

When she was gone, I opened my phone and nearly threw the thing in the pool. I'd never hit a girl before, but it was a good thing that Val was out of sight, because the feral anger I felt in that moment as I read through the messages to Clover she had penned was unlike anything I had ever experienced.

JOSH

Your mom's family sounds like a bunch of backward ass hillbillies

CLOVER

lol yeah kind of, but they're not all bad

JOSH

I get back in town next week

CLOVER

You do?

JOSH

I just want to feel you in my arms

My body flooded with heat. It was the first time we'd talked about physical contact.

CLOVER

I want that too. Really bad.

JOSH

Can I kiss you

when I get home next week

CLOVER

please don't make fun of me

JOSH

never, baby

CLOVER

I've never been kissed

JOSH

can I be your first?

CLOVER

I would like that so much

JOSH

Will you be at the So Long Summer Bash at the country club? Next Saturday?

CLOVER

Yeah, my mom goes every year

JOSH

I'll be there

CLOVER

really??

JOSH

I wouldn't miss it for the world. I can't wait to hold you all night and tell you how beautiful you are in person. You know that, right? You're the most beautiful girl I've ever seen.

CLOVER

you can't say stuff like that

JOSH

yes, I can. It's true. I think about you every night.

you make me so hot.

CLOVER

omg

JOSH

do you think about me like that?

you don't have to be ashamed, baby

CLOVER

What if I said yes?

JOSH

I'd say I want to do a lot more than kiss you one day

I'll meet you behind the club just before the fireworks. near the rocking chairs.

CLOVER

okay. I'll be there.

That was the last of the conversation between Val and Clover. My teeth were grinding so hard I was surprised they didn't chip.

My neck was warm and the veins in my arms were practically pulsing.

My phone lit up. It was her. And in the time I'd spent passed out, this little thing between us had become so much more real, and the worst part was that nothing Val said was untrue.

CLOVER

Josh?

It's me, I wanted to say. *It's fucking Bennett. The boy you've known your whole life. The boy who's been hiding behind a mask for the last four years. The boy who's been here all along.*

JOSH

yeah?

CLOVER

I love talking to you.

JOSH

I love talking to you too

CLOVER

and sometimes I think I might love you

Fuck, fuck, fuck.

There was no pain more raw than hearing the person you loved say those three words to you only for them to be meant for a version of you that doesn't exist. But I was delusional, and I convinced myself that the only lies in all this were my name and a few small details. She was still talking to me. This was still just Clover talking to Bennett. But without the bullshit of expectations and fear and shame.

So, when I typed out my response, I told her the truth. It was selfish and wrong and cowardly. All it would have taken was one message. One message to set the record straight. She could be mad at me for as long as she wanted, and I would let her. I deserved that. It would be okay, because I would have stopped this lie before it bled into our real lives. But I wasn't the good guy. I hadn't been for a very long time, and I doubted I ever would be again.

JOSH

I love you, too, Clover. I love you so much.

CHAPTER 24

Clover

I wake up on Sunday morning to an empty bed. I know I made a fool of myself last night, but if Bennett were just here, we could talk about it. Or at least mutually pretend that it never happened. But he's not here and all I feel is embarrassed. It's a familiar feeling in terms of Bennett.

He doesn't get home until late that night and he's too chatty. Like if he can just fill any silence, there won't be room for us to discuss anything else. And this sets the tone for the rest of the week. On Tuesday, my mom drives down to campus and we go out for Chinese food. She's so busy at work and fills me in on gossip. I inhale the familiar rose scent of her perfume, which I always find comforting.

"How's my little overachiever coping with the course load?" she asks.

"A's across the board," I tell her. "Well, pottery is a close call."

She guffaws. "Pottery? You didn't even like making the Christmas ornaments your class would make every year when you were a kid."

"Those arts and crafts projects were pandering."

"Sure, sure, sure."

"I don't know. It's nice to be bad at something that doesn't matter."

She seems happy to hear that. It's a time every week when my brain has to actively concentrate and create and problem solve.

I do not tell her about Tate or how he missed Monday morning class, because that doesn't seem unusual, until suddenly, he's missed Wednesday and Friday too.

I guess it's just as well, after I shut him down on Saturday night. He was persistent, which I didn't find unusual at the time, but now in hindsight, I have that sinking feeling in my gut, like when you've just narrowly escaped a car accident.

Even though Bennett is mostly gone, I find small traces of him. A few bottles of my favorite conditioner on my desk. I've noticed too that my drawer of snacks is always magically full and so are my vitamins. I text him to thank him for the conditioner—which I shouldn't accept but can't make myself refuse. His only response is to like the text.

Pizza Tramp has been a Wexley mainstay since the eighties—at least that's what the student guide said on the tour I took last spring. After working a few hours overtime last night, I didn't get home until four in the morning, so when I wake up starving, I stumble over to Briar and Daisy's room and drag them both off campus for an appropriately greasy meal. Damn the cost.

Outside, the wind is howling and the place is swarming with students bundled up in Wexley Bears merch on their way to the stadium. After I order our pizza (pepperoni and banana peppers), we wait for a table to clear and are lucky enough to snag a booth next to the pinball machines.

When my name is called, I run up to grab our pizza and practically collide with the person reaching for the tray next to mine. "I'm so sorry," I say on instinct as I take our food and attempt to disappear.

"Not even a hello?" the person asks.

I spin back around, and Tate stands there, a peculiar expression on his face.

"*You're* the one who ghosted me this week," I remind him, even if my stomach sinks at the sight of him. My drunken memory of Saturday night is full of feelings but lacking hard facts, so even though I feel gross standing so close to him, I can't fully articulate that to him.

He dips his chin in acknowledgment. "Ahh, yeah, I should have warned you. I got an internship that I couldn't turn down, so I had to get into the evening class."

"Understandable," I say, trying to hide my relief. "You'll be glad to know I finished shaping my vase and it almost looks like something that resembles a receptacle."

He laughs with that inviting grin that feels like a reward. God, he's good. "Well, I'm glad to hear you're surviving without me, even if my ego is just a little wounded."

"Right," I say with a stiff smile just as someone calls his name from the bar. "I guess I'll see you around."

His gaze flickers down to my hand, where my ring should be, and he nods before disappearing into the crowd.

I glance down at my naked finger. I'd misplaced the ring a few days ago. I hadn't mentioned it to Bennett because I'd hardly seen him and I wasn't in a hurry to admit that it could be missing.

With our pizza in hand, I weave back into the maze of tables and return to our booth to find that our party has doubled.

"There she is!" Julian sits wedged up against the wall with his arm slung behind Bennett, who gives me an apologetic glance.

"Hey," he says as he glances up and then casts his gaze downward. "I told them we could grab our own table."

Daisy reaches across the table and pats his hand. "Why would you do that?"

On one side of her, a very disgruntled Briar rolls her eyes. Tex is doing his best not to crowd the bench seat, but the fact that he is shaped like an upside-down triangle and eats protein like it's his job is making things difficult.

"Stop trying to tear our family apart," whines Julian.

"Julian," I say with a wink as I set the pizza down. "I'm glad to see you still consume half of the oxygen of every room you walk into."

"Hey, I could be in your bed with my harem right now."

Bennett gives him a shut-the-fuck-up look as he slides out of the booth with his receipt to get their pizza. He stands up right in front of me, our toes almost touching, and I tilt my head up.

"Hey," he says, and runs the backs of his fingers down the side of my arm. Then he leans down to kiss me on the cheek, and I shiver in response. It's been a week since we've touched and I didn't realize how famished I was for him. Then I see the blank stare on his face, because oh, right, we're in public and we're married.

Behind him, Julian seems very entertained. "My stomach is going to eat itself," he yells over the swell of the restaurant as pregame coverage starts to play on the televisions suspended in every corner.

Once he leaves, I scoot into the booth, where Julian yanks me in for a hug.

"I can't believe I wasn't invited to the wedding," he moans. "I would have made the perfect addition to your accomplices."

I roll my eyes and then glance over to Briar and Daisy. "He means wedding party." I give him a stern look that I hope gets the message across.

He nods and then slings an arm over my shoulder.

Daisy smiles. "So you're Bennett's cousin? Does that mean you got a front-row seat to these two falling in love?"

Julian barks out a laugh. "If that's what you want to call it, then yes, I did indeed."

Daisy smiles again, but her eyes crinkle in an uncertain way before turning to Tex. "So it's Tex?" she asks. "As in Texas?"

"Oklahoma, actually."

My head tilts to the side as Bennett returns with two more pizzas.

"The nickname is Julian's fault," Tex explains. "And my real name is Miles, if you prefer. I certainly do."

"You don't let me call you Miles!" Julian protests.

But Daisy's eyes light up and she launches into something about a ballet scene from *Oklahoma!* and Tex seems genuinely invested, while Julian lures a skeptical Briar into a conversation about a podcast he's been listening to about scammy influencers.

"I feel like our kids are meeting for the first time," Bennett says as he covers his slice of pizza in red pepper flakes.

"There's a lot at stake here," I tell him. "Though I think Briar is going to be the toughest to crack. I haven't even cracked her yet."

"Julian loves a challenge."

I reach past him for a napkin and he catches my hand. His finger runs over my ring finger. "Your ring," he says, voice almost strangled. "Not really your style, I guess?"

That was the furthest thing from the truth. I'd grown quite used to spinning the ring around my finger during class. The fit was just a little loose, so it made for easy fidgeting, but I loved the style. Simple and yet unique. "Um, no, I guess . . . I must have taken it off when I went to bed."

"Do you think you lost it?" he asks after a long silence. "When's the last time you remember having it on?"

I don't want to hurt him and I know that lying about this now can only lead to more hurt. "Um, Saturday night, I guess. I remember spinning it around my finger while we walked to the party. I usually take it off for pottery, but when I wasn't wearing it, I assumed that I left it in the dorm."

He nods to himself, his fist tightening on his drink.

"Shit. I guess it's possible that I dropped it somewhere between the party and the dorm on my way home." The guilt is heavy and real. But it was so dark in that house and I was not in control of my faculties at all. It could be anywhere really. And that's not even considering the likelihood that someone just picked it up and pocketed it.

"I'm so sorry," I finally blurt, irrational tears welling up in my eyes. "Oh god, I feel awful." My voice trembles slightly. I feel like I've been careless, and not just with an object. "I know you said it was fake, but I hope you didn't spend much on it," I tell him. "Can I buy a replacement? Do you remember where you got it?"

He watches me for a moment before the tension in his shoulders eases and he gives me a reassuring smile. "Don't worry about it. Like you said, it was fake."

"I'll order something cheap online," I tell him. "Or maybe I can make it over to an antique store in the old downtown."

He nods again, and under the table, his hand wraps around my thigh and squeezes, turning my insides warm. It's a touch that is for no one else's benefit but ours. "I'm sorry this week has felt so off," he tells me.

"It's okay," I say softly.

"I wanted to talk to you about walking home so late by yourself," Bennett says quietly. "I'm going to start meeting you at the end of your shifts."

"You don't have to do that," I tell him, even though I am way too eager for a reason to spend more time with him after the last week. "I always have my cell phone on me."

"Don't fight me on this." His hand is still on my thigh, not as high as it was, but the contact still has me a little lightheaded.

"Okay, fine. My next shift is on Monday night."

His eyes trace my lips, and I nearly lean in to kiss him, because that's what married people do, right? We're in public. It would be no different than any other public kiss we've shared.

"Ah, Clover, there you are."

The voice pulls my attention from Bennett, and Tate is standing there, his hands braced on the end of our table. His brown eyes practically sparkle, and he looks right past Bennett, only giving a quick glance to Briar and Daisy. "Ladies."

I clear my throat, and Bennett's grip tightens, the tips of his fingers digging into my thigh.

"Tatum Farris," Bennett says, his voice dry and taunting.

"Ben, I didn't even see you there. Only have eyes for this one, I guess," he says with a nod toward me. "Oh! Clover! Is this skirt chaser the lucky man? This guy really knew how to get around last year. Put the rest of us to shame."

My mouth opens, but it takes only a second to regain my composure and force a smile despite how unsettled I suddenly am.

"But that's all old news, I'm sure. You're a married man now apparently. Shocking, honestly." He chuckles. "Might need to send out a little dispatch to the female population of Wexley so they know you're off the market. I can think of two dozen women at least who will be very disappointed to hear the news." He looks back over to me. "He really has kept you a secret, hasn't he?"

Shame unfurls in my belly. The idea of being a secret that Bennett wants to keep buried, combined with him having a whole life last year that I know nothing about, is quickly filling me with anxiety. My appetite disappears and my throat feels like it's becoming more and more narrow with each breath.

"Tate, don't you have some incel support group you're late for?" Julian asks lazily.

Tate ignores him. "Clover, I meant to tell you. We found a ring at the house after the party. In my bed, actually."

Bennett stiffens beside me, and everyone's attention turns to me.

I glance over to Daisy and Briar. "I passed out for a bit before you guys came back for me."

Tate snorts. "Nothing to be ashamed of, sweetheart. Bennett here has been in beds all over town. In this place alone, I could probably count a few."

I smile, teeth grinding, through the embarrassment and the subsequent anger. I am furious that I'm supposed to be married to Bennett and somehow the entire campus knows him better than I do. Including that girl at the house party I went to with Daisy who practically curled around him like a snake. The image of him in our bed with other girls draped all over him. It adds fuel to the fire.

"You said you found a ring?" I ask sweetly. "Can you send me a picture of it?"

"Sure," he says, glancing to Bennett. "I'll text you."

"Good luck with that Bailey & Parsons application," Bennett says.

Tate's mouth flattens into a thin line, and he gives a short nod before leaving. The silence at the table is heavy as we continue to eat.

"We better go," I say, and Tex shoots to his feet to make way for Daisy and Briar to exit.

I scoot toward Bennett, but he doesn't move. His pupils zero in on me, severe and searching. I don't know what he wants from me.

Am I supposed to say that it's okay and I don't mind that he apparently slept with a quarter of the student population last year? Should I tell him how angry it makes me, even when I have no right to be?

Whatever reaction it is that he wants, I don't plan on giving it to him.

"I'll see you later," I say breezily, and he finally relents.

I walk right past him and out the door, into the chilling fog.

CHAPTER 25

Clover

"Wait!"

The three of us are halfway down the sidewalk when I turn to see Bennett jogging toward us, pulling his arms through his jacket.

"You guys go ahead," I tell Briar and Daisy.

"Are you sure?" Briar asks, and if I weren't dreading whatever is about to come next, I would feel touched by her hard-earned affection.

"I'm good," I tell her.

Daisy gives me a tight hug, and I let myself sag against her for a moment. She steps back and earnestly says, "We're just across the hall if you need us."

Suddenly, I remember our discussion in the laundry room a few weeks ago. Forgiveness is only done willfully. It doesn't just happen.

"Can we talk?" Bennett asks once he catches up to me. "Please?"

I suck in a deep breath and nod.

"I'm parked not far from here," he tells me. "Come on. You gotta be cold."

I follow him the two blocks to his car, staying just a step or two behind. I can't bring myself to look at him right now or even talk, because suddenly I'm fifteen again and it's that last day of summer.

I was wearing a dress I loved and had been saving for a special occasion. It was white with straps that tied into bows.

Josh. We'd spent all summer talking back and forth, about topics from the insignificant to immense. From the moment I met him, we had this sudden and intense bond. A lifeline. He was someone I didn't realize I needed until he was there, from his first text in the morning to the last person I said good night to. And everything that happened in between.

I should have been more savvy. More suspicious. But talking to him felt as natural as breathing.

I was in Texas when he messaged and asked if we could meet. He said things that made me blush. Things I'd only dreamed of a boy saying to me, much less one I was in love with.

I couldn't get home soon enough. I kept imagining the colors of the fireworks reflecting off the white fabric of my dress as we met—and maybe even kissed—for the first time.

The So Long, Summer party at the Cannon Beach Country Club was the most beloved event of the year. Even when it rained, I remember people jumping into the pools and dancing in the muddy grass.

That year, we were gifted clear skies. Bennett had gone ahead with his friends, and I went with my mom and Sydney, who curled my hair. The three of us sat in her bathroom and they both seemed to know something was up.

"I'm meeting a boy," I finally said, unable to contain my excitement. "He goes to CBHS and his name is Josh. We've been chatting for a while, but he's been out of town all summer."

Sydney gasped as she unwound my curl from the barrel and then held it coiled in her hand as she waited for it to cool. "Our little Clo has a gentleman caller!"

Mom looked wary and Sydney dropped my curl to smack her on the shoulder. "Beth, come on. No one meets in person anymore."

"And we're meeting at the rocking chairs out back, Mom," I told her.

"That's basically as public as you can get," Sydney said.

Mom sighed and looked between us. "No wandering off. And you come and introduce us to him after you two meet. Don't think I won't be watching."

Sydney laughed and pointed two fingers at her eyes and then at me. "We will be watching, Josh. Whoever you are."

When we arrived at the club, Mom and Sydney veered off to the champagne wall and I headed for the rocking chairs that overlooked the cliffside golf course. On my way, I took a lemonade from a waiter and whispered a thank-you.

The thing with the rocking chairs was that all the teenagers congregated there while they slipped alcohol and joints back and forth among one another.

On the ground level below was a temporary dance floor with string lights hung overhead, heavy round bulbs and paper lanterns.

Bennett was there with his friends, clustered against the nearby railing. He kept running rough hands through his hair and he looked about as restless as I felt.

His eyes darted over to me a few times, but the way he acted toward me in front of his friends didn't feel as important to me anymore. I had someone, and he was going to be there soon.

That's not to say I wasn't anxious. Josh didn't run in any of the same circles as the Calvin Prep kids. What if he was nervous to show up here? Maybe he worked part-time as a valet or in the kitchens and didn't want me to know. That would be a relief, actually. To know that he lived on the edges of wealth just as much as I did.

I opened my phone to check my messages, but the last message was from this morning.

JOSH

morning angel

CLOVER

Good morning! I can't believe by this time tomorrow we will have met.

He hadn't said *I love you* again, so neither had I, and the more distance I got from the confession, the more foolish I felt for it. But he hadn't really given me any reason to feel that way.

Bennett's friends—Valerie in particular—kept glancing back at me and laughing. It was something I was used to, but it still hurt.

Over the summer, Bennett and I had found a middle ground. A sort of quiet contentedness. But then after I came home from Texas, he was cold and arrogant. I felt cheated out of a week of normalcy. Bennett usually loosened up over summer break, like those warmer months were a time of truce. I would have been pissed if I weren't so full of anticipation.

The sunset burned against the horizon and the blue night sky crept into the high points of the atmosphere above.

I checked the time. Josh was an hour late. I hate that younger version of myself for holding on to hope. For not just leaving then and there.

Forty-five minutes later, the maintenance staff at the club was preparing for the fireworks.

Bennett's friends had dispersed a bit, though he'd remained, talking to some guy until he was all alone.

I'd kicked off my wedges and sat on one of the rocking chairs with one leg tucked under me. The distance between us was loud and I looked up, searching for stars, trying desperately to avoid Bennett as I came to terms with the fact that I was being stood up.

"Clover, you need to go," he said.

I lowered my gaze, but he was standing with his back to me, hands resting on the stone railing ahead of me.

"I can sit wherever the hell I want, Benny."

He shook his head and then turned around, taking a step closer to me with a pained expression. Desperate.

"Oh, Joshua!" a female voice called in a falsetto. "Josh!"

Slowly, I stood, my head turning to where all Bennett's friends were inching closer to us. My mouth tasted sour as a terrible feeling began to dawn on me.

"There you are, Josh!" Valerie said as she flung herself against Bennett's side, tugging on his arm before turning to me.

Oh my god. I looked back to Bennett, a vein bulging in his neck, anguish burning in his normally cool blue eyes.

It was all a lie. Every message. Every word.

Josh wasn't real. Bennett had made it all up. This went beyond teasing and high school politics. This was cruel.

I wanted to disappear. I wanted the ground beneath me to open and just swallow me up.

The first firework went off with a whistle. I flinched as it exploded into the sky, soaking us in red.

The whole group of Bennett's friends were laughing. People who laughed at me already for reasons I had either learned or pretended not to care about. I wasn't actually rich? My mother worked for the Graves family? She was the help? I refused to be embarrassed by that.

But this—this . . . I was trembling with anger, tears spilling with every blink.

"Josh!" people started calling. "Josh! Josh! Josh!"

It was turning into a chant. A taunt.

"Hey, Clover," Valerie cooed. "Were you waiting for someone?"

I looked to Bennett, hoping to find an answer there on his face, but his gaze was trained on the ground, staring at my discarded shoes as he shook his head softly.

I could practically hear his thoughts in my head. *You need to go.*

So, I finally did. I ran down the steps and through the dance floor.

"Clover!" someone called. Sydney, possibly.

Fingers wrapped around my arm, tugging me back.

Bennett stood, shocked, like he hadn't expected to catch me. Like he had no plan for what he might actually say to me.

"Why?" I asked through a sob as every secret I'd shared—big and small—raced through my head.

His brow softened, and the words were there, waiting to be spoken. Words that could never justify but maybe explain.

Then he stumbled forward as his friends—Valerie in the lead—came to a halt behind him, still laughing obnoxiously and crooning, "Josh! Oh, Josh!" back and forth to each other.

Bennett's expression hardened into something careless. Indifferent. "Because I could," he said. "Because you were *that* desperate."

It was me against them in that moment. People who had been born into privilege and opportunity and me, a girl who had dared to live among them. And then there was the boy—the boy I'd once called my closest friend. The boy I'd fallen in love with over a lifetime and then all at once.

"What's going on here?" my mother shouted, parting the crowd of cruel teenagers.

The fireworks continued overhead as she put the pieces together, her eyes wild and full of anger and disappointment.

"Did you send him pictures, Clover? Did he ask you for anything like that? Baby, you have to tell me."

I stood there frozen just as Sydney joined us, her arm coming around me, and my mother took my silence as an answer.

Mom turned on Bennett, the closest person she'd ever had to a son, and drilled a finger into his chest. "Predator!" she shouted and despite the music and the pyrotechnics, the word echoed.

Sydney's arm dropped away from me as she stepped toward Bennett and then in front of him.

Something irrevocable passed between the two women.

Mom took me home immediately. I never went back for my shoes. A valet drove us home and we went straight to the guesthouse.

She held me for hours as I sobbed into her chest until I fell asleep in her bed.

I woke up the next morning to the news that we would be moving out by the end of the week.

Sydney offered to continue paying my tuition, but Mom declined, and it was the only relief I felt for quite some time, knowing I would never have to return to that place.

When we make it to Bennett's car, he opens the door for me, but I don't take the hand that he offers.

He gets in and fat, slow raindrops begin to hit like pellets against the windshield the moment he closes the driver's side door.

"What you've done over the last few years with other people is none of my business."

He turns to watch me, but I hold my head straight, watching the wet leaves blow off the trees overhead.

"Clover, I've rehearsed this apology in my mind over and over again since that night." He sighs, and from the corner of my vision, I can see his hands twisting his steering wheel. "And I saw that look on your face again just now. That—that look of embarrassment. Of being caught off guard. And it took me back to that night all over again. I've wanted to say I'm sorry since the moment I saw you at the diner, but the words I managed to string together in my head were never right or big or—god, I was such a fucking awful human. Sometimes, I still am."

I turn to him now, but I don't know what to say. I had resigned myself to the fact that the whole ordeal would live in the past and we would dance around it until the end of the semester when we would get a divorce. After that, maybe we would be polite. Wave to each other from across campus. And we'd never have to confront the hulking shadow of our past.

"I need you to know, Clover, that everything I said to you—everything I shared with you—as . . . as Josh, was real. I meant it all."

My heart thunders in my chest as I remember the heaviest words of all. The words that have haunted me since that summer.

My cheeks are wet and I'm crying without even realizing it. "Why did you try to meet me?" I ask, my voice cracking.

He shakes his head. "That was Val. I passed out at a party while you were in Texas and she got into my phone and . . . she's a vicious bitch, okay? But all of this? It was always my fault."

"You had a whole week to warn me."

He looks down at his hands, now in his lap, fingers twisting, as he searches for what he wants to say. "I was a coward. I kept holding out hope that something would work out. That I would find a time alone with you to confess and that I could make you understand." He pauses for a long moment. "I'm just so fucking sorry. I have regretted it every day since."

My chest heaves and I have to breathe through the threat of sobs burning in my chest. "I forgive you," I tell him. "I think I did the moment you showed up at the courthouse. But I'm still upset with you. I wish you would have told me about last year."

It's unfair. I know that in every possible way. But I'm jealous and angry for always feeling like I'm on the outside when it comes to him.

His head rolls back against his seat and no tears fall, but his lashes are wet as they kiss the thin skin under his eyes.

"Can you take me home, please?" I am exhausted on every possible level, and the only thing I want is to lay my head down and close my eyes.

He lifts a hand, fingers flinching as he reaches closer to me, and then pulls away. "I can do that," he says. "I can do that."

CHAPTER 26

Clover

On Monday night at the library, I am exiled to the top floor where the only lights are motion activated and where books go to die.

I step off the elevator with an empty cart and a massive list of call numbers for books that need to be pulled from the shelves because they are too old, no longer relevant, or a combination of both. The bold font at the top of the page reads: **BOOKS TO WEED**.

Things with Bennett aren't just magically better. I feel less anxious around him, but we are not suddenly fixed. It's not our past that I feel myself holding on to. In fact, forgiving him out loud was easier than I thought. But I can't stop thinking about every girl before me and how they compare. Were they thinner? Wealthier? Taller?

I know it's unreasonable. He doesn't owe me the details of his past. The fact that both of us have agreed not to get involved with other people right now is a courtesy more than anything. But I feel caught off guard and gullible.

The lights above flicker on as I push the cart down an aisle, looking for some local history texts. My finger passes over each label as I scan for call numbers starting with nine four one.

I make it through three rows of shelves before my brain is circling the drain again. I don't want to feel this way. My eyes burn with the threat of tears. Without fully meaning to, I spent the last three years keeping careful boundaries around myself and only ever feeling anything in small, rationed measures. Now, I don't know what to do with all this unfiltered, raw emotion.

The elevator on the other side of the floor chimes as the door opens. The lights in the ceiling tiles come to life as someone walks up the neighboring row.

My heart hiccups in my chest. *Please don't be a murderer.*

"Clover?"

He's here.

I have to remind myself that I am still upset.

"What are you doing here?" I hiss, searching for a window in the stacks so that I can see him.

Bennett's head darts into view and since I'm on my step stool, we stand eye to eye. It reminds me so much of Midnight Yell. "I came to walk you back to the dorm. Like I said I would."

I check the time on my phone before putting it back in the pocket of my skirt. "I still have forty-five minutes left in my shift."

His lip twitches as he tries to disguise a smile. "I guess it's a good thing I like books."

"Whatever. I have work to do. Go entertain yourself." I step down and slide the stool over before mounting it again with my list at the ready. "Or maybe you can find a warm body to do that for you." Okay, that was unnecessary, but I never claimed to be mature.

"Oh, we're going to play this." The lights start up again as Bennett walks down his aisle and turns the corner onto mine.

The numbers on my paper blur together like a lost language as he approaches, but my finger never stops running over spines. I cannot let him make me feel this way. He takes up so much space in my brain and heart.

"You're still mad." His voice is suddenly behind me, and I'm pretty sure that if I turned around, he would be right about at boob height.

I pull a random book down called *Deadly Outlaws of Oregon* and open it to a random page as I pretend to be on some official library mission.

Strong, elegant fingers reach around my shoulder to pluck the book away from me before placing the title on the cart.

"Hey! I'm going to have to reshelve that," I tell him.

"I'll help you," he promises. "I'll even reach up there so that you don't have to get back on your little booster stool."

I turn around, huffing a bit as I do. "There is nothing little about my stool."

"Uh-huh." He's very close, and even though I don't fall, he holds his arms out just in case. "It's a very big stool," he tells me. "Do you think the smaller stools go around saying *it's not the size of the boat; it's the motion in the ocean* because of how big your stool is?"

"Are you comparing my stool to a dick?"

He lights up with a delighted grin. "Clover Rowan Walsh, how vulgar of you to assume such a thing."

I roll my eyes and bite down on my lips so I don't smile. "I need to get back to work." Holding on to this anger feels so much easier than the alternative.

He glances at my sheet and then back to me. "I don't think those books are going anywhere. And we need to talk, Clover."

I suck in a deep breath and he steps closer so that there's no space between us. His hands move to my waist. Every other light has turned off and it's only us in this small puddle of light.

"You're mad at me," he says, his chest pressed against my thighs and abdomen and his face tilted up to me, the sharp edge of the knot in his throat bobbing.

The silly furrow in my brow gives me away. He reaches up and uses his thumb to smooth the wrinkle like he can erase every worry. I wish it were that simple. I want it to be that simple.

He narrows his eyes and doesn't speak again until he's certain he has my attention. "Let me be abundantly clear. I am not sleeping with anyone, and I haven't since we got married. Even then, there hadn't been anyone since I left campus in May."

A small bit of relief loosens the tense ache in my chest. "Fine," I say. "But you can do whatever or whomever you want."

"But that's not actually true, is it?" He doesn't flinch. He doesn't utter another word. Not until I respond.

I swallow hard and then shake my head once.

He traces my collarbone and then his touch tickles along the side of my neck until his fingers are pushing through my hair, cradling the base of my head. "We're shit at communicating. But I need you to hear me when I tell you that I can't stand the thought of you with anyone else."

I want to ask him if he will still mean that after this semester, when this unholy union ends in divorce, but I'm not nearly brave enough.

He rocks forward and rests his head against my abdomen so that I am acutely aware of how heavily I'm breathing.

How can I expect myself not to touch him? When he's right here, clinging to me.

My fingers card through his thick brown hair, and he practically inhales me, his arms squeezing tight around my middle as I drag my nails over the nape of his neck. His grip loosens and then one hand is ghosting over my hips until he reaches the hem of my skirt.

The blue of his irises is different from mine. His are deep and bottomless, reminding me so much of a lake we visited as children with our moms, tucked away in the mountains of Washington surrounded by a formidable wall of ancient trees. His lashes kiss as he blinks up at me, his hand sliding up the back of my thigh.

A not-so-subtle gasp pulls into my lungs. My blood is pumping a chaotic symphony as I wonder if I was mistaken in skipping tights in favor of the slouchy wool of the knee socks I chose today. Maybe it would have been easier to stop this before it turns into something that can't be undone.

"You are mouthwatering," he whispers. "Do you know how incredibly difficult it was to behave when I had you in my lap a week ago?"

His confession is contagious, and the feel of him is dizzying and calming and leaves me wanting to say every true thing I've ever thought. "I'm jealous," I whisper. "I was and I think I always will be, and I'm so fucking angry at you for making me feel that way."

His hand continues to stroke my thigh, moving higher with every pass until his palm is on my ass and one side of my skirt is bunched up around his wrist.

I don't want to talk anymore. I want us to be lips and hands and teeth, but if I don't just say this, I might let it fester until the jealousy is bigger than anything I can control. "And it's silly," I continue, "because how bizarre is it to be jealous of people you hooked up with at a time when you weren't even in my life?"

"It's not silly." He is genuine and seems to come from a place of absolute understanding.

"I have no claim over you," I tell him. "And our marriage isn't even real."

"It feels pretty real to me right now."

That sends my heart galloping, because what if? What if this really was it?

"Has there been anyone else for you?" His voice is throaty and demanding. "Before me?"

I nod slowly. "Two other guys. One from high school and one from the weekend I toured campus. Just them, though."

"I. Hate. Them." He makes a strangled noise. "I hate them for touching my wife."

Those two words sink into me like sharp canines, turning what had been a gentle, swirling sense of desire into something more urgent and—

His fingers knead into me and the smallest of moans slips past my lips.

I felt so brazen that night at the party. It was all liquid courage, of course. But it had felt so simple. I wanted him. His body seemed to want me back.

But now, the jumble of emotions is messy and unsure. I spent so many hours today imagining all the things he found desirable about every person he'd been with.

The self-doubt running through my brain comes to a halt as he brings his other hand to my ass and uses the leverage to lift me, forcing my legs around him as my body slithers down until I'm seated against his waist.

"Ben—"

The rest of his name is lost to the collision of our lips, his tongue rolling against mine in a bruising kiss.

I wrap my hands around his neck and relish the pleasure of his hard abdomen between my legs. He spins us around and my back is pressed into the other side of the stacks. My ass rests partially on the edge of a shelf. It gives me enough leverage to shamelessly rock against him, the contact sending a shudder through my body.

"Fuck," he gasps into my mouth.

My two prior sexual encounters were very . . . to the point, and neither included anything that was remotely satisfying for me. Now I am drunk on the possibility of there being more to sex.

Still holding me close, Bennett lowers me to the floor and drops to his knees between my thighs. His hands slide up my ribs and cup my breasts. My skirt is rucked up around my hips, showing a glimpse of my dark red mesh underwear. His breath is ragged as he feasts on the sight of me while I linger on the taut swell in his jeans.

With a smirk, he catches me staring and thrusts forward against me. The contact is so teasingly brief that it's painful and he has the nerve to laugh.

"Take that sweater off," he tells me as he drags a finger down my sternum and pulls down on the V-neck. I reach for the hem but then hesitate for a moment. He's settled in between my legs, otherwise I might squeeze them shut to hide what I know is a growing wet spot on the gusset of my underwear. The fluorescent fixture above us feels like a spotlight and I wish we could crawl into a pocket of shadows.

"Do you want to stop?" Bennett asks in the most casual way. The same as he might sound when inquiring about my day or if I need a ride. It's neutral. Pressure free. A flash of a fuzzy memory hits me as I recall the weight of Tate's hands on me and how, now, in comparison, that felt all wrong.

This is nothing like that. I see my hesitation for what it is: embarrassment. Nerves.

"What if you don't like what you see?" I ask.

He smirks again and then leans down, brushing a strand of hair out of my face, with his elbows braced on either side of my head. "If the situation in my pants doesn't speak for itself, every little glimpse of you I have seen over the last two months has set my brain on fire. I am so turned on by you, Clo, and I guarantee you that nothing in my imagination will ever match the perfect reality that is the body beneath me right now."

"Why do you have to say things like that?" I ask. "Why do you have to sound so sincere?"

"Because seeing you again, Clover . . . it's a second chance I never thought I'd have and I don't plan on leaving anything unsaid anymore."

"I don't know how to give that back to you," I tell him, and it's easy to forget that we are splayed out on the top floor of the library in the middle of the forgotten stacks that no one bothers to visit, while the study rooms and computers below are full of students who are desperately cramming for midterms.

"I don't say these things for them to be reciprocated." His lips meet mine, and my mouth parts for him.

His kisses are slow, like melting wax, and my body relaxes underneath the weight of him.

"Now, will you let me see you?" he asks.

He helps me take off the sweater, his fingers lingering on my skin, and when I'm free of the cozy knit, he tosses it off to the side.

"Perfect," he says, his hungry gaze roving over my sheer, dark red bralette embroidered with dark green vines. My pebbled nipples are visible and he guides me back, one arm wrapped around me and supporting my spine as he kisses along my throat and then down my chest, leaving intermittent bites followed by his soothing tongue. "That's my girl. Always matching."

It's a silly thing to splurge on, but matching my undergarments has always made me feel quietly confident and I love that he notices.

My hips involuntarily grind into him as whimpers escape every time his teeth scrape against my skin. "Not always," I rasp. "But most of the time."

Bennett rewards me with a few torturously slow thrusts, and when I mewl in response, I'm glad that the lights will serve as a warning should we find ourselves with any company, because I don't think either of us can stand to be interrupted right now.

His lips close over my mesh-covered nipple and I have to bite down on my lips to stop myself from crying out. He places a single finger over my lips, his dimples ornamenting his flushed cheeks. "Can my pretty wife stay quiet for me?"

I nod furiously, and his finger drags down the bow of my lip before he's pulling down the cups of my bra and suddenly there's no barrier between his tongue and his teeth and the sensitive peaks of my breasts.

My hands are roughing through his hair, pulling and tugging, and I love watching him ruined and messy.

I immediately forget my promise to be quiet when he kisses down my sternum and nibbles at the underside of my breasts. He claps a hand over my mouth to muffle a loud gasp while he continues to tease me until he's hovering at the waistband of my skirt and tugging at it with his teeth.

"What are you—" I can't bring myself to ask. The thought of his mouth moving any lower is too much. "I've never done . . . that."

The smile that spreads across his lips is downright devious. "I won't lie, kitten. The thought of being the first person to put their mouth on you is making my cock leak."

The vision of that makes my whole chest flush, and the silly pet name stirs something warm deep inside me. "Can we ease into that?"

"We can do whatever you want, Clo. But just so you know: Tasting you is in my top rotation of fantasies. But we can stop for now if you want."

"No," I say quickly. "I'm just not ready for that . . . I think."

"Will you let me make you feel good?" he asks. "Before I walk you home. It doesn't have to be oral. I might be a spoiled little rich boy, but I do have other talents."

I press a hand to my cheek and my skin is as on fire as I feel. "Okay."

He peppers my chest with kisses as he settles on his side next to me and I'm so swept up in the moment that I don't even think to suck in my stomach as his fingers glide down it and under my skirt, toying with the elastic waistband of my underwear and the little green rosette there.

His hand slides farther down and he cups me, applying a cruel amount of pressure. Too much and not enough.

"Look at me, Clo," he whispers.

Those blue eyes are on me, his chin nodding with encouragement as one finger slips through the seam of my warm center.

"You're so wet."

"Please," I beg, and before the word is fully out of my mouth there's another finger dragging upward, moving in little circles.

My spine arches up, pushing my chest forward and stealing his attention. "My god," he says, his teeth tugging on the lobe of my ear before finding my nipples and doing delicious things with his tongue.

His fingers slide down for a minute, penetrating me slowly and *holy shit*. I'm still jealous as hell, but the one benefit of Bennett sleeping his way through his first year at Wexley is that he knows *exactly* what he's doing. The guy I slept with last year over winter break used his hand on me like it was a jackhammer. But the way I stretch around Bennett sends a tingling warmth down to the tips of my toes.

He pulls his hand free for a moment and I'm on the verge of babbling and begging him not to stop, but he shocks me to my bones as he sucks on both of his fingers, his eyes rolling back. "I could drown in you."

This is so filthy and every part of me is on fire as I watch him. The things I want to do with him—want him to do to me—are the sort of salacious acts I've never even dreamed of acknowledging. Before now.

His hand is back again, pulling my panties to the side, because he can't seem to be bothered with my waistband. This time he moves with relentless confidence and ruts against my hip.

His fingers find my clitoris again and the pressure is—

Oh. *Oh.*

"Just like that," I tell him.

And he follows instruction flawlessly. Which is honestly shocking, considering what a brat he can be.

The warmth in my belly tightens into a scalding heat, and this feeling—it's nothing I've shared with anyone else before. No one has ever seen me this undone and vulnerable.

I'm rocking into his hand now, chasing a spark as he grinds into my hip.

"Good girl," he whispers in my ear through a thick moan. "My sweet girl. That's it, Clo. Let go."

His praise and permission are what send me over the edge. My muscles tighten and seize. I'm panting and his fingers continue to stroke me in lazy circles as I ride out the contented high. I'm hardly even aware of the way his hips convulse against me.

My eyes open, burning against the light, and I expect to see him wiping his hand on my skirt, but he brings his fingers back to his mouth. His throat vibrates with a satisfied hum like he's just treated himself to a taste of honey.

"I—that was—" His lips brush mine and there's a faint earthy taste to him.

"May I please walk you home now?" he asks with his face burrowed into my neck.

I nod and watch as he gently pulls my bra up, putting me back together again. "But what about you?"

"There's nothing to take care of," he says. "That was the single most erotic thing I've ever seen and I humped your leg like a fucking dog." He laughs to himself and kisses my forehead. "God, I should be embarrassed. But I'm not. That's what you do to me. That's how badly I've wanted you."

I roll over onto my side so that we're facing each other and he gathers me in a tight embrace.

"Do you know what time it is?" I ask.

He takes his phone out of his back pocket. "Twenty past one."

"I think I just got paid overtime for coming."

"Coming on the clock is a very good use of library payroll if you ask me."

CHAPTER 27

Bennett

Once I touch her, I can't stop. I walk her home and make her come on my fingers like it's my life's purpose. That night she uses my chest as her pillow and the next morning I wake up to her hand sliding down the front of my boxers. She says it's something she's never done before. I give her the slightest direction with my fist around hers and suffice to say, Clover is a quick learner.

When we get out of bed, Clover stands in front of her drawer of underthings, and I hover over her and peek at the collection I've been dying to see.

"Can I pick?" I ask her.

She glances back to me and rolls her eyes, but her cheeks blush as she obliges.

This quickly becomes my favorite part of every day. As a patron of the arts, I decide it's my duty to add to her collection and find myself checking the tags to find her sizes when she's in the shower.

On Halloween, there is a Married Mixer party as well as trick-or-treating in Haystack Hall. With Clover's workload, I am given the task of sourcing our costumes, which is probably a mistake because I dress us as Marv and Harry, the Wet Bandits from *Home Alone*.

"Do you think we can fool around later while you're still wearing the bald cap?" I ask her.

She snorts and pats my cheek. "Only if you're good."

Oh. I suddenly understand the good girl/praise kink thing, because the idea of being good for Clover sends a thrill of excitement straight to my dick.

The mixer doesn't last long and soon everyone over twenty-one is heading out for the bars. We leave, but not before getting a picture with Sandra and Greta, at their request. They are dressed as *The Price Is Right* contestants. Even Miss Linch is in the spirit. Her boyfriend is a gender-bent Matilda and she is dressed as Miss Trunchbull.

When we head back to the dorm, we are held up by a vampire flash mob in the quad.

Haystack Halloween is in full swing upon our arrival and we give out the full-size candy bars I stocked up on. Dylan the RA is mysteriously missing in action, so between our rush of overgrown trick-or-treaters (many of whom thank us with mini bottles of liquor) and Briar's grilled cheese operation, our hallway is a constant press of dubiously clothed college students.

We decide to close our door when we run out of candy and the most exciting thing happening in the hall is a few guys drunkenly arguing about whether you can use a Christmas stamp to mail things during other times of the year.

"Trick or treat, Bennett," Clover whispers into my ear as she pushes me back against the bed. Her tongue travels up my neck before her teeth tug at the lobe of my ear.

"I was good for you, wasn't I?"

She nods into a long, hungry kiss before stepping back so that she's awash in the light from the projector, the opening scene of *Hocus Pocus* playing out behind her. Slowly, she strips out of her costume, which is so sexy and fucking unhinged, too, because she leaves on her bald cap and singed beanie the whole time. Last year I went to a *Star Wars* burlesque show with Julian and Tex, but a striptease from my wife dressed as Joe Pesci is unmatched.

The feathers dusting her jacket go flying and soon I am given my treat. She wears the bra and underwear set I snuck into the bag with her costume. The underwear is a sheer black thong, and the bra is a skimpy little thing with white ghosts barely covering her nipples.

"Boo," she whispers as she saunters over to me and straddles my lap.

I hit pause on the movie, a freeze-frame of an aerial view of Salem, leaves gusting from the trees.

"I'm very greedy," I tell her as the tips of my fingers dig into the round globes of her ass. "Entitled, too. And there's still one treat I'm dying to taste."

The pulse in her neck flickers erratically.

I wet the pad of my thumb on my tongue before bringing it down to make tiny, teasing circles on her delicious clit. "I'm going to put my mouth here," I tell her. "And every time you're nervous or uncertain, I want you to dig those lovely fingers into my hair and pull. I want you to ride my face. I want you to use my mouth. Because I can imagine no greater fate than to be used by Clover Rowan Walsh."

It takes a bit to warm her up to the idea, but eventually, she gives this to me—shy at first, and then with hips bucking into my eager, eager mouth.

After two grilled cheese sandwiches and a random collection of candy, we wrap in blankets as the movie plays on the screen in front of us.

As I fall asleep, my mind is an echo chamber of self-doubt. *I don't deserve her. I don't deserve her. I don't deserve her.* But again, I'm greedy. Too greedy to let her go.

The next morning, we are a tangle of limbs and the sky is dark with heavy clouds. The projector is still on, and I reach behind me where it is propped on the headboard to turn it off.

Just as I successfully slip back under the covers without waking the soft, warm body beside me, there is a rattling knock at the door.

Clover jerks awake, disoriented. I make soothing noises in her ear and then slip out of bed, yanking on the nearest pair of pants.

I'm still mumbling a string of expletives when I open the door and find my mother standing there in her beloved Gucci trench coat. Her frown deepens and she pushes past me before I can warn either her or Clover. "Excuse me if I don't feel the need to be invited into a dorm room I am apparently paying for."

Clover skitters to the back of the bed with our duvet clutched around her chest, and my mother stands there, speechless for one of the very few times in her life.

"Oh," she finally says, and then looks to me. I can see all the many possibilities shuffling through her head. "Clover," she says as her expression softens.

"Um, Mom, could you give us a sec?" I ask.

She jumps a little, noticing Clover's state of undress, and then backpedals out of the room. "Of course."

We get dressed in a quick, hurried silence before calling my mom back in.

"I can't stay," she says immediately, "but Roy noticed that I was being charged for a dorm this semester on top of your town house and when the school said it wasn't an accounting error . . . I, well, I came here to see for myself. Which I wouldn't have had to do, but you haven't answered my calls for a few days."

The tips of my ears warm, I turn to Clover, who is sitting in oversize sweats and a T-shirt in the farthest corner of the bed with her legs crossed. The rise and fall of her chest is more rapid than it should be. I want to crawl over to her and promise everything is fine and that she isn't in trouble, but her cheeks are flushed with embarrassment.

"It's my fault," she blurts.

I shake my head and step between my mother and the bed.

"This is what's going to happen," my mother says in that calm voice she uses when an employee is having a meltdown. "The two of you are going to come over for dinner tonight. Whatever is happening here"—she waves her hand at the bed—"is not my business. But I do feel that I am owed an explanation about why I am paying for both a dorm and town house."

I glance back to Clover, deferring to her. "Sure," she says. "Okay."

I nod. "Okay."

CHAPTER 28

Bennett

I try to convince Clover to skip her afternoon catering shift, but she says she can't afford to miss shifts, and I don't think me offering to literally pay her to quit at least one of her jobs will help.

When we pull through the gates of the family estate a torrential downpour is flooding my windshield, coming down so hard that we can't even hear each other. Clover's head is on a swivel as she tries to catch a glimpse of the property, but there's no visibility.

I park in the circle drive in front of the main house and turn to her. "You ready?"

Her eyes are hollow with fear, but the smile she gives me is soft and encouraging and I think it's more for my sake than hers.

We run the short stretch to the house in the rain and let ourselves inside.

Our longtime chef, Mallory, is putting the finishing touches on her chicken tortilla soup, which is the perfect thing on a day like today. It takes her a moment to look up, but when she does, she nearly drops the glass ramekin in her hand. "Oh! My! Word!" Immediately she hustles around the island to pull Clover into her arms.

At first, Clover is stiff as she looks over to me, but after a second, her body relaxes into Mallory, who has known both of us since we were in elementary school.

"You are so grown up," Mallory tells her, hands gripping Clover's upper arms. "It's *so* good to have you home."

Home. Clover and that word. They're synonymous, I realize.

After a brief, surface catchup, Mallory kicks us out of her kitchen and sends us to the nook where we usually eat because the actual dining room is cavernous in comparison. Beth always said that it was so funny that in a house this big, we were always searching out the smallest, coziest spaces.

Mom is already seated with her laptop.

I lead Clover around the table and hold her chair out for her. It's something I would probably do anyway, but for some reason it is important to me that my mother see that I can take care of Clover.

Just as I sit down, Mallory sets the table with our soups and Mom puts her laptop away.

"Mal," Mom says, "you should head out. The weather is only going to get worse."

"All right," she says as she walks back in with a fourth bowl and sets it down. "You just leave the dishes for me in the morning."

Mom rolls her eyes. "I'm capable of doing dishes for four."

"Four?" I ask.

Clover looks over to me and I shake my head to let her know that I have no idea who the fourth could be and that my mother has gone rogue.

The doorbell echoes through the house and I stand to answer it, but my mom is already up and moving.

"This feels weird, right?" Clover asks.

"Yeah, I—"

Clovers freezes, lips parted. "Mom."

What the fuck?

Beth stands shoulder to shoulder with my mother. Just the sight of her stings still.

It's fresh in my head. Her calling me a predator, fireworks going off. My mom moving from Clover's side as the scene unfolded.

"Beth," I practically whisper.

I never thought I would see them both in the same room again.

A few weeks after the ordeal at the country club, Beth wrote me a letter. She left it for me in our mailbox. She said that after the dust settled, she got the whole story from Clover. Beth apologized for saying what she did, but she was still disappointed in me. She told me she loved me and she always would, even if we weren't in each other's lives in the same way anymore. That night, I went home and showed the letter to my mom. She read it silently and nodded to herself before giving it back to me. And that was the last time either of us acknowledged Beth or Clover to each other.

My mother mourned their exit from our lives in a way that was distinctly her. After a while, we settled into a new normal. She fell deeper into work. Traveled the country visiting as many Graves Coffee locations as she could. She began to look into expanding the brand.

Clover stands and hugs her mom.

"Hi, baby," Beth whispers, and then she comes around the table to place a warm hand on my shoulder before we're all sitting down, letting our soup go cold.

When it's clear no one knows where to start, Beth breaks the silence. "Sydney came to see me at work today and said that you two had something to share with us."

My eyes are on Clover. Her lip is nearly bleeding from how hard she's biting down. "We're married," I say without looking away from her.

Something clatters at the other side of the table, but I don't look away because the only reaction that concerns me is Clover's. I pull her hand into my lap and she turns to our mothers and begins to explain.

To their credit, there are only a few interruptions. When she mentions the ceremony, I can see them both trying to mask their feelings about missing the wedding of their only children.

It's my mother who speaks first. "This isn't about the money. I'm not upset about that." The fine lines around her eyes and mouth are heavy with worry. "Honey, you do know that I offered to cover your tuition at Calvin Prep?"

Clover nods.

"Of course, your mother refused," Mom mutters.

"Syd, don't start this right now," Beth tells her in a clear, even voice. "She wasn't happy there. And who would expect her to continue after what she went through?"

"I'm just saying," Mom says, "it's a good school, and I would never let my pride stand in the—"

"My pride!" Beth digs in. "None of what I did was in the name of—"

"Stop!" Clover shouts.

That startles them both into silence.

"Need I remind you that Bennett and I are both adults? Sydney"—Clover's voice softens—"I'm sorry this put you in the position to be paying double housing this semester. I—I honestly didn't even think about Bennett keeping the town house and what that would mean, so—"

"Clo, it's fine," I tell her. "What was she going to do with that money? Put it in an account and watch it grow instead of putting it toward something important like helping you stay in school?"

"He's right," my mother says softly.

"I wish you would have come to me," Beth tells her.

"Mom." Clover's voice falters. "I—I love you, but there was nothing you could have done."

Beth straightens her shoulders, her lip trembling for just a moment. "There are payment plans, Clover. Perhaps we could have gotten you a housing waiver so you could commute and—"

"With what car, Mom?" Clover gives her a soft smile. "This was the best solution."

"Bullshit," Mom scoffs, her eyes narrowing in on me. "You should have just asked me for the money. You know I wouldn't have said no."

I nod, because it's true. Sydney Graves can hold a grudge as well as she can hold a board meeting, but she would never say no to something like this for Clover.

The truth I can't say out loud—not in front of all of them at once—is that deep down I *wanted* to marry Clover. I wanted to save the day. I wanted to be the solution.

"Speaking of money," Beth says, "it goes without saying, that when all this is . . . resolved, Clover will not be taking a penny from either of you, but you, Bennett Andrew Graves, should know better than to elope without signing a prenup."

"You said it. Not me," Mom mumbles.

I would let Clover drain every single one of my accounts dry. In fact, the thought of her carelessly spending my money turns me on in a way that I can't think too much about in front of our mothers. "All right, well, now you both know." And it honestly pisses me off.

Our little bubble has burst. Reality is creeping in, getting too close, and I don't like it. Admitting all this to our mothers feels like we're just a couple of reckless teenagers, but I love Clover. I loved her even when I didn't know how to. I don't care that this started as the means to an end or that this was always meant to be temporary, because I'm not letting her go. Not without a fight.

Beth and my mom both look ready to say more, but something in my expression discourages them.

"I think we should heat up this soup," Beth eventually says. "We can all sleep on this new information. It's been a lot for one night."

I can see in the way her lips purse that my mother wants to protest, but she eventually nods and I help her gather up the bowls to put in the microwave.

We both stand there in the kitchen, waiting in silence for the timer to go off.

"You should've asked me," she says quietly. "I cannot believe you let Clover think that her only option was to tie herself down like that."

The soup is done but I'm standing there, frozen with guilt and anger and . . . Why would I expect anything less than her disappointment? There are so many things she could say to me in this moment that could bring us closer together, but instead, she's pushing me just out of reach.

As we eat, there are a few words of praise for Mallory's recipe, but those are the only sounds other than metal clinking against glass.

Beth excuses herself first and Clover walks her to the door while I clear the table rather than talk to my mother.

When Clover returns, she hovers beside me in the kitchen and tries to take over, but there isn't much for her to do. She's fidgeting and antsy. I know she's eager to leave.

"Almost ready to go," I whisper to her.

The doorbell rings and we share a brief look before both heading to the door as my mom files in behind us.

A very damp Beth steps inside. "There's a tree down in front of the gate. I don't think any of us are going anywhere tonight."

CHAPTER 29

Bennett

Beth takes one of the rooms downstairs, and Clover and I are left to the second floor.

My mother walks her to a guest room and leaves her with one of my old T-shirts and sweatpants. She makes a point to lead me out of the room and close the door behind us.

"We *are* married," I remind Mother. "Should I go out to the—?"

She shakes her head. "Just take your old room for the night."

We say good night and I think for too long about whether I should hug her, but then the moment passes.

I've been sitting on the edge of the bed for less than two minutes when there's a knock at my door.

Clover steps in, wearing only my T-shirt. The neck is stretched and it hangs down to the middle of her thighs, pulled taut over her hips. "It felt weird being in bed by myself."

I hold my arms out for her, and she shuffles in, crowding between my knees. She lets me envelop her and after a minute of simply listening to me breathe, she looks around and asks, "What happened to all your stuff?"

"My mom moved me into the guesthouse when I graduated."

She snorts. "This place isn't big enough for the two of you?"

I lean back so I can see her as I tuck a lock of hair behind her ear. "I think seeing it empty just made her really sad after a while."

"Can we go see it?" she asks. "Is it very different?"

"You'll get all wet," I tell her.

A mischievous grin curls along her lips. "Oh no."

There are spare Wellies and some rain shells in the mudroom, so we both bundle up as best we can and make a run for it.

The guesthouse is beyond the pool and closer to the cliffside. It might be significantly smaller than the main house, but the view is superior.

We splash through puddles and mud, but the boots do a good job of protecting our feet. When we both stumble into the dark house, we're soaked from the sideways rain blowing in off the water and we quickly strip out of our gear.

I flip on the gas fireplace while Clover flicks on a few lamps and turns in slow circles. "The couch is different," she says, walking around the dark green leather sectional.

"Yeah, I couldn't be responsible for a white couch."

She laughs, standing behind the couch, her arms spread across the back. "Neither could my mom, honestly. She flipped the cushions so many times that I wondered if the inside of the couch led to another dimension."

I tried not to change the house too much. Just a few pieces of furniture so that my mom would walk in and think I at least tried.

"I haven't really spent much time here," I tell her as I crowd behind her. Skin, damp from the rain. The threadbare T-shirt does little to separate us, and all I want is to touch her.

The back wall of windows facing the cliffside is open air from the first floor to the second mezzanine. The lightning illuminates the sky in an unpredictable rhythm, spilling into the house.

Clover arches back against me, her lovely ass pressing into my groin.

With one arm curled around her waist, I use my free hand to push her hair aside so that my teeth can sink into the soft flesh of her neck. She emits a low, throaty moan. I decide that if I had to choose one last sound to hear on my deathbed, it would be that.

"Ben," she whines, an arm reaching up, fingers winding around the back of my neck.

My erection was already coming to life when she stepped into my room wearing this T-shirt, but now it is fully stiff in the cleft of her ass.

She turns in my arms and pushes me back just enough so that she can lift the shirt over her head.

I almost complain about undressing her being *my* job, but she leaves me breathless without a complete thought in my head.

Her underwear only just covers her. A small navy scrap of fabric with thin strings pulled over the curves of her hips, nearly disappearing into the mouthwatering crease there. The curve above her pubic bone makes me feral and has me thinking obscene, irresponsible things about making her belly swell.

The bra is a flimsy mesh thing with strips of navy fabric that run through the center of each cup, just wide enough to cover her hardening nipples.

"Do you have any idea how many hours of my days have been spent wondering what you're wearing under your clothing? From the first day of school when you got dressed in our room. I could write an entire essay about your propensity for matching underthings."

"Really?" she asks in a way that says she's got me right where she wants me.

She pulls me back to her by the waistband of my wet jeans, and my hips jerk forward as I watch her delicate hands undo the buckle of my belt and then my button and fly.

My mouth is on her, biting and licking and teasing. She yanks the collar of my T-shirt and pulls me down on her, so that we're both tumbling over the back of the couch, laughing and moaning into each other's mouths.

"You're still wearing too many clothes," she says.

With one hand, I yank my long-sleeved shirt off. "You could tell me to bark and I would say how loud."

She grins devilishly.

"Woof," I say as I dip my head down to run my tongue between her breasts, then pull her nipples into my mouth one by one, swirling my tongue over the fabric. Her fingers dig into the leather of the couch, and I rut into her, the seam of my boxer briefs damp with pre-come.

"I don't want this to stop," she tells me, her moan echoing and competing with the rattling of thunder.

I don't know if she means us or what we're doing, but I'm foolish enough to hope that she means both.

I gather each of her wrists in one of my hands, pinning them above her head, into the corner cushion of the sofa. Reluctantly, I abandon her tits. Her eyes are calculating as she searches my face for any sign of doubt.

My free hand slides up her ribs, cupping her, and I could study the broad expanse of my hand on her milky skin for the rest of my life and still find new subtle beauties. "If you're looking at me to say no—if you're looking for someone to stop—you won't find that here."

"I want you," she keens beneath me.

I grind into her, and she gasps.

"Fuck, Ben—Bennett, I need you to be inside me. Please."

The pleading goes straight to my already hard cock. I sit back on my knees a little, her wrists still pinned in one hand. My other hand runs down her middle, and when my fingers rub against her folds, pushing the fabric against her clit to tease her, I find that she has soaked right through her panties.

"You're dripping for me," I tell her. Lightning flashes across the sky, giving me a perfect view of the color in her cheeks. "There it is," I whisper. "My favorite color."

"What?" she asks on a desperate breath.

I free her wrists for a moment to caress her cheek with the back of my hand. "The color of your blush, love."

She burrows her cheek into the cushion.

I click my tongue and grip her jaw, bringing her back to me as my fingers press into her again. "No hiding."

Her kiss is violent and punishing in retaliation for how I am winding her up. "I've only done this twice before."

"I know," I tell her, cradling her face with both hands now. "And I promise to make this so good for you that you forget their names."

She hums against my lips and scrapes her nails down my shoulders before wrapping her legs around my waist and pulling me flush against her. My arms drop down to brace myself, and I buck against her in several quick thrusts until we're both moaning and rambling.

I can't wait any longer. I promise to whatever god is listening to make this girl come over and over again for as long as she will let me, but right now I need to feel her tight, wet heat on my cock like my life depends on it.

She cries out the moment my body is no longer on top of hers. I kick off my boxer briefs and sit back down, my cock bobbing against the planes of my abdomen.

Clover scrambles to her feet and I take hold of her hips, spinning her around, a groan on my lips when I see the cheeky back of her panties. I want to sink my teeth into her plump ass. But I have one thing in mind as I yank the sinful little garment down and pull her onto my lap. She reaches back and unhooks her bra as her legs straddle my thighs and her luscious, dimpled rump strangles my dick.

"I'm on the pill," she tells me.

My teeth are clenched as she rolls her hips against me. "I'm clean. I got tested at the beginning of the semester and I haven't been with anyone else."

"Good," she says. "Good. I'm okay if we don't use a condom. But only if you are."

"You're sure?" I ask, my arm reaching around so my fingers can dip into her slick core.

"Ab—solutely," she tells me, practically choking on the word. "I've—I've never done this position."

"I swear on my life I will fuck you in as many places and positions as you want. There are so many things I want to see you experience, but I need . . . *godfuckingdamnit*, I need to see your face. I need to see what you look like when you come on my dick." The way her brows furrow. The way she licks her lips. I need to see it all.

"Okay, okay." She turns, our skin barely breaking contact, and she is right there, hovering over me. Her bare pussy brushes my dick for the first time, and both of us are panting, breath hitching.

With a curious, hungry look in her eyes, her fingers wrap around the base of my length. She sits up higher on her knees with one hand splayed on my chest.

Helpless to the temptation, I catch her nipple in my mouth.

The head of my penis nudges her clit, and she practically purrs as she repeats the action twice, three times, using me for her pleasure.

She's lost for a moment before her gaze connects with mine, and she's naked to me in every way. I see it all. The nerves, the lust, the excitement, and the slightest hint of worry.

I move her hand to my other shoulder and stroke myself a few times before pushing against her center.

With an encouraging nod from me, she begins to sink down.

My jaw drops, lips forming an O, and we only break eye contact when she looks down to watch me slowly disappear inside her. There's something so raw and heady about watching her fascination as a sharp, high-pitched moan cracks in her chest.

"That's it," I rasp. "You're doing so well."

Once I'm fully seated inside her, I hold her hips still for a moment, eyes fluttering, throat swallowing as I try to gather myself.

I've had plenty of sex, but this feels significant. Monumental. A defining moment, and one I never thought I would have the privilege of experiencing.

"I have wanted this for so long." My voice is gravelly and desperate.

She pushes against my bruising grip and rolls forward as she nods with her eyes closed.

Wonder. There's no other word to describe how it feels to watch her.

Fuck. I can't tell her I love her when she's sitting on my dick. That's no different than a starved man complimenting the chef. I can't do that. But I want to.

My hands move up to her waist, and she falls forward, her arms draped over my shoulders. She slides up my cock, and then down. I let her feel her way through this for now and experiment with what feels good. I let her take it slow. For now.

"How do you feel?" I ask.

"Full," she whimpers. "But so"—her breath hitches—"good."

"You're so tight for me, sweet girl. So warm and"—I thrust up into her as I smooth her hair, petting her—"perfect."

She arches back, giving me a lovely view of her, the fire crackling behind her, lovely tits on display for me. Our bodies rock back and forth, finding a rhythm, and she falls forward again so that she is pressed flush against my chest.

With my arms wrapped around her waist, and her sweet moans filling my senses, I need to fuck her.

I snake one arm up her spine and pull her as close to me as she can possibly be as I begin to drive up into her at a relentless pace. I want to fuck her so hard that she wakes up in the morning and can still feel me there between her legs. It's reprehensible, I know. I wonder if that's why I hurt her before I knew how to love her; so that she would think of me even if it was for all the wrong reasons.

"Oh my god!" she cries as I maintain my pace.

She says my name over and over again like it's a prayer. "Bennett, Bennett, Bennett, Bennett."

I slide down in my seat and slow just enough so that my thumb can find that pleasure spot. With her hands on my shoulders, she drops her hips down on me, her inner walls clenching until I'm seeing stars.

"I can't—" she chokes out. "You're going to make me come."

She rides me while I concentrate on her clit with one hand and cradle her jaw with the other. Her forehead is drawn in concentration as her hips create tight circles. The color in her cheeks has spread to her chest, and my thumb sweeps across her parted lips.

"Look. At. Me." I grunt as each word lands on a thrust. "Look at me when I make you come, Clo."

"Yes," she says, her lids heavy and eyes glazed. "Yes."

What else could I ask for in this moment? What else would she say yes to? *Stay*, I beg silently. *Just stay.*

I hold her gaze, pupils blown, as she begins to clench, her muscles spasming. My attention on her clit is unwavering.

She is beautiful in every way. Her hair curls into its natural waves after running through the rain. Her round cheeks are that perfect shade of pink. My favorite color, though I'm starting to think the color of her nipples is a close second.

"Right there," she says, and I even commit the way her toes curl to memory.

Then as if she herself has been struck by lightning, her body stills, jaw slack for a moment as she falls apart with a throaty moan. A string of my name and curse words and then my name *as* a curse word streams past her lips as I drive into her once more. She makes slow, lazy circles with her hips as her body jerks with the aftershocks of her orgasm.

After a moment, she looks down to me with a soft, astonished laugh. She pitches forward and kisses me, her tongue lashing out against mine as she starts to move with purpose again.

But I can't hold back any longer, not after seeing the way her brain broke from the orgasm I gave her.

My fingers dig into her waist as my hips snap upward, driving into her.

"Come for me," she whispers in my ear. "I want to feel it all."

My balls are tight and full as one hand comes up to fist in her hair. My rhythm begins to stutter as that distinctly hedonistic pleasure begins to tighten in my belly like a snake preparing to strike.

"I'm coming, I'm coming." I'm grunting and I chant over and over again as I spill inside her.

The lightning and thunder crash back and forth like a chaotic symphony, mimicking the unwieldy beating in my chest.

I pull Clover to me, so that her heartbeat can regulate my broken one, and because I need to feel her skin on mine every day for the rest of my life and I'd like to get a head start right now.

"Oh my god," she breathes against my neck. "I didn't think it could feel like that."

It's impossible for me not to fucking preen at her praise. "Does this mean I win?"

"What?"

"Against the others?" I ask.

"Oh, you win," she says. "First place, the gold medal, top of your class. And what about me? How do I stack up?"

"To who?" I ask.

"All the other girls."

"Again," I say. "To who?"

With a growl, I lick her cheek.

She giggles, her hair tickling my neck. "You freak, what are you doing?"

"Marking you, obviously. I don't need any other guys to come sniffing."

With an arched brow, she leans back and laps her tongue up my neck and along my jaw. "Mine," she says.

"Say it again."

Her blue eyes sparkle in the dark and she nuzzles into my chest. "Mine," she whispers against the scar. "Mine."

We stay like that for a long time, my dick softening and then becoming hard again. We go again, because I'm twenty years old and what's the point of being young if you can't take advantage of the recovery time?

We take a shower in the downstairs bathroom and strip the beds upstairs of their bedding so we can sleep on the couch in front of the fire.

Wrapped in a shroud of duvets and throw blankets, I hold Clover to me as she traces the scar on my chest.

The storm outside has quieted to a steady rainfall, and we're both humming with contentment.

"When did you do this?" she asks, her finger drawing circles around the bumblebee tattoo on my chest.

"My eighteenth birthday."

She looks up from under those soft blond lashes. "For Grandpa Dean?"

"Sort of." I tighten my grip on her, because there is so much I want to say to her right now, but I need to know that she is solid and she is here and she's not going anywhere. "And for you."

"For me?" Her voice is soft and full of astonishment.

I nod and kiss the top of her head. "The patch of clover. Do you remember how many bees it would attract?"

She nods.

"You were always the clover and I was always the bee." When I got the tattoo, it was something I never imagined being able to tell her. In fact, it felt more like a memorial of what was and what could have been, more than anything else.

She sits up, propped on her elbow, and I feel the loss of the contact instantly. I compensate by bringing my hand up to cradle her face instead.

I take a deep breath. Even if she doesn't feel the same way, I am lucky to have the opportunity to say these words to her. I have to tell myself this or else I'll just close up, and how would that make me any different from my mother?

"Clover. I have spent most of my life loving you. Even when I didn't know what the feeling was. I don't know who I am without loving you, and when I said it back to you when we were teenagers, my only regrets were that I didn't say it first and I didn't say it as . . . me."

Her lips part.

"Wait," I say. "Just please let me get this out. I need you to hear this and if you still want to say whatever it is you're about to say afterward, then please do."

"Okay." Her eyes are bright and awake now.

"I never thought I would have you back in my life. I never thought I would be so lucky. I didn't deserve it and I still don't."

Her brow furrows and I have to resist the urge to smooth away her worries with my thumb.

"I want this to be the beginning. I want to take you on dates and spoil you and eat grilled cheese with you. I want you to make fun of me and I want to be bad at things with you. I want to go to those stupid painting parties with you. I want to travel with you and watch you see something amazing for the first time. I want to be there when you take over the world by day and then listen to you make those little, sighing giggly noises you make in your sleep by night."

"I do not make—"

My arched brow silences her and she shrinks back with a coy smile. "I want to wake you up in the filthiest ways you can imagine. I want to be old and horny with you. I want our kids to be so embarrassed by us and then I want their kids to feel the same. I don't deserve it. I don't deserve any of it. But I am greedy and spoiled and I am here begging for something I will never be worthy of: you."

My chest is heaving after not taking a single breath as I wait for her response. For her to tell me that life isn't fair and you can't have everything you want.

"Are you done?" she asks, like I'm a child who's just thrown a tantrum.

I nod, and she flings herself at me so hard that we nearly break both our noses.

"Shit, that hurt," I tell her.

She brushes her nose against mine gently this time. "Pain builds character."

When she tries again, her lips are soft and slow, the perfect antidote to my manic confession. "I love you too." She presses her forehead to mine. "Sometimes I hate you for making me feel this way."

"Oh." The balloon of hope in my chest begins to deflate.

"But I don't want this to end either."

She presses a hand to my heart, her palm warm and calming.

It's all so goddamn poetic. Sharing each other fully, physically and emotionally, in the place where it all began. Our lips join in slow and lazy kisses until we fall asleep wrapped up in the certainty of each other.

When I close my eyes, I go back to the beginning and relive it all over again in my dreams. This time, the painful parts are easier to bear, because now I know that in the end, Clover Rowan Walsh loves me.

CHAPTER 30

Clover

When we wake up in the morning, we christen the kitchen table with my leg slung over Bennett's shoulder. I feel self-conscious at first with the morning light pouring in, but the way his eyes darken as he watches me helps to push the doubt out of my head.

In a matter of eight hours, we have already had more sex than I had ever had in my life before last night.

The whole drive back to campus, I keep looking at him, like he might disappear or like last night was just my imagination. I'm sore too, but it's something I feel oddly proud of.

Sydney was in a virtual meeting when we left, and my mom had already gone to work. There was a note for us on the marble table in the foyer, propped up against the arrangement of fresh flowers.

Benny and Clover—
I would like to take you both out on my birthday.
More to come.

—Mom/Syd

I miss my morning class, but I get to talk to my mom on the way to pottery during her lunch break. Without Sydney and Bennett listening in, her questions are endless. She asks if we're planning on living together next semester, which seems like a subtle way to see if we plan on staying married. Are we romantically involved? Do we share a bed? Are we being safe? Have I been refilling my birth control? What was it like seeing him again? Are there any pictures from the courthouse?

I don't have answers to everything, especially the questions concerning the future.

Last night, I told Bennett I loved him and he said it too.

That felt real and solid, but in the light of day, it's all sort of nebulous and uncertain. I'm scared that asking those black-and-white questions will lead to more questions neither of us knows how to answer.

I can't help but think I cornered him into marrying me, and I don't want him to think that we have to stay married in order to be together.

But then . . . the thought of ending this feels like undoing something meaningful. The thought has me losing my breath.

I do love him. That, I know for certain.

Sublime is the most decadent restaurant on the coast, and many Portland natives drive out here just to experience their twelve-course tasting menu and the moody views. The restaurant is built almost like a theater with stadium seating. All the tables are half circles so that each diner can face the water, and of course, because the reservation is under the name Graves, we are seated at the most secluded table.

"Does this feel like a trap?" I ask as the hostess leads us to our table.

Sydney is already there waiting for us. She wears a green silk dress with a high neck.

I sit between Bennett and Sydney as a sort of buffer, I think. When the waiter comes by to explain the theme of tonight's menu, I nod along but can't help letting the push and pull of the waves quiet my mind.

My nerves leading up to tonight were fried. It's like we're children again, waiting to be grounded. I do feel bad about the rent and dorm fees, of course. I shared this with Bennett when he first got the calendar invite from Sydney, and since then, every time he's seen me getting lost in my own thoughts, he comes up behind me and whispers, "We are adults. No one is in trouble."

But it does nothing to assuage my guilt or the constant feeling that I have disappointed our mothers.

My stress translated into my indecision over what to wear. Nothing I tried on was right, and though Bennett swore I looked great in everything, he begged me to let him treat me to a new outfit. As much as I wanted to give in, I refused. The thought of going to dinner with Sydney in a new dress paid for with a Graves family credit card only made me feel like more of an opportunist.

After sharing my options with Daisy and Briar, Daisy picked up on my dissatisfaction and opened her closet to me without any prompting. Our shapes are quite different, but there was still a lot to work with.

The second-to-last dress I tried on was a slim-cut black dress Daisy wore for her high school graduation. On her, it had come just past the knee, but for me, it hits mid calf and is perfect for Sublime's cocktail attire dress code. The bodice is boned, but the fabric has some give to it and forms to my figure effortlessly. The corset back helps with the sizing, and also allows me to go braless. (Something Bennett is a very vocal fan of.) The sleeves hang off my shoulders with silky, feminine, soft pink bows that drape down the length of my arms.

With it, I wear a pair of black Dior heels my mom gave me for Christmas. She'd purchased them while she and Sydney were on a work trip to Singapore earlier that year before everything went tits up. I'd begged her to return them, but she simply shook her head and told me to take good care of them. I'd worn them to senior prom, which I stayed at for exactly forty-five minutes, and now again tonight.

All evening I wait for the inevitable lecture, but it never comes. Even Bennett loosens up, which is not something he typically does in his mother's presence. We spend one whole course laughing at the suggestive shape of the squash we are served. The waiter blindfolds us for another course consisting of a flight of foams. We are supposed to guess the flavors, and every single one tastes like ass to me. I say so without realizing the waiter is still there and Sydney nearly slithers right out of her chair from laughing so hard.

The head chef comes out to woo both mother and son, and I am reminded of what it was like to go places with them both growing up and how the world seemed to bend to them. But more so, I am struck with the realization that in just a few years, Bennett will be stepping up to run the Graves Corporation alongside Sydney until she's ready to retire. The boy who was raised to be a king. It's hard not to feel insignificant and daunted by how hard I will have to work to achieve just a fraction of that kind of success one day.

Sydney covertly sneaks me a glass of wine over dessert, and it immediately warms my cheeks.

"The gift!" I remind Bennett. "Did you leave it in the car?"

"Oh, yeah," he says, and squeezes my thigh. "I'll be right back."

The moment he leaves, Sydney looks down at me, all nostalgia and concern. "Thank you so much for coming out to celebrate," she says. "I'm sure it won't surprise you to know that I don't really have much of a social life." She scoffs. "It was quite the blow when I realized my only true friend worked for me until she didn't."

"I think she misses you too." The moment I say it, I wonder if it's some sort of betrayal to my mom to be out with Sydney and Bennett without her. But it is true. Mom had no choice but to work as hard as she could to provide for us, but sometimes I wonder if all the extra shifts were an attempt to fight off the loneliness.

"I tried to get her to come back." She shakes her head. "But of course, the two most stubborn women in the world had to become best friends."

"Maybe Bennett and I will just have to lock you both in a padded room until you come to a resolution."

"Well, I would need to have my calendar cleared for a good, long while, I think."

I take another sip of wine, because there's nothing more I can say to fix the two of them until they decide to even try.

"Clover, before Bennett comes back . . . I want to let you know that I would like to cover the cost of your living expenses and any other academic fees you incur until graduation. We don't have to tell your mother either. You can just tell her that you received a grant or something if you're more comfortable with that, but—"

"I can't accept that, Sydney. I just—this whole thing was a mistake to begin with and no matter how hard I try to justify it, I am using Bennett." My head is shaking so hard I'm nearly dizzy. It's moving, truly, but the thought of taking money from her makes me feel like I've been cornered. "I have to find my own solution. I can't let this go on."

Sydney takes both my hands in hers. Her skin is smooth and

supple and it makes me miss the hand cream she always kept in her purse. "Clover Rowan, you listen to me. You are the closest thing I have ever had to a daughter, and I refuse to let you struggle when I am so capable of helping you. I'm honestly ashamed for not thinking of becoming an anonymous benefactor or something sooner. Your mother refused any help from me when I let her go. She wouldn't even agree to a severance package, and where did that get her? What moral high ground did she gain in denying herself that?"

She lets go of my hands to reach into her purse and places a card on the table. "This is my personal family attorney. She litigated my divorce from Bennett's father. I have already been in touch with her and have told her to expect your phone call. I plan on covering all of your legal fees and will not settle for anything less than supplementing your expenses and anything else you require."

Tears are swelling in my eyes and I blink rapidly in an attempt to stop them before they fall.

"Oh, Clover," she says, anguish in her voice. "Promise me you'll take what I'm offering you."

"Okay," I whisper. I know that divorcing Bennett will feel all wrong, but it will also give him the freedom to be with me without any sort of obligation. It will let him choose me. It will let us grow into a relationship and do this the right way.

Bennett returns with his mother's gift. He's quiet and almost uncertain as he watches her take the bag, but she's always had that effect on him. Buying something for Sydney Graves is no simple task.

Sydney gushes over her gift, an antique glass fisherman's buoy in rope netting. She has a small collection of them and we happened to see a cranberry-colored one in an antique shop window in downtown Wexley.

"You know," she tells us as we walk out to our cars. "They would use gold to create this particular color, and it's quite the rare find."

She gives me a kiss on the cheek and then a rare hug to Bennett. His body is stiff, and with how affectionate he is with me, it's easy to forget that he and Sydney have always been a little physically distant.

The moment we get in the car, I buckle my seat belt and sink into a light sleep.

Bennett is silent as we walk up to the dorm, and I make a mental note to pester him when we're in bed to see what's on his mind.

As soon as he unlocks our door I shuffle inside and kick off my heels before flopping down on the edge of the bed.

But Bennett remains quiet as he begins opening and closing drawers and haphazardly throwing clothes into his gym bag.

I laugh because I'm a little nervous and because he looks like a little boy planning his big runaway. "Going somewhere?"

"This whole thing was a mistake, right?" he asks.

"What?" I'm on my feet now, reaching for him, but he rolls his shoulder back before walking past me to the bed. He picks up the small clutch I took to dinner and rifles through it, tossing my lip gloss and a tampon on the bed.

"What are you doing?" I reach for the bag, but he holds it out of my reach like a fucking bully.

He huffs, his frustration with the size of the bag growing, and eventually just shakes it out. My debit card and IDs and the rest of the contents flutter to the bed below. And then finally the crisp ivory business card Sydney gave me not even an hour and a half ago.

He holds it up, practically waving it in my face. "This," he says. "You're letting my mother pay you off in exchange for divorcing me. Is that it? Is that how much you love me? I wonder what the exact price tag is on that, Clover? Have you done the calculations? I know you love your numbers. I heard you talking before I sat back down at the table."

I yank the card out of his hand, and I immediately regret taking off my heels because I would love a few extra inches right now so that I could at least attempt to get in his face. "Sydney is not paying me off. What the hell are you on about?"

"A mistake," he says. "Isn't that what you called us?"

"I'm using you, Bennett!" I shout back at him, neighbors be damned. "Don't you see that?"

"At first, yes. And I deserved that." His hands are in his hair, tugging against the roots. "I still do, but you can't tell me that's all that this is now."

"Of course it isn't, but you have to know that we did this all wrong." My voice loses its edge. "This is our chance to fix it. I'll have my housing taken care of next semester, so we can get divorced after finals. That was always the plan."

"Well, pardon me for thinking the plan changed when I tore my damn heart out and served it to you on a silver platter, Clo."

"Everything between us can still be true," I tell him. "We don't need a marriage certificate for that."

"What if I do?" His voice is desperate and on the verge of cracking, his cheeks ruddy and eyes wide.

"You don't. Bennett, don't you get it? If you divorce me, then we can take our time and get to know each other. You won't be obligated to me like you are now."

"I know you," he says through gritted teeth. "I've known you and loved you all my life. I have taken my time for twenty years, but I am *done* living without you, Clover. Do you know what happened after that night at the country club? I cut each of those so-called friends out of my life. One by one, I found their dirtiest, most vile secrets and I promised them that if they even so much as thought about you again, I would make their lives miserable. For the next two years, I went to school and I came home. And then I did it all over again the next day. I was a fucking hermit until Julian became my roommate last year."

I'm glad to hear it. I'm glad to know that his life changed after that. Mine certainly did. But how does that make a difference right now? "What do you want me to say to that, Bennett? Thank you? I never asked you to punish yourself, and I refuse to stay in a marriage that you entered to nobly settle some sort of moral debt with me. My god, *I used you*. How many more times do I have to say it for you to understand? This marriage is built on a collapsing foundation."

"You are my wife," he grinds out painfully. His eyes are ringed in red and the vein in his neck is pronounced and pulsing.

I want to sit him down and lay his head in my lap. I want to comfort him. But I need him to see reason first. "You don't have to let this be a bad thing. We can do this the right way. Hell, Bennett, we can date and be a normal college couple if you want. And we can do all that without me wondering what will happen if one day next semester you decide that this isn't what you want."

"*You* are what I want. I don't want a divorce. I don't want to date a normal college girl. I want to date my wife. I don't care how or why we got here, but we are here and it is everything I have ever wanted, and now you're trying to take it away from me. My mother might not have said that her financial support was contingent on our divorce, but I know that woman. She is in my DNA. She doesn't want this for us."

My lungs feel like they're filling with fluid, like I'm drowning from the inside out. "I don't think I want this either," I whisper, because for as long as this marriage continues, I will fall asleep every night knowing that I bullied him into this.

He's sitting on the edge of the bed now and I go to stand in front of him. "Bennett, if you love me—if we are meant to be—then one day we can do this all over again. We can get married in a church or on the beach or in that same damn courthouse. Our moms can be there. And it won't be happening because I need *something* from you. It will be because all I need is *you*."

He shakes his head. "You have me. Wholly and completely. You have me, Clover, and you're cutting me loose. All I need is you and you're asking me to let you go because you think that's what you're supposed to do." He stands, his chest so close that I have to tilt my head far back to see him. "Fuck. That."

Without another word, he shoves a few more things into his bag and hikes it over his shoulder before slamming the door so hard the windows shudder in their frames.

The room is empty.

Our bed is empty.

I am empty.

CHAPTER 31

Bennett

Tex and Julian go easy on me at first. When I arrive on their doorstep—well, technically it's mine, too—there are no demands to explain or assumptions that I am a fuckup.

I mean . . . I am. Why else would Clover not want to see this through? Why else would my mom want us to get a divorce?

But they just crack open a bottle of Macallan that one of Tex's uncles gave him for his graduation. I tell them everything slowly over the course of a few days. I tell them there is a universe in which she loves me, but it can't be this one, because how can she love me and want this to end?

I miss classes for a week, and that's when Tex and Julian attempt to stage an intervention.

"We're not going to let you throw your whole semester away," Tex says as he takes the Xbox controller out of my hands just as I'm about to walk me and my horse off a cliff in *Red Dead Redemption*. You know, for fun. Yesterday was *Grand Theft Auto*. I went into public lobbies and wreaked havoc on prepubescent boys until they blew me up.

"The least you could do is leave the horse out of this," Julian tells me as he hits the power button on my remote. "Besides, this isn't how you win her back, you dumb fuck."

They listen to me bitch and moan and eventually they push me into the shower.

It's the second-to-last week before fall break and I've been back to all my classes for the last two days. I have no idea what the fuck the professors say, but I'm there and Tex assures me that is worth something. In the evenings, he forces us all to study together despite Julian's protests. Something about mirror neurons. We make dinner together—which mostly consists of dino nuggets and pizza rolls. I usually clean up, and every time I go to throw something away, Tex reminds me of the elaborate recycling and composting system that he has miraculously trained Julian to memorize.

I spend most of my class time scrolling back and forth between two photos.

Both are from the courthouse. One is posed with our judge in the background, likely talking to his court reporter. Neither of us is smiling in the photo. We look like a couple of Victorians who are perfectly still and somber because the old-timey camera's exposure is too long to hold a smile.

In the second photo, though, Clover is looking away like someone is calling her name and my attention is on her with the ghost of a smile.

I zoom in to see her ring on her left hand, and suddenly the most vital thing to my survival is getting it back.

CHAPTER 32

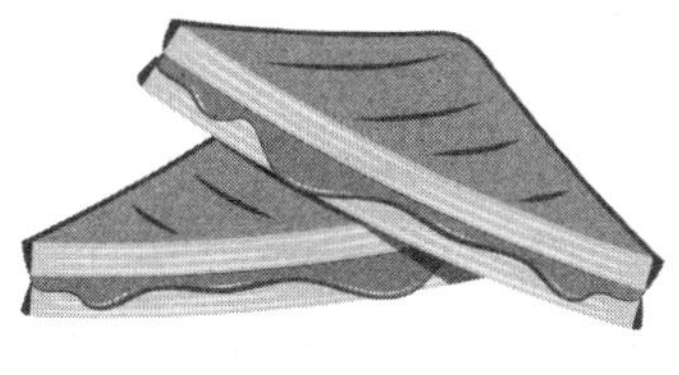

Clover

At first, I'm convinced Bennett will come back. It takes me forty-eight hours to realize that he won't and that waiting around for him won't change that.

I wouldn't have thought it was possible to feel lonely in a two-hundred-square-foot room, but when Bennett leaves, everything about our space feels cavernous and drafty.

The threat of bombing the semester and losing my academic scholarship is the only thing that gets me to classes, and the reality that I will have to figure out my own housing next semester is enough for me to show up to work. Even if I am a husk of a person.

Pottery is the only class I am managing to enjoy, and I think I'm going to miss it next semester. I'm probably not even qualified to move on to Pottery 2, but I guess it couldn't hurt to find out. It would be something to look forward to, at least.

I won't take Sydney's money. That is one thing I have decided for sure. No matter how all this plays out, I can't live with the idea that Bennett would even think I would choose money over him.

On Wednesday night after my library shift, I drag my body down the hallway just as Briar is packing up her grilled cheese operation for the night.

"Hey," she says. "Bennett out of town?"

I turn to her, my key card in hand, and my resolve immediately crumbles, tears spilling before I can choke out a reply.

"Okay. Fuck. Crying. Not really my wheelhouse." She turns over her shoulder and waves her arms. "Daisy!"

A moment later, I hear an "Oh!"

Daisy steps around Briar, pulling her baby-pink headphones around her neck.

The second I see her I only start crying harder.

"Hey, hey," she says, rushing to me as she gives Briar a what-did-you-do look.

Briar shrugs, untying her apron and hanging it on the back of the door. "All I asked is if Bennett was out of town, I swear."

Daisy guides me into their room and onto her bed. "Take a breath. Just breathe." She smooths calming circles over my back and points to her pink mini fridge with her free hand.

Briar returns with a very cutesy can of prebiotic soda and opens it for me, encouraging me to take a sip.

The breathing is working, and after a few hiccups, I take the water and concentrate on the cold trickle down my throat. I pat dry my warm cheeks and manage to say, "Thanks. Sorry about that."

"What's going on?" Daisy asks. "I'm guessing it's about Bennett."

Briar sits down on my other side, and she's not physically

comforting me, but something about her posture makes me feel like she's standing guard for me.

"He left," I tell them through a shaky sigh.

Daisy's eyes go wide for a second before she schools her expression. "Like, temporarily?"

I shake my head because talking is making it all so much worse.

"But you guys are like the picture of domestic bliss," Briar says, and there's a hint of sadness in her voice, like our relationship failing is upsetting to her on a personal level. "Honestly, the only example of a healthy marriage in my life."

The words are right there, sitting on my tongue. I know I shouldn't. The semester is almost over. But Briar and Daisy are the only friends I have on campus, and I want to trust them. Maybe I can at least finish this semester with the knowledge that I've made two friends.

"It was a lie," I whisper.

They both sit silently, waiting for me to explain.

With their questions and all the relevant background information, it takes almost an hour and a half, three grilled cheese sandwiches, six snack-size pouches of fruit chews, four and a half Diet Cokes, and a trip to the ice machine downstairs to refill our heavy-enough-to-be-murder-weapon water cups.

When my story is complete, the three of us sit in a row on Daisy's bed wearing under-eye masks and considering toenail polish colors for me because it is something small that we can control. After Daisy and Briar paint five toes each, we huddle around a phone and watch ridiculous, brain-rotting videos.

Daisy closes her eyes for just a minute sometime around five and ends up with her head in my lap atop a fluffy, lip-shaped throw pillow.

Briar opens a fresh pouch of fruit chews and rolls them all together into one mega fruit chew ball. She takes a bite, and then turns to me. "We could apply for a three-person room."

"What?" I hear her just fine, but I must be misunderstanding. Most of the time, Briar has me wondering if she even likes me. Surely, she isn't suggesting that I live with her and Daisy.

"It could be fun," she says. "And a little bit cheaper."

"That's—that's really kind of you, Briar."

She snorts. "Don't make me take it back."

"Maybe you should talk to Daisy first."

"About what? Every night will be a sleepover for her. In fact, if I didn't ask you to move in with us, she'd probably do that thing where she puts her hands on her hips and scolds me."

"Well, I should at least think about it, right?"

"Sure. I think the late housing change request is the Tuesday after Thanksgiving, so you have a little while."

We sit there in silence, my eyes finally becoming heavy.

"I'm surprised he hasn't come back yet," she says.

"Who?"

"You know who. Bennett. That time you were sick . . . he was practically manic. And ever since the beginning of the semester, he has waited up for you to get home from your late nights at the library. I would always see him with the light on. It only took a few weeks to pick up on the pattern."

I shake my head at her. "But . . . the lights were always off when I got back."

She looks at me pointedly, and I realize that he probably turned them off just before I normally arrived home.

"I am the last person anyone should take relationship advice from," she starts. "But it sounds like you both want the same thing in different ways. And he spent all those nights waiting, right? So maybe he just needs to cool down. I think if you want to backpedal things a little, he would be willing to wait some more."

Backpedal. I hate the sound of that. Like we've gained progress and would just lose it all if we simply relabeled our relationship.

"Why does it matter to you so much?" she asks. "The whole not-being-married thing."

"Because what if someday we actually want this for real?"

"And it doesn't feel real now?"

I pause, trying to parse out how to respond. When I think of the moments that were supposedly fake, I have to admit that even those made me feel something. Every touch and kiss led us here. I can still feel the carpet of the library on the backs of my thighs and picture the sight of the gas fireplace flickering shadows across the room. That was all very much real to me.

"Of course it does," I tell her.

"So then what's the point of waiting? Why does it all have to happen in some sort of order? You've got now. Right this moment, and that's as far as life's guarantee goes." She studies me as I feel my brow furrow, and my memories channel back to the dozens of times Bennett would smooth his thumb over my forehead, like he could erase my worries.

"My aunt," Briar says. "She would always say *don't save the good stuff.* Clothes, dresses, dishes . . . whatever. Because we could just die. We could just wake up one day and think it's any other day and we could leave the new dress with tags in the closet for another, better day, but that day might never come. And then you're well and truly fucked."

"That . . . is so depressing."

She nods. "Yeah, life is pretty bleak. But I think you gotta ask yourself: Is Bennett the good stuff? Is he the dress with tags? Is he the fancy-as-shit china? And if that's the case, what are you waiting for?"

I let that settle for a minute. What am I waiting for? Is this really about reserving the someday possibility of marrying on our own terms? Or is this about waiting for the perfect day—the perfect season of our lives—that might never come?

I spend the next night in Briar and Daisy's dorm. We pool our resources and make a rather comfy bed of blankets and pillows. Daisy and I help each other study for our Geology 1 class, which we take from the same professor at different times. Every once in a while, we help Briar with her seemingly endless customers. And by the time I fall asleep, I can clearly see how simple it would be if the three of us did take the roommate plunge. Especially considering that I would have my own bed and wouldn't be relegated to the floor.

On Saturday morning, Mom picks me up after I ask if I can spend the night at home and catch up with her.

"Lucky me," she says as I buckle my seat belt. "A slumber party with my favorite girl."

"Can we make pizzas for dinner?" I ask. "The ones with the pesto on top."

"Looking for some comfort food?"

"Something like that."

I begin to tell her what happened while we eat dinner on the couch.

She lets me curl up against her, and to my surprise she doesn't immediately advocate for me and Bennett to get a divorce. She frowns when I mention Sydney's birthday dinner and our conversation, but I can't tell if it's because she wasn't included or because Sydney offered me money. Probably a little bit of both.

The conversation happens in waves. We watch thirty minutes of a movie, and something new occurs to me. It's not until we're falling asleep in her bed that she finally says her piece.

I've been waiting for her to express her disappointment and say all the things she couldn't say in front of Bennett and Sydney, or anyone else for that matter. Instead, she kisses my forehead and says, "Love isn't really concerned with timing, is it?"

CHAPTER 33

Bennett

The Thursday night before fall break is always casino night at 1919 Hemphill.

I don my navy Tom Ford tux—the same one I got married in.

Tex flew home earlier today, and that's for the best because he definitely wouldn't go for my plan. Julian, however, is more willing to test fate.

When I park around the corner, I pull the rest of Tex's bottle of Macallan out from under my seat. I throw back about two fingers and hand it to Julian for him to take a sip before I have one more.

"We'll be in and out," I tell him. "The ring is in Tate's room. I know it."

Julian pops the top back into the bottle of scotch and rolls it under his seat. "Here's to not getting our asses beat."

"All I need you to do is roam around without drawing any attention and just let me know if Tate heads upstairs. I'll text you when I have the ring and we'll meet back here."

"Let's *Ocean's Eleven* these motherfuckers," Julian says.

It's a waste of time to bother with the line at the front door, and anyone who knows us probably won't let us inside anyway, so we sneak in through the back gate and walk through a haze of marijuana smoke to the back door.

Some girl calls my name, but I don't bother to see who it is. It's not *her* and that's all that matters.

Inside, I know where to go.

"Good luck," my cousin says as we split up just outside the kitchen.

I work through the crush of bodies to get to the front of the house. Most guys are dressed in suits and the girls are in the kinds of dresses and gowns that are held in place with copious amounts of double-stick tape. There are costume boas and stray feathers on every surface, and there are even girls walking around dressed as Playboy Bunnies with trays of shots and edibles.

In front of the staircase is a red velvet rope and a shit-faced freshman who is supposed to be keeping people off the second floor.

I look around for options. Behind me are two brunettes dressed like showgirls with giant feather headbands.

"Hey," I yell over the music, and hike my thumb over my shoulder. "What if I gave you both a hundred bucks each to distract that sad excuse for a bouncer over there?"

The short one peers past me to get a look. "Make it three hundred total," she says, and her taller companion practically spits her drink out at the brazen counteroffer.

"Done." I open my wallet and take out four crisp one-hundred-dollar bills. "Here's an extra hundred to make him disappear for the next thirty minutes."

"You're on!" says the short one as she drags her friend with her and stuffs the money down the front of her sparkly minidress.

It takes a record forty-five seconds of pawing at the guy's chest, and it is abundantly clear he never stood a chance.

As they drag him off into the living room, the tall one glances back and blows me a kiss.

I duck under the rope and run upstairs as discreetly as possible. My phone vibrates with a notification, and once I'm out of view in the hallway leading to Tate's room, I check my messages.

JULIAN

found Tate playing cards

he is not happy I'm here but I just threw down enough money to cover a semester's worth of tuition so he would shut up

these guys are pumped to win all my money

And they prob will

Is high stakes Texas Hold'em different than regular stakes Texas Hold'em

What about going unnoticed did Julian not understand? It was honestly foolish of me to expect him to even do that.

BENNETT

the only advice I have for you is to know when to hold 'em and know when to fold 'em

JULIAN

I didn't know you were funny

I pocket my phone and let myself into Tate's room, flipping on the lights. The last time I was in here, Clover was drunk and it was dark except for a small desk lamp. But with the overhead lights on, I find Tate's room to be much cleaner than any college guy's room typically would be. The place is likely maintained by a housekeeping service.

The only thing breaking up the dark hardwood floors and navy blue walls is the white trim and wainscoting. His bed is made, and the walls are ornamented with lacrosse team photos and trophies. There are a few pictures from high school of him at parties with other guys—big fish in little ponds.

Of course, it would have been too fucking easy for the ring to just be sitting there on his desk under a spotlight.

I start with the two nightstands on either side of his bed. The first side is full of random junk and a few unmarked pill containers.

It is impossible to be in this room and not think of her. The weight of her in my lap and how I had just wanted to keep her safe.

The other nightstand is full of condoms and lube and an old, cracked cell phone. After rifling through the dressers, desk drawers, and his closet, I kneel next to the bed and look underneath. There's loose lacrosse equipment, and a deflated basketball that I remember the guys pelting one another with last year in the backyard when everyone was high and bored. The last thing is a Nike shoebox in the exact middle of the space under the bed, and I think that's gotta be it.

After pulling it out, I sit down on the edge of the bed. I flip back the lid to find the box is full of nothing but trophies. Thongs, a few bras, some Polaroid photos from a camera that seemed to get passed around last year. Mostly girls with glassy eyes laid out in the basement in various states of undress. Some are aware—though barely—and others are just passed out. It's fucking disgusting. My stomach turns at each new discovery, and eventually I just shake out the whole damn box, which is pointless—

Until something knocks against the cardboard and the ring . . . Clover's ring falls out into my waiting palm.

The relief I feel is nothing compared to what it will be if I'm able to win her back, but it's still so fucking sweet.

I shoot off a quick text to Julian and his response comes a moment later.

BENNETT

Got it.

JULIAN

Good, because I can't lose any more money tonight.

BENNETT

meet you at the car. Be careful.

I give the room one last look, wondering if I should bother piecing back together the mess I'd made. But then I shake my head as my focus settles on his little spread of trophies. No, let him fucking see that I know what a piece of shit he is. Anger, sudden and violent, practically strangles me.

A lacrosse stick is poking out from under the bed and I make a split-second decision to take it with me.

I take the stairs two at a time with the ring tucked into the breast pocket above my heart. The drunk first-year has reclaimed his station at the foot of the stairs.

"What the—" he yells after me as I hop over the velvet rope and make a beeline to the basement door. I have one last piece of unfinished business.

The night is still young, so the basement is relatively quiet except for two couples sequestered in opposite corners. Neither of them even looks up as I make my way down the stairs. At least they don't until the moment I swing the lacrosse stick into the scoreboard, shattering a handful of incandescent lights.

I go for the slate next, but the plastic head of the stick cracks, which is fine, because mounted to the wall right beside the scoreboard is a metal baseball bat with the Wexley logo. Likely from the seventies.

A girl screams somewhere behind me, and I almost apologize for startling her, but hope that my little display encourages her to abandon whatever poor decision she is about to make.

It takes a few solid hits, but once the slate cracks, it begins to fly off in brittle chips.

Footsteps thunder up the steps to the main floor, and I know my time is running out.

But god, this feels fucking great. With every thwack of the bat, the former versions of myself slip further away. The guy who had to catfish his way into Clover's heart because he was too chickenshit to do it for himself. The guy who slept his way through freshman year just to feel something. The guy who is starved for affection. The one who didn't deserve Clover and is only as good as what he can offer her.

Those versions fall apart like pieces of slate until all that's left standing is a slightly drunk guy who is wildly in love and would do anything to keep the girl. Whether that means divorcing her so we can start from scratch or picking up right where we left off and doing everything in my power to make this work. Couples therapy. Cheesy date nights. Matching shirts like Sandra and Greta. Whatever it takes. If I have to live in that deteriorating dorm building for the rest of my life just so I can keep Clover, I will.

The bat crashes through Tate's name and then his body count when I hear footsteps trampling back downstairs.

"What the fuck?" Tate shouts.

I spin around on my heel and prop the bat on my shoulder. I am ready for a fight.

The only problem is that so are the five other guys standing opposite me.

I've been in a handful of brief tussles and come out the winner, but these odds feel like a death wish. And yet I am willing to pay the toll for the opportunity to destroy the legendary scoreboard.

Swinging my bat down and using it as a cane as I strut over to Tate, I wonder if I'll lose any teeth tonight.

"Allow me to get things started," I tell him as I draw my fist back and let it smack into his jaw. The sound of skin hitting skin is barbaric and juvenile but only makes me hungry for more.

The first few hits I land are solid, and I even manage to brandish the bat and connect the metal with someone's gut before it's yanked away and thrown out of play.

My mouth is warm and metallic and full of blood. Someone gets me in the ear, and I feel like I'm underwater. I stomp on a few feet and let my fists swing recklessly. It's not like I'm likely to hit someone on my side. After all, it's me versus everyone.

I'm laughably proud of myself for staying on my feet as long as I do, but once my vision begins to blur and my knees hit the ground, I know I'm fucked.

I'm on my back and trying to curl in on myself as the punches and kicks continue to land, when things start to go dark.

The last thing I remember is bright lights turning on and a familiar voice screaming my name followed by a series of threats and curses.

CHAPTER 34

Clover

The automatic doors are too slow as I step past a few half-sober students waiting on rides. My erratic pulse and the blood rushing in my ears push me toward the check-in desk.

"I'm here to see my husband," I say, breath ragged, to the worn-down-looking woman behind the counter.

"Clover!"

I whip around at the sound of my name and Julian is rushing toward me from the waiting area. His jaw is bruised and the tux he is wearing for whatever reason is rumpled.

"They sent me out here to wait while they took him for a CT scan. They were being really weird about having me back there, so I told them to call you." His eyes narrow with meaning. "His wife."

I nod quickly and turn back to the woman behind the desk.

"Name?" she asks dryly.

"Bennett Graves."

She sighs through her nose and scrolls on her computer. "Have a seat. Someone will be with you shortly."

Julian leads me to the only two free seats, next to a guy who apparently superglued sunglasses to his face.

"What the fuck happened?" I ask Julian. "The only thing the hospital said when they called was that he'd been in an altercation and that he appeared to have a concussion."

He shakes his head, and for a moment, I'm scared he's going to feed me some sort of bullshit, but then he starts talking. "It was like six on one."

Julian tells me that they were at 1919 Hemphill and how they were supposed to be in and out. When Bennett hadn't met him outside, Julian got worried and went back for him. He found him in the basement, the scoreboard shattered, and a whole circle of guys ganging up on him.

"My god," I say to myself. "What was he thinking?"

"Nothing good," he says. "I swear, he's been trying to punish himself for the last two weeks."

I sink back in the chair, hands covering my face, because I have spent a decent amount of time since he left hoping that he was hurting as much as I have been. "Why were you guys even there?"

Julian grimaces as he reaches into the interior pocket of his jacket and hands me a hospital baggie with Bennett's wallet, phone, watch, car key, and three rings. One is his Graves signet ring, one is his thick gold wedding band, and the third is . . . mine. A thin gold band, holding an oval stone.

I take the bag and hold it to my lap, tears forming and throat tightening. "He—he went back for my ring? It's not even real. Why would he do that?"

The look Julian gives me is almost peeved with one brow shooting up. "Really?" he asks. "You think Bennett Graves gave you a fake ring?"

My cheeks flare just as a nurse opens the swinging doors to the ER and calls out, "Clover Walsh?"

"Over here!" Julian says as he pushes me forward.

I shove the bag of valuables into my tote and head for the nurse. When I look back, Julian is right where I left him. "You're not coming?"

The nurse answers for him. "Only immediate family and one visitor at a time."

"Is he okay?" I ask frantically, already forgetting about Julian as I follow her into the chaos of the emergency room.

"He's awake," she tells me as if that means anything, but it is a relief I suppose, and I'm suddenly wondering if there was a time when he wasn't awake.

She walks at nurse pace—which is a different measure than normal human speed, because nurses walk like someone is chasing them down a dark alley.

Barely stopping, she motions to an open door at the end of the corridor and says, "The doctor will be with you shortly."

When I walk into his room, Bennett is sitting in bed in slacks and no shirt. His chest and face are covered in bruises and the center of his bottom lip is split.

Bennett's gaze is slow and lazy as he looks me up and down. I realize I left the dorm in exactly what I was wearing. Lilac-and-white-checkered boxer shorts and a sweatshirt Bennett left behind that says *Proud Dad* with the Wexley seal beneath it. (A birthday present from Julian.)

There is a nurse standing at the computer near the hospital bed and he glances back and shakes his head at me. "Sorry, immediate family only. No girlfriends."

Something fierce and protective pushes against my chest. "Excuse me, but that's my husband."

If I didn't already have an inkling that Bennett is on pain meds, I would now based on the warm, goofy smile he gives at the word *husband*. "And that," he says with entitlement, "is my *wife*."

I find myself smiling back at him, and wishing I had the ring on my finger to prove it.

The nurse rolls his eyes and mutters something about babies having babies before telling me, "He's not allowed to fall asleep for another three hours. And don't even think about defiling this hospital bed."

"Gross," I mumble. I'm guessing the staff at Wexley Medical Center has seen some shit.

I go to sit in the armchair beside his bed, but Bennett pats the side of his mattress with one hand. The other is held against his body in a sort of awkward way like it might be injured.

"What the hell were you thinking?" I ask him as I hover at the edge of the bed.

He pats the space next to him again more insistently. "I'm surprised you even answered your phone."

"Ah, there it is," I say as I sit down beside him and kick off my strawberry-print slippers before putting my feet up. The constant static in my head that I've been living with for the last two weeks quiets the moment my skin touches his. I'm left wondering what fight could have been worth losing this. "I was starting to think the pain meds had made you docile."

"You're the one who wants a divorce." His words slur over the last syllable.

For the first time this semester, I finally have the upper hand. He's seen me make a drunk fool of myself and has nursed me back to health, and now it's his turn to lose his inhibitions and embarrass himself.

He drops his head down on my shoulder and with our height difference, I can't imagine he's that comfortable, but I just lean back and let it happen.

"I stole your ring back."

"So I heard."

His chest shudders with a huff. "I think they gave it to Julian. He's probably already used it to propose to a paramedic."

I don't bother telling him that I actually have both of our rings, because that might lead to a conversation about them that he's in no condition for. And me? Well, I'm just a coward.

"I also heard about your little fight with the scoreboard."

"It was a real donnybrook. Not with the scoreboard. Just all the assholes I ran into afterward. The scoreboard stood no chance against me."

"What the hell is a donnybrook?"

"A brawl," he says, like I'm ridiculous for not knowing. "It was on my SAT."

"I can't tell if this proves or disproves that you have a concussion."

He shrugs and reaches past me for the Jell-O on his tray.

"I got it." I take the cup and tear back the foil lid before handing it to him with the plastic spoon stuck inside.

He takes a bite and then holds a spoonful out for me.

I side-eye him, but he's just watching me expectantly, so I open my mouth and take the gelatin peace offering.

"Maybe I should get the shit kicked out of me more often."

"We might not want to make a habit out of that." I should be mad at him for doing something so violent and stupid and then getting caught up in a fight on top of that. But some very basic part of me wishes he'd been able to put the other guys in the hospital.

"I'm guessing you had a run-in with Tate."

He scoffs. "More like he had a run-in with my fist."

"What a big tough guy you are," I tell him in a baby voice.

His normally charming smile is a little lopsided. "I threw the first punch," he admits.

"That must have felt good."

"Felt great."

Bennett finishes off the rest of the Jell-O as the doctor comes in, scrolling through one phone with another in his other hand. He's short with a head of black curly hair.

"Graves?" he asks without looking up. "Bennett?"

Beside me, Bennett nods, but the doctor still hasn't looked up, so I answer for him. "Yes," I tell him. "That's right."

"Next of kin?" He glances up to me briefly, the bags under his eyes dark and heavy.

"She's my wife for now," Bennett provides as he yanks my hand into his lap, my arm pressed against his bare side.

The doctor pauses at that, but lets it go. "I'm Dr. Roshan. Your CT scan came back clear. You've got a sprained wrist and two broken ribs. The split lip and the bruises should heal in the next few weeks, but I'm going to recommend you take an anti-inflammatory."

"So, he's okay?" I ask eagerly.

"Anyone who gets in a six-on-one fight is not okay, but physically, he is fine. We'll keep him here for another two hours of observation." He scrolls through something on his phone.

"He had open-heart surgery as a baby, though," I tell the doctor. "For a congenital heart defect. Doesn't he need to be observed or—"

Dr. Roshan nods. "We did see that in his records. We ran an EKG and everything appears to be fine."

"You're sure?" I ask.

"I'm sure." He gives me a patient smile before continuing. "Looks like one of the nurses dug up your emergency contact info from the files the university shares with us and someone left a message with your mother."

Bennett groans, tossing his head back against his pillow. "Fuuuuuuck me."

That elicits a laugh as the doctor backs out the door. "Moms." He shivers. "Fear in the hearts of men and all that. Push the nurse call button if you need anything. But for the love of god, use it sparingly. My staff's patience is running thin tonight. We had a handful of frat guys come in earlier after shooting off firecrackers from a turkey fryer and they got caught trying to steal boxes of grippy socks."

"Well, look at that," I tell Bennett once Dr. Roshan is gone. "You're not even the most interesting patient in the ER tonight."

"I am *very* interesting," he says. "Hey, is that my sweatshirt?"

"No," I blurt. "Yes. But you left it and we're still married, so isn't it communal property or something?"

"Looks better on you, anyway."

He pulls me to him with his good arm, my cheek resting against his warm chest.

"Maybe we shouldn't—the doctor just said you have two broken ribs. I don't want to put any weight on you."

"I don't care," he says.

"Why did you do it?" I whisper. "The scoreboard."

He's quiet for long enough that I look up to make sure he's not asleep, but his gaze is focused on the small window at the top of his door. "I needed to know I could be good."

"Bennett." I take his chin in my hand and force him to look down at me. "Bennett, you *are* good. Do you hear me?"

"If that's true, then why aren't we staying married?" His words are fuzzy, like they're sticking to the roof of his mouth, and I notice that the drip of pain meds they have him on is nearly empty, but the question still chips away at my heart. He makes it sound so simple. But can it really be that simple? Is there a world where we just do this damn thing and give it a go? Will we ruin our chances of being truly happy if we don't take a step back?

"Let's watch TV," he says.

I grab the controller attached to the bed.

He eyes the nurse call button mischievously and presses down on the red circle before I have a chance to yank it away.

"Bennett!"

"What?" He's too pleased with himself as he wiggles his toes. "I didn't get any grippy socks."

We spend the next two hours watching old episodes of *Baywatch* on the tiny grainy television suspended in the corner. When the nurse gives him the all clear and says the doctor will be in to discharge him as soon as he can, Bennett falls asleep the minute the door shuts behind her.

It's with him practically curled around me and his left wrist in a black brace that Sydney finds us.

She opens her mouth to speak—likely to demand answers—when she sees that he is passed out and instead slumps into the chair beside the bed.

"I'm so sorry you had to deal with this," she whispers, shaking her head. "I got in late last night and didn't realize my phone was still on airplane mode. I couldn't believe how peaceful things were." Under her anorak, she wears jeans, clogs, and a baggy white T-shirt that probably costs more than I make in a week. There are bags under her eyes and new lines that I don't recall spidering out from the corners.

I give her a weak smile as I slither out from under the weight of Bennett's arm and step into my slippers.

"You should go get some sleep," she tells me as she takes in my appearance. "I saw Julian out in the waiting room. He says Benny hasn't been staying at the dorm."

I shake my head, my arms wrapped around my middle.

"Did you talk to him about the—"

"Yeah. It didn't go very well."

"He'll come around." She offers me an unconvinced smile. "How about you call me over the break so we can get your housing sorted?"

"Actually, I—thank you, Syd. Really. It means a lot that you were willing to help, but I'm applying for a three-person shared dorm room with two of my friends. It should be more affordable, so I won't need to take you up on your offer."

"Oh, sweetie, I'm so glad you've found some girls to room with you, but I'd still like to—"

"No." It comes out firmer than I mean for it to, but in the case of Sydney, that's probably for the best. "I . . . it's important to me that I do this on my own."

She studies me for a moment, and I can practically see the opinions forming in her head. "I told Julian to make sure you get home okay."

"Thank you." I have the distinct feeling that I am being dismissed, though she probably thinks of it as being relieved.

I take my bag from where I left it on the counter next to the sink and turn back to Bennett. There is so much I need to say, but he is asleep, and needing to say something isn't the same as knowing how to say it.

"You'll tell him I said bye?"

She pulls me to her for a hug and a kiss on the head. "Of course, Clo. Go get some sleep."

Bennett is still wedged against the bed rail, maintaining the space I left empty. "Okay."

When I step out into the hallway, I stand there for a moment, my back pressed against the wall, trying to find the courage to walk back in there so that I will be the first thing he sees when he wakes up.

But Sydney is here now. He doesn't need me, especially when he might not even remember me being here in the first place.

CHAPTER 35

Bennett

Today is my fifth day home and my only visitor has been Julian on Monday when he dropped my car off along with a half-eaten Edible Arrangement.

He plopped down on the guest room bed. (I hadn't wanted to go back to the guesthouse. I couldn't see it and not think of her.)

"I got hungry," he said with a shrug.

In exchange for eating half of my get-well Edible Arrangement, I grilled him over and over again about what Clover seemed like after she left my room.

When I woke up, she was gone from my bed and the lights in the room were low, the TV still on as my mother dozed in the chair beside me. For a moment, I thought I'd dreamed up the whole thing, but when I finally charged my phone I saw her texts.

CLO

hope you're feeling better.

CLO

I gave your stuff to Julian, but I still have our rings.

I didn't want to tell her I would come get them from her. It felt too much like admitting defeat, so I told her thank you and decided to follow her lead. In response, I got radio silence.

On Thanksgiving, it's just Mom and me. Despite being in the same house for the last week, my mother and I have managed to give each other a wide berth, but today—one of the few days that Sydney Graves actually cooks—that is less possible.

There was a time when this holiday always meant me, Clover, Beth, Mom, and Grandpa Dean eating in sweatpants and nibbling on these little frozen quiches Beth bought every year that I loved. We ate cranberry sauce from a can and bought pumpkin pies from the grocery store. It always felt like the most normal day of the year. But now with just the two of us, it almost feels lonelier to observe the holiday at all.

My mother seems to feel the same way because she picked up a rotisserie chicken for us to share and is making two baked potatoes and green beans in addition to a pistachio dessert salad that Beth used to make and a small pumpkin pie. And all the other hallmarks of the holiday without it feeling like too much for only two place settings.

"I had hoped Clover might join us," she says as I pass through the kitchen. "Maybe even Beth."

I grip the edge of the countertop until my knuckles turn white to stop myself from saying something truly shitty.

She turns off the faucet and glances back at me. "Did you hear me?"

"I did." My voice is clipped. "I don't think paying off my wife to divorce me really sends the one-big-happy-family-holiday-dinner message."

As she towels off her hands, she comes around the kitchen island to stand beside me. Sometimes I forget that I overtook her in height in middle school and she has to tilt her head back to make eye contact. My mother has this innate thing about her that people refer to as *presence*. She has the ability to make even the largest men feel small.

"Benny," she says, "you can't be serious. I offered to pay for her housing and other miscellaneous expenses. Clover shouldn't have to resort to marrying you just to survive her first year of college."

"Ah, right, because I am without a doubt her worst and last alternative."

She looks taken aback, like I've slapped her. "I never said that. When did I say that?"

"You know just as well as I do that not every message needs to be spoken in order to be heard, *Mother*." I practically spit that last word at her feet.

She softens, her tactics switching as she assesses me like an opponent. "Honey, Beth and I used to talk all the time when you two were just little things about how it would be such kismet if you fell for each other."

"Right," I say, my voice dripping with disdain as I start to walk off. "You've probably always thought Clover was too good for me."

Her fingers wrap around my forearm and yank me back with a surprising amount of force. "Bennett Andrew Graves, I have never thought such a thing. Perhaps you're conflating your opinion of yourself with mine. It's easier to have someone to blame, isn't it?"

My only response is to gasp. Fuck, that cut deep. I want to rage at her, and spout off all the things she did wrong with me and how she failed to be the affectionate mother I never thought myself worthy of. But everything hurts too much. My body. My defective heart. It all throbs.

"You pushed her away from me. You gave her the one thing she needed." My voice is vibrating with anger. "The thing that would set her free. And now I have to just hope that one day she will come back to me."

"Benny, she didn't take the money."

My mouth opens, but I don't have the words. I don't—

"She was adamant. And you should know, she hasn't even contacted the attorney I put her in touch with. That's not to say she won't, but—"

"But she's had over two weeks," I say mostly to myself.

My mother reaches up and pushes a wayward lock of hair off my forehead. "I want whatever you both want, okay? And if this is it? Then I'm here for it. I'm sure Beth is too. I wish you'd gone about it all a little differently, but I'm not trying to tear you apart."

"It sure as fuck felt like that."

She flinches at that. "I love you two so much. I need you to see that all I was trying to do is create options. Money can be such an awful thing. But if I can use what I have to give a girl like Clover some agency, I will. I won't apologize for that, but my offer to her was never meant to be anything more."

I think she's telling the truth. I want so badly for that to be the case.

Her hand rubs up and down my bicep. The contact is the kind of warmth you can't help but lean into.

"And I'm sorry," she says, her voice cracking. "I *truly* am. I went about this all wrong. I should have spoken to you first. This should have been something we approached Clover with together."

"Thank you," I mumble. I feel so fucking raw still, and I need to take a step back to process this and decide what to do next.

"Dinner will be ready in about an hour," she says. "Why don't you go rest for a little bit?"

"I still look that bad, huh?"

"Healing always looks worse than it feels."

I take a handful of crackers and prosciutto from the makeshift charcuterie board she's set out before sinking into the couch. Clicking through the channels, I skip right over the football and land on a cheesy Christmas movie about a time-traveling duke.

I need to get back to campus on Sunday and talk to Clover. I've been a useless piece of shit since I left the dorm. It's on me to go to her and make this right, and that starts with a call to the family attorney.

The thought of watching her walk away and just hoping that we can make things work is enough to make me nauseous. She would have to choose me. But would she ever truly be mine otherwise?

The only way Clover Walsh—the girl who I've loved for most of my life—can truly be mine is to let her go. I've had it wrong this whole time. I'm the patch of clover and she's the bee. Now the only thing I can do is patiently wait for her to land.

CHAPTER 36

Clover

I held on to the rings on purpose. Julian didn't question me when I handed him Bennett's other things. I knew that if I gave them both back to him, that would be it.

When I got home that morning, I slept for a few hours wearing my ring as well as his on my thumb. That afternoon, Daisy dropped me off in Cannon Beach at my mom's house on her way to the Portland Airport, and the house was so much quieter after living in a dorm for the last three and a half months. It was even more unsettling than having the dorm room to myself.

When my mom got home, she recruited me to help her clean out her closets—a project she'd started weeks ago and had abandoned. Mom had the next day off, so we stayed up until the job was done and then the next morning, we woke up and attacked another closet. It was therapeutic in a way.

Mom worked on Thanksgiving and after her shift, we grabbed dinner at the Driftwood Diner. I was glad to see that Marianne had the day off. We went home and Mom went to bed while I fell asleep on the couch watching a surprisingly sexy Christmas movie about a young Santa finding his Mrs. Claus. I spent the day wondering what Bennett was doing and thinking that most married couples probably don't spend their first holiday apart. I was happy for the time with my mom, but every night that week, I found myself reaching out for a warm body that wasn't there.

Mom drives me back to campus early on Sunday morning. The rain follows us along the coastal highway, and without any more closets to clean out, the low humming thoughts I've had all week long are pushed to the forefront of my mind.

"Mom?"

"Hmmm?"

"What if—do you think you and Sydney could ever be friends again?"

She ponders that for so long that I wonder if she heard me.

"I didn't think so for a long time," she finally says. "I still don't know. But we were soulmates in that way that friends can be." Her grip on the steering wheel tightens for a moment. "But it's hard when money is involved. We were best friends, but I was also her employee. You know what I mean, Clo?"

I nod, and suddenly I'm second-guessing myself. I've been inching closer and closer to the realization that I want to be Bennett's wife and that maybe it doesn't matter how something starts, only how it grows. But the money of it all. It's a burden that he will never understand the weight of.

"It's a power dynamic. And it's one that she abused when she fired me. But then . . . if someone had called you that. A predator . . . or something just as insidious. Wouldn't I have done the same thing to them if I had the ability to?"

We listen to music for the rest of the ride and as we pass the welcome sign for Wexley, I say, "I love Bennett."

"I know," she says softly.

Tension I didn't know I was holding on to unwinds as I exhale and sink back into my seat. Of course she knows. "I don't know why, but staying married to him feels like cheating. Like—like I tricked him into this."

She snorts, shaking her head. "I have watched that boy fall in love with you for the last ten years, baby. I don't think he cares how you two got here. Just that you did."

The car slows as she pulls up to the parking lot behind Haystack Hall.

"And if you're concerned about me and Syd, we are two grown women. We will be just fine."

"So, you wouldn't be disappointed if—oh my god, I can't believe I'm saying this—if we stayed married?" How is it that I feel suddenly thrust into adulthood and still so concerned with my mother's approval? Will it always be that way?

She turns to me, smoothing a hand along my hair. "The list of things you could do to disappoint me is microscopic. Taking a chance on love? A love that's built on forgiveness? I'm proud of you for that, and honestly, I'm taking notes. Syd and I both should."

I practically vault myself over the center console to give her a hug.

☘ ☘ ☘

When I text Bennett to ask him to come over, he responds and says he can't be here until this evening.

I play it cool and tell him that will work, but I have about ten hours to burn until then.

I clean and organize the room. I study for finals for as long as my brain will allow me. I spend time in the pottery workshop, adding the last glaze to the paperweight I made for my final—a very blob-like octopus.

After I pace in her and Briar's room for a solid hour, Daisy suggests I take an everything shower, and she even stocks me up on some of her pricier scrubs, hair masks, and skincare.

In the thirty minutes leading up to six o'clock, I panic.

I'm doing this all wrong. Bennett deserves a grand gesture. Something public and romantic. Not a quiet night in our little dorm room with its warped floorboards and peeling paint.

With three minutes to go, there's a knock at the door.

He's early.

I count to ten before opening the door so it's not completely obvious I've been standing here, hovering and waiting. "Hi."

For a moment, he says nothing. He wears black jeans and a black T-shirt under a baggy charcoal sweater. His face is scruffier than normal, and his left eye has a shadow of a black eye. His collar reveals just the edge of a fading bruise.

"Thanks for coming," I say simply to break the silence.

He takes a deep breath and nods to himself, like he needs the self-assurance. His eyes look everywhere except at me.

My stomach clenches into a fist. This doesn't feel like the reunion I was hoping for. Not at all.

"Hey. I'm glad you texted. And um, thank you again for coming up to the hospital last week. I know it—"

"Of course."

He hands me a manila envelope that I hadn't realized he was holding until just now.

I take it hesitantly and begin to pull the papers out when I see a header that reads: The Law Offices of Bailey & Parsons.

I've never had a punctured lung, but I wonder if this is what it feels like. Almost as if air is leaking from your body at a rapid rate, but you're not able to replace it with oxygen. Slowly, I look up and finally—finally—he is looking right at me.

His face is colorless, and I realize he's given me just what I asked for.

"They're signed," he says quietly, taking a step closer as a cluster of boisterous students pass behind him. "So you can look them over if you want. I can send them in or you can if you'd rather do it for yourself."

I'm shaking my head and the only word I can manage is: "Why?"

"Why am I divorcing you?" He swallows, his Adam's apple working. "Because there isn't anything I wouldn't give you. I meant what I said. I love you, Clover. It fucking hurts." He pushes a hand through his overgrown hair. "Shit. It terrifies me to think of a life without you. The only thing that scares me more is making you stay and never knowing if it's because you wanted to or because you felt you had to."

He pauses to give me a moment to form a response, but I'm just—I'm gutted. But I'm touched too. It's tragic, really.

He did this for me. He gave me what I thought we needed even if it was the last thing he wanted.

"That's why I couldn't get here sooner. I had to wait for the paperwork to come in and I know you don't care about the money, but there's—just please. Let me have this one thing, okay? Let me know that you're going to get through school without having to work two jobs and constantly stress about the next bill. I need—"

"Come in," I blurt. "Please just come inside."

I stand back and hold the door open for him and he sees my not-so-grand gesture. No, it's quiet and it's private and it's just for us.

"What is this?" He looks from me to the couple of candles burning on his side table that I brought from home. I spread a fleece blanket out across our bed and there on a paper plate are two grilled cheese sandwiches on a tray I borrowed from Briar that I am almost positive she stole from the dining hall. Beside it is a small jar with a handful of flowers I yanked out of the landscaped flowerbed next to the Haystack Hall sign.

"Don't laugh, okay?" I toss the folder on the bed and then take the rings out of my pocket before falling to one knee. When I look up to him, a nervous laugh bubbles up. "God, you're even taller from down here."

His eyes are wide as he sinks to his knees in front of me.

"What are you doing? No! This is *my* grand gesture."

Bennett cradles my face in his hands and pulls me to him so we're just a few breaths apart.

"Will you marry me, Bennett Andrew Graves?" I ask for the second time in my life. "Well, really, *stay* married to me. Will you stay married to me?"

"No open flames!" a voice barks from the hallway.

We both turn to catch Dylan as he walks past.

"If I see those candles again, I will confiscate them," he says in an almost delighted voice.

"That guy is the worst," Bennett says.

"I heard that," Dylan yells.

Briar follows just behind him. "Leave the lovebirds alone, narc," she snaps before slamming our door shut.

"Thank you!" I call before turning back to Bennett, his hands still on my face and stroking my cheek now. "Bennett, I love you. I want to shred these divorce papers into a million pieces and spread them across the state of Oregon so they can never be pieced back together again. So, what do you say?"

"This isn't what you actually want, though." His gaze roves over my face, searching for answers. "I have faith," he says urgently. "I have faith that we can find ourselves here again. I love you, Clover. I've never been so certain of anything in my life. After you and your mom left, all I wanted was to forget you. Every memory of you was a fresh pain, and even when I found ways to dull the ache, it never went away. *You* never went away. And that's how I know that for me, it will always be you, so I can wait. I can wait to see if you feel the same."

I sniff, but it does nothing to stop the tears once they start to spill. With my hands balled into fists, I pound against his chest. "You stupid, gorgeous jerk! I'm going to have to start writing down rules again. No grand gesture stealing! This was supposed to be my big moment to tell you how much I love you, but now you've made me cry and I can't beat that."

His pupils flare with excitement and he steals a quick kiss from me. "Try."

"Fine. You're the worst and I love you, okay? I love that you always rub my forehead when I'm worried and that you have a smart mouth and that you do nice things but only when you think they're in secret. And when I think about waking up and not being your wife, I feel completely empty like someone has gone and cut out all the most important parts of me. And that part of me is louder than the voice in my head that says we're too young or that we got here for all the wrong reasons. Because we're here. We're here, Ben. And I don't want to be anywhere else with anyone else. I don't want to let us go just because we did this all backward."

I'm rambling now. Bennett said all the right words, and I'm rambling. But I mean it. I mean it all. "I want to eat black-market grilled cheese with you and watch movies on our projector, and I want to have a song. We *need* a song. Couples have songs. When I get dressed every morning, I want to count the hours until you're undressing me. I want to carve our names into this bed. I want to decorate a Christmas tree with you because it makes me so sad to think that we might not. I want to kiss you on New Year's Eve and I want to buy each other stupid things on Valentine's Day and I want to fight with you over chores and stealing blankets and—"

"We can do that. We can do all that," he whispers. "I'll buy you a Christmas tree pretty enough to be in a Hallmark movie."

"I don't care how fucking pretty the tree is, you snob."

"I'm not a snob," he retorts.

"Oh, really?"

He grins. "Maybe a little bit of a snob."

"Are you really going to leave me hanging?" I ask him.

His hands drop away from my face and he takes my ring from me. With great care, he holds my left hand and presses my palm to his lips. He leaves a kiss there and then one on the tips of each of my fingers. "You're sure?" he asks, the ring hovering above my finger. "I'll love you all the same no matter what answer you give."

"Bennett, if you don't put that ring—"

He steals another kiss as he slides the ring on.

I moan against his mouth and his hand immediately moves to the back of my head to deepen our kiss, but I pull back only for him to growl in return.

"Let me at least get this ring on you," I tell him. "These are my vows to you: We've spent all our lives growing together. Becoming new versions of ourselves. But if I have to figure out this life thing and get over the miserable fucking pain of being exposed and vulnerable, then I don't want to do it alone. I want to do it with you. I pick you, Bennett. I pick you every time."

His smile is broad as he holds his hand out to me.

I press his palm to my chest right above my heart, and even though our anniversary will always be a humid day in August, today, I decide, is when we really begin.

Then, because I have been frustratingly horny for weeks and because this wedding is in the privacy of our dorm room—our home—I pull his finger into my mouth, my tongue running along the length and the metallic taste of his ring lingering.

"Fuck," he whispers, eyes wide and hungry.

In an act of lewdness, I suck on his finger as I pull it out of my mouth, his ring right where it's supposed to be.

I bring his hand to my cheek again and nuzzle into the warmth. "With this ring, I thee wed."

His eyes are hazy and love drunk. "I do. Till death do us part. To have and to hold. All of it," he says. "All of it. Forever."

"All of it forever," I repeat back to him.

"So . . . we never did get a honeymoon," he says.

"Finals first," I tell him. "Honeymoon second."

His hand skims the hem of my T-shirt, and my body responds immediately with goose bumps. "Well, we should probably study. For the honeymoon, obviously."

"It's the responsible thing to do." I inch closer to him so that my lips skim against his with every word. "We might even have to pull an all-nighter."

EPILOGUE

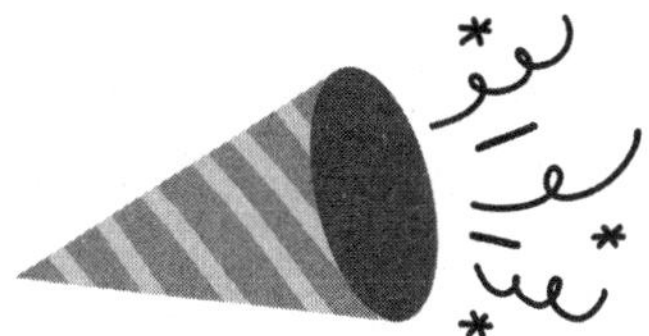

Bennett

My wife is so fucking hot.

"What was that?" asks the man to my left.

I shake my head. Shit. I hadn't meant to say that out loud. I'm at a cocktail table, sandwiched between a master coffee roaster and some guy whose only personality trait is debating the most sustainable form of disposable cups. But all I can think about is my wife on the other side of the room and how her throat arches when she laughs, throwing her head back.

My mother's annual New Year's Eve party is legendary, and invitations are highly sought after, which means it's a networking circle jerk. And now that I'm within a few years of taking up an official position at the Graves Corporation, I can't attend something like this without fruit flies like these two buzzing around.

I track Clover as she moves across the room from my mom to her mom and finally to Julian, who has been shotgunning vodka and Red Bull for two hours straight.

My super fucking hot wife is in her new dress tonight. When she tried it on for me last week, I bent her over the guesthouse kitchen table before she could try on the next one and that was how she decided this dress was the winner.

It *is* a great dress, but so is every other thing Clover puts on her body. A short, white little slip with a sheer overdress dripping in pearls and sequins with flared sleeves. Turns out I have a thing for Clover in white. It reminds me of getting married and that reminds me that she is my wife. *My wife*. Damn. And when I think about that, I can hardly keep it in my pants.

Unfortunately, though, all I'm able to imagine as she laughs with Julian is what the hem of said dress looks like pushed up around her waist.

She glances over her shoulder at me. The gold and silver New Year's Eve headband tucked into her tousled waves reflects the light of the dance floor.

I am gratuitous in the way my eyes rake over her body. Her tongue swipes across her lower lip in response.

She slinks toward me like a shark hunting its prey, hypnotizing me.

"Excuse me, gentlemen," she says as she approaches our cocktail table. "I need to steal my husband before he dies of boredom."

Beside me, each man takes a second to register her blunt statement.

I choke on a laugh and hold my arm out for her to take.

"Thank you for saving me," I tell her, my lips pressed against the crown of her head.

"Things seemed dire. Stage five boredom. Terminal. A real killer."

"I might require a full body exam to ensure I'm in the clear."

"I will be very thorough when we get home," she swears.

I guide her toward the ballroom exit. "I'm afraid it can't wait."

She pulls the cuff of my jacket back to check the time. "We have eighteen minutes before midnight."

"Say no more."

Clover

We are less than discreet as we sneak up the grand staircase at the front of the club. The moment we step into the upstairs hallway and are free of the knowing smiles of the valets at the doors, Bennett crowds me against the nearest wall.

His mouth is hot on my neck as he licks and nips a path to my jaw. "You have to stop wearing white," he says.

My hands tug on his hair, and I'm thankful for the extra inches these platform heels give me, because I'm tall enough to drag my tongue along the notch in his throat as I smooth my hand over the hard swell in his trousers.

"Fuck," he groans. "Forget I said that. Wear all the white. I've had a chub for the last thirty minutes just from watching you sip your drink. Your tongue and that straw. Jesus Christ, Clo."

"Well, it's not every day that I consume a beverage in the most pornographic way possible, but you were basically ignoring me to schmooze with those corporate coffee bros."

He gasps, delighted. "You were seducing me? It was all a ploy! I've been seduced!"

"Well, just wait until you see this," I tell him as I push back his chest to create just enough space between us to open my clutch.

His eyes widen as he sees my panties stuffed inside. "You're in trouble now," he says as he shoves the scrap of nude lace into the pocket of his suit jacket. "I'm collecting these as evidence. You're not getting 'em back until tomorrow at the earliest."

He tugs me farther down the hallway, checking every doorknob until we stumble into a smaller party room full of unused centerpieces.

I push his jacket off his shoulders and throw my headband in the same direction as my clutch while we trip over each other, all mouths and tongues and swallowed curses until I'm perched on the ledge of a giant picture window. The room is dark, so we can see clear across the golf course and over the cliff to the waves breaking against the deep winter sky.

Bennett checks his watch again. "Ten minutes."

"How did we waste eight minutes making out?"

"I wouldn't call it a waste," he says as his hand travels under the hem of my dress to cup my bare center. One finger slides in with ease and he moans. "You've just been walking around like this? Wet and waiting . . . straight to jail."

His fringe tickles my neck as he sucks on the sharp edge of my collarbone. "Or you could just fuck me."

"I'm getting there, *wife*. I gotta make these ten minutes count."

A soft whine shakes in my chest as he swirls his finger right—*fuck*—there. "Does it make me a bad feminist if you calling me your wife makes me feral?"

He drops to his knees, hands rubbing against the back of my thighs as he hooks one leg over his shoulder. "Considering we agreed to both change our last names to Walsh-Graves, I'm going to say no. Besides, fuck the rules, wife."

He sucks a bruise onto my inner thigh, and I hold the back of my hand against my open mouth to stifle a scream.

"Graves-Walsh," I tell him in between breathless pants as he pushes my dress up for me to hold and his mouth closes over me. "It's alpha—*oh god*—alphabetically correct!"

"Do you really want to argue about this right now?" he asks, breaking away from the very important duty of eating me out like a fucking buffet.

"Arguing as foreplay," I grit out.

"What happened to just foreplay as foreplay?"

He uses the flat of his tongue to do ungodly things to me as my brain becomes a jumble of crossed wires. "I can't . . . I can't believe I didn't want you to do this to me at first." All it took was one mind-numbing orgasm with his head between my legs on Halloween and then another right after finals finished for me to get over all the worries and fears I had about being on the receiving end of oral.

I yank his hand up from where his fingers were digging into my hip to check the time again. "Shit. Three minutes."

Bennett moans and hums into me as the watch-wearing hand squeezes my breast, his thumb harshly rubbing my nipple.

It's so goddamn tempting to keep him there on his knees, riding his handsome face with those perfect dimples while I lecture him about why I am right when it comes to our hyphenated name. Instead, I slide my leg off his shoulder and pull him up to me by his tie, because the last time I was here at the Cannon Beach Country Club watching fireworks was a nightmare and I am determined to replace that memory with something better and sweeter. Something I want to hold on to and remember forever.

My fingers deftly unbuckle his belt and make quick work of his zipper and fly. He hisses when I reach into his boxer briefs and pull his weeping cock free.

At my back, the first firework erupts into the sky, illuminating Bennett's flushed cheeks.

"Fuck," I cry. "We have to finish this later. I can't miss the fireworks."

"You won't," he says sternly as he spins me around, my arms

hooked around his forearm that sits in the arch of my back, pressing my chest against the window.

"What if someone sees us up here?" I ask.

He slides his erection through my arousal before thrusting his hips forward with a grunt.

I'll never get tired of how it feels to be full of him. To share this intimacy with him as husband and wife.

"They won't," he says on another thrust. "All anyone can see from down there is two newlyweds who snuck away to enjoy the fireworks in private. No one out there knows that I'm fucking you with your panties in my pocket."

From below, we can hear the ten-second countdown, and Bennett drives into me on each number.

"Two," I whisper.

One is lost to his lips as he stills for just a moment, his free hand gripping my chin, my head turned to the side so that we can ring in the new year with a kiss.

Our mouths part on a gasp, and he ruts into me, his hand taking mine and leading downward. He directs my movements, teasing my hot, wet center until I'm at a tipping point.

"You are so fucking stunning," he says. "In your little white dress . . ." He grunts into my neck. "I'm going to—" he starts.

"Me too," I tell him as I throw my head back against his chest.

His grip on my hip tightens and I fall apart on the next stroke.

My body is pliant and shuddering as I convulse with pleasure. He follows with a few slow thrusts, wringing the orgasm out of me.

I'm still crying his name when his climax pulses inside me. He pants into the crook of my shoulder as I clench around him.

My hand comes up to cup his cheek and direct his attention. "Look."

A chorus of my favorite kind of fireworks shoots up into the air. The kind that flies impossibly high and then erupts into a shower of light.

I can feel him grinning against my neck. "Do you remember the last time we were here together and saw fireworks?"

He nods wordlessly, his throat swallowing against my shoulder.

"I can't make myself regret it," I murmur, the show playing out in front of us in a beautiful display.

His arms tighten around my waist. "I was a little shit, but I'd make every mistake all over again to have you as my wife."

"It all brought us here," I tell him as the grand finale burns in the sky. "And now we have forever."

"Not even forever is long enough for me to love you, Clover Rowan Walsh-Graves."

"Well, Bennett Andrew *Graves-Walsh*, we'll have to make do, won't we?"

Acknowledgments

Working on this book was the most fun I've had in a very long time, and that's largely because *The Undergrads* series has been a reunion tour with some of my favorite people in this business. The band is back together, y'all.

Alessandra Balzer, we are so back, baby! I love this series, but I especially love it because it brought me back to you. You were the first editor to take a chance on me, and I learn something new and invaluable with every book we work on. Thank you for seeing the vision for *The Undergrads* and for taking a leap of faith on something new for both of us. We're college girls now!

The whole team—old and new faces alike—at Macmillan has been an absolute dream to work with. Thank you for the warm welcome. I have felt right at home since the very beginning. An extra-large helping of gratitude to Jen Besser, Donna Bray, Bess Braswell, Molly Ellis, Morgan Rath, Nellie Kurtzman, Sam Fabricatore, Mary Van Akin, Lavell Nero, Jennifer Healey, David Briggs, Ilana Worrell, Mariam Chaduneli, Celeste Cass, Tim Greco, Meg Miguelino,

Meaghan Leahy, Bryn Goldstein, Brad Wood, Tom Stouras, Christine Jaeger, Patricia Doherty, Alison Lazarus, Lauren Monaco, Gillian Redfearn, John Edwards, Jen Edwards, Holly Ruck, and Sage Daughtery. If I ever revisit my college days, it's my greatest hope that I'd have each of you on my dorm floor.

Aurora Parlagreco! The minute there was a handshake on this series, I begged for you to design the covers and, like always, you did not disappoint. I am so thankful to be working with you again. This has been such a collaborative process, and I cannot thank you enough for working with me on this series. Your thoughtful creativity continues to blow my mind.

John Cusick, you are my "yes, and" man. My "we'll make it work" man! Thank you, thank you, thank you for continually making my dreams come true.

The world of Wexley is full of romance, but it's also about first adult friendships and how those relationships are canon events. I owe a huge thank-you to my friends, including: Ashley Pierce, Sierra Simone, Kristin Trevino, Veronica Trevino, Ashley Lindemann, Kate Fasse, Ashley Brown, my pookies, the BU who has so kindly adopted me, John Stickney, Andrew Smith, Karra & Doug Rybicki, Morgan & Lee Moore, Luke & Lauren Brewer, Erica Rusikoff, Josh Taylor, Carly and Jess at UTC, and, lastly, my mom and best friend, Gail Murphy. An extra-special shout-out to all my college friends from Wesleyan. Like Clover, I was a nontraditional student, and you all truly gave me a college experience I could call my own.

Thank you to Ashley Lindemann, Flavia Vazquez, and Tiara Cobilis for keeping the Julie Murphy lights on. You're both magic.

And to my Ian. My very own college sweetheart. The most surprising and somewhat unlucky series of events brought us together in that classroom, and I wouldn't change a single thing.